DOCTOR WHO

THE DAY OF THE DOCTOR

THE CHANGING FACE OF DOCTOR WHO
The cover illustration portrays the Tenth and Eleventh
DOCTORS, and the DOCTOR as he appeared during the Time War.

DOCTOR WHO

THE DAY OF THE DOCTOR

Based on the BBC television adventure *The Day of the Doctor* by Steven Moffat

STEVEN MOFFAT

BOOKS

9 10 8

BBC Books, an imprint of Ebury Publishing
20 Vauxhall Bridge Road,
London SW1V 2SA

BBC Books is part of the Penguin Random House group of companies
whose addresses can be found at global.penguinrandomhouse.com

Novelisation copyright © Steven Moffat 2018
Original script copyright © Steven Moffat 2013

Steven Moffat has asserted his right to be identified as the author of this
Work in accordance with the Copyright, Designs and Patents Act 1988

Doctor Who is a BBC Wales production for BBC One.
Executive producers: Steven Moffat and Brian Minchin

First published by BBC Books in 2018

www.penguin.co.uk

A CIP catalogue record for this book is available from the British Library

ISBN 9781785943294

Editorial Director: Albert DePetrillo
Project Editor: Steve Cole
Cover design: Two Associates
Cover illustration: Anthony Dry
Production: Phil Spencer

Typeset in 10/12 pt Adobe Caslon Pro
by Integra Software Services Pvt. Ltd, Pondicherry

Printed and bound in Great Britain by Clays Ltd, Elcograf S.p.A.

Penguin Random House is committed to a sustainable future for
our business, our readers and our planet. This book is made
from Forest Stewardship Council® certified paper.

MIX
Paper from
responsible sources
FSC® C018179

In memory of Sir John Hurt, who saved the Day

Contents

FEED CONNECTING
FEED CONNECTED
FEED STABLE
PLEASE ADJUST FOCAL LENGTH IF REQUIRED.

Oh, sorry, I'm early. You can skip this bit.

No, really, I'll see you after the first chapter. Just turn the page.

Look, seriously, I just put my teacup on the SEND button. Please move on.

Oh dear, you're still here. The trouble is, you see, I'm writing this live. The longer you keep reading this bit, the longer I have to keep writing it. You're delaying the book for everyone.

Oh, and now you're all giggling. I knew releasing a book on psychic paper was a mistake. But this lot, they love a gimmick. Please just turn the page. Or, if you're listening to the audiobook version, fast forward. And those of you reading on one of those computer tablet things, please understand you are the only species in the universe who thinks they're a good idea.

Oh for heaven's sake. If you're going to loiter about, I suppose I might as well do some introductions. Apologies for any typos— as I have been trying to explain, this section of the book is being written live, and I am connecting with the page in front of you through a psychic time-space link, and of course maintaining so many cognitive-paper-interfaces across the multiple time zones required for thousands of individual readers can play havoc with your spelling. Also I just spilled lemon sherbet on my keyboard, and the R is a bit sticky. But we'll soldierrrr on, eh?

Sorry, but who's talking? Please, don't talk while I'm wrriting, it's tremendously rude.

Thank you!

Oh, someone just closed the book, and put it back on the shelf. I think they were in a bookshop. Well that's not very encouraging, when I'm just getting started. Never mind, we're better off without them. Oh, they're off to the Crime section now. Probably more their level, quite honestly.

Okay, the rest of you, eyes on page, we're all in this together. Please don't skip forwards or backwards, because I hate having to repeat myself. Especially in advance.

Now, the Doctor Papers, *which form the bulk of this book, will* <u>not</u> *be written live. These bits are only live because I got a tiny bit sloppy about the deadline. In fact, I regret to inform you, that I'm writing to you from ten years in the future. Yes, I know, very poor, but there's nothing like seeing your own book on sale to remind you to write it.*

We're going to start with Chapter Eight. Bit unusual, I realise, but this being the story of the end of the Time War, there really is no correct order in which to tell it, and the events on Karn are as good a place to start as any. Also I like the number 8. It's bobbly, like two jellies on top of each other.

This chapter is known as The Night of the Doctor. *It is a document from an unimpeachable source; written by one of the participants in that strange drama. The circumstances of its composition are complex and disputed, but the identity of its author should become clear in the reading. Indeed, this is your first challenge, students. Read with close attention. Our subject is authorship. Question 1 is: Who is speaking? See you afterwards for a full discussion of this, the first of the* Doctor Papers. *Or the eighth. Whatever.*

What follows is the true story of how the Time War ended. Though not necessarily in that order.

(By the way, these pages should be appearing as italics. If not, please just give three light taps on any verb, and the page will reboot. And if you don't like any aspects of my prose style, give the book a good shake. That should help you work off your irritation.)

Chapter 8

The Night of the Doctor

On the day I killed him, the Doctor was a happy man. Though since what made him happy was a distress call from a terrified woman who died less than seven minutes later, my conscience is clear.

At the time, he was in his eighth and final incarnation. My memory of his appearance is a little hazy, but I have a general impression of dark hair, urgent blue eyes, and a choice of clothing that was probably intended to be swashbuckling. I think there were long boots, possibly a waistcoat, and certainly one of those overcoats with the kind of collar that young men turn up against the wind in the hope that someone might use the word Byronic. He wasn't young, of course: no one can be called young on the day of their death, when they are as old as they will ever be. But the voice echoing round the creaking, wooden cathedral of the TARDIS console room was young enough, and more than adequately terrified.

'Hello, please, hello, can anyone hear me? This ship is crashing, please, is anyone there, can anyone hear me?'

It should be remembered, this was at the heart of the Time War, that endless savage conflict between the Daleks and the Time Lords that threatened every moment of the time continuum. It is strange to reflect that the deadliest conflict history will ever know began between a race of traumatised mutants sealed into tiny battle tanks, and an enclave of time-travelling academics, who had sworn never to interfere in the affairs of the wider universe. However, the day came when the Time Lords of Gallifrey decided that the Dalek mutants posed a threat to all reality, and so attempted to use their time-travel abilities to cancel them from existence. The attempt failed, and the Daleks used their own time-travel machines in a similar attempt to cancel out the Time Lords. And so time became a weapon in a war that could never end, and the conflict spread not only through space, but backwards and forwards through history. Days became battle lines, and century turned on century, and divergent time streams found themselves fighting each other for the right to exist. It was said, one soldier could die a thousand times in one day of that war, and discover he'd never been born the next. And so, when the Doctor heard that cry for help, there would have been countless billions across the universe suffering in exactly the same way. But this young woman had an advantage over all the others who, in that same moment, were also screaming and begging for their lives. She happened to be in earshot of a man who mistook himself for a hero.

The Doctor had always loved distress calls. They appealed to his vanity. He lived for the thrill of stepping through a door, and seeing all those faces turn towards him in hope and wonder. The danger, too, was delicious. More than delicious; over time it had become necessary. Danger is the only true palliative for a guilty man. And certainly the only drug strong enough for the Doctor.

Setting aside his tea, it took him seconds to track the signal to a little gunship, tumbling towards a red planet. There was one life sign on board, and all the engines were phasing. Clearly, there was no possibility of deflecting the ship's course, and a tractor beam would almost certainly shatter the hull, so a manual extraction was the only possibility. He would have to materialise on board, introduce himself as dramatically as possible, and get her into the TARDIS. She would be so happy and excited to see him. He wondered, briefly, how it would look if he took his teacup with him, but decided the risk of spillage was too great.

'Please, please, somebody, please!'

The fear in her voice would have broken any heart. The Doctor grinned. For the very last time, he slammed the levers, roared the engines, and sent the TARDIS spinning to the rescue. Although there was no one else to hear, he laughed and whooped. If anything sealed his fate, in that final hour of his existence, it was his laughter. I never wanted to hear that laugh again.

The owner of the voice was a young woman, called Cass Fermazzi. She was clever and brave and doomed. In later years, when I was able to return her remains to what was left of her family, I learned that she had grown up on one of the farm planets of the Gazrond Belt, and had stowed away on a star freighter at the age of fourteen to see the wonders of the universe and found there were no wonders left. Instead there was a war that threatened all reality. At first she ran, but one day, helping an old soldier die in a crater full of mud snakes under a burning moon, she realised there was nowhere left to hide. The following morning, the kindly medtech who closed the soldier's eyes unclipped the bandolier from around the dead man's chest and gave it to Cass, perhaps mistaking her for a friend or relative. Cass took the bandolier, tightened it around herself, and decided to start running in the opposite direction.

Three months later, she was crewing a gunship. Four years later, she had survived the Nightmare Child, wept at the massacre of Skull Moon and fought in the ruins of the Ulterium. On the last day of her life, she and her crew successfully repelled a Dalek fleet from the feeding hives of the Vantross, but then, as they flew to safety, found themselves under attack from one of the Time Lord battle cruisers, now as indiscriminate in their slaughter as the Daleks themselves. They were blasted from the stars for no better reason, Cass realised, than that they were blocking the view of the retreating Daleks.

She'd been the only one who didn't panic. She'd teleported the crew to the safety of the nearest planet and, with no one left to teleport her, and realising that a safe crash landing was now an impossibility, she'd finally asked for help.

'Help me, please. Can anybody hear me—help me!' She slammed the overheating console with both fists.

'Please state the nature of your ailment or injury,' said the medical computer.

'I'm not injured, I'm crashing! I don't need a doctor!' Cass screamed.

'A clear statement of your symptoms will help us provide the medical practitioner appropriate to your individual needs.' A simulated face appeared on the screen and made an attempt at an encouraging smile only marginally less comforting than the cratered surface of the planet now filling the viewplate.

'I'm trying to send a distress call, stop asking about doctors!'

It was a feed line that the hungriest ego in the universe could hardly be expected to resist.

'I'm a doctor,' came a voice behind her, 'but probably not the one you were expecting.'

Cass spun round and saw a man, who was making a particular point of leaning casually against the wall. A thousand questions lit up in her head, but he was already stepping forward to the console. 'Where are the rest of the crew?'

'Teleported off.'

'But you're still here?' His hands were now busy at the controls. Was he checking she was telling the truth?

'I teleported them.'

'Why you?'

'Everyone else was screaming.'

He looked at her, and smiled like she'd passed a test. 'Welcome aboard.'

'Aboard what?'

'I'll show you!' And suddenly he had taken her hand (when did she tell him that was okay?) and she was yanked out of the command chair.

8

The ship howled and creaked, and the main corridor was twisting and flexing, so it felt like running inside a thrashing snake. There was the harsh stink of molten metal and she could feel the heat of the floor thumping against her boots. Her sleep pod was ablaze and everything she'd ever owned was gone.

'Where are we going?' she managed to ask.

'Back of the ship!'

'Why?'

'Because the front end crashes first, think it through!'

A joke? Was he joking? Was this man wasting breath on jokes, right now? And where the hell did he come from anyway? And hang on, did that mean he had a way off the ship? She felt a dangerous surge of hope. And in that moment, with a stomp of iron, the rest of the corridor disappeared. A blast door had slammed across in front of them, blocking their path, and finally Cass Fermazzi knew she was going to die.

'Oh, why did you do that?' she heard him muttering. But he sounded only mildly irritated, like a man trying to reason with a fugitive bar of soap in a bath.

'Emergency protocols,' she found herself explaining, like it even mattered now.

There was a silver rod in his hand, and he buzzed it at the door. 'What's your name?' he asked.

Was he making conversation? Did he seriously think she was in the mood for a chat?

'Cass.' Oh, apparently she was.

'You're young to be crewing a gunship, Cass.'

No, she wasn't telling him her life story, this was not the time. 'I wanted to see the universe. Is it always like this?' Why was she *talking* to him?

'If you're lucky,' he grinned, and then the door was grinding open. Cass barely had time to wonder how he'd done it, before he'd grabbed her hand again, and they were stumbling to a halt in front of—

What the hell was that?

9

It looked like a tall blue crate, wooden, with panels and barred windows. Absurdly there were the printed words Police Public Call Box above a pair of doors, and was that really a light on top? And there was something else! Although Cass had never seen this box before, something stirred inside her like a race memory. Even a new-born knows to love the sunshine and fear the storm, and with that same ancient certainty, she knew what this battered old crate meant. To her, to everyone. It was purest evil.

He was pulling her towards it now. Instinctively, she pulled back.

'It's all right,' he was saying, reaching for the blue doors. 'It's bigger on the inside.'

And then she understood the fear she felt. 'What did you say? Bigger on the inside, is that what you said?'

'Yeah, come on, you'll love it.'

'Is that—' The word choked in her throat for a moment. Even on a crashing ship, moments from death, it was a word that felt too dangerous to speak out loud. 'Is that a TARDIS?'

Oh, the look on his face. A wounded infant. The memory of better days and lost magic. 'Yes,' he said, 'but you'll be perfectly safe, I promise.'

She wrenched her hand from his. 'Don't touch me!'

He started to reach for her again, but the look in her eyes stopped him cold. 'I'm not part of the war,' he said. 'I swear. I never have been.'

'You're a Time Lord.' He was, it was so obvious. The arrogance, the presumption.

'Yes, but I'm one of the nice ones!' Oh, and now he thought he could be charming. Could they never understand what they were?

'Get away from me!'

'Look on the bright side. I'm not a Dalek.'

She looked at him, and felt the universe shift ...

But no! This is too much. I am old, and perhaps I am getting carried away. Truthfully, no one can ever know for sure what was going through Cass's mind in that moment, but I do

10

think I can guess. For us all, there is a hill somewhere on which we would gladly die. If we are blessed, one day we will find it beneath our feet. That day had come for Cass.

'Dalek, Time Lord, who can tell the difference any more,' she said, and stepped backwards the through the door. She slammed her hand on the red button, and activated the incursion seal. Her ship, like all the others, had been proofed against Time Lords, and now was the time to see if it worked. She watched him through the plexi-panel, buzzing away with his silver rod. The door was shuddering, but it didn't open. 'Cass! *Cass!*'

'It's deadlocked. Don't even try!'

'Just open it. Please, I only want to help.'

To help? How could he think that anyone would believe that? 'Go back to your battlefield—you're not finished yet, some of the universe is still standing.' Oh, the joy of saying those words, of seeing them impact.

'I'm not leaving this ship without you!'

Those pleading blue eyes, that hunger to be trusted. More than that, to be worshipped, to be adored. Oh dear God, was she supposed to think he was a hero now? They were all the same, those vain, wilful children with their two hearts. But was he really going to stay, and burn with her? Well, if that's what he wanted! Cass Fermazzi smiled and felt the last moment of joy she would ever feel, as she said: 'Then you're going to die right here. Best news all day.'

The ship was grinding and shrieking round her. The heat and light grew fiercer, but now it was exciting.

'Cass!' he was shouting. 'Cass!'

Yeah, she thought, smiling into his silly, anguished face— say my name. Say my name, Time Lord, and die.

Which is exactly what the Doctor did, though not for the last time that day.

'And here he is at last,' someone was saying, 'The man to end it all!'

11

The Doctor tried to move, tried to open his eyes, but nothing happened. He didn't recognise the voice, but whoever it was, she had to be talking about him. It was always about him, when people talked that way.

'My sisters, the Doctor has returned to Karn.'

Yep, there you go, he was right. Him! He wondered if he should pop one eye open and make a joke, people loved that. Or even sit bolt upright with a big smile. But when he tried, still nothing happened.

No, wait, what did she say? Karn? That rang a bell. He decided he should probably make a note, but then remembered he didn't have a notebook. Or a pen. Or, in fact, the ability to move any part of his body. He decided to make a mental note instead, but promptly forgot what he was thinking about. Damn, why hadn't he made a note?

The voice again: 'This has been foretold. We have always known in our bones, one day he would return here!'

Ah, this was sounding very him. A long-awaited return! Probably a prophesied battle against an ancient foe, rising from some sort of terrible depths, he shouldn't wonder. All in a day's work for the Doctor. He decided to leap to his feet, swish his coat about a bit, and choose someone to make him tea. But the world stayed dark, and the rocks stayed cold against his back. Perhaps Cass could help him. He'd just saved her life, hadn't he? She'd probably be with him in a moment. One good turn deserved another.

Now a hand was stroking his face. It was a very warm hand. Or was it that his face was very cold? Oh, that was interesting. He couldn't remember why he was so cold.

The voice, close now, warm breath on his face: 'Such a pity he's dead.'

Oh! Dead, was he? That was going to make things a bit more diff—

Being dead, the Doctor was unaware of his final journey across that barren world, and only the crows of Karn saw him borne into the cave where he and I would stand face to face, at the very end.

Ow! Someone had slapped him, and there was a bitter aftertaste on his lips. He was somewhere else! Sitting on a stone floor! The wind was gone, so maybe he was inside. A cave, going by that dripping sound. There was movement around him; the smell of smoke and the crackle of burning torches. Now he heard a low murmur of female voices. Was one of them Cass? Of course! Cass must have dragged him to safety, after he'd rescued them both from that crashing ship. If only he could remember exactly how he'd done that. He decided to open his eyes as soon as he remembered how.

'Cass!' someone shouted. Good! Obviously she was here somewhere, and safe. 'Cass, Cass!' It was a man's voice, high with desperation, and so cracked and full of terror that it took him several seconds to recognise it as his own. The shock opened his eyes.

She was old, and robed in scarlet. Her face was creased and weathered, but her stare glittered, as she squatted in front of him like a wise old ape. In a line behind her, against the fire-lit rock, stood several more scarlet robed women, younger, but as pale and hollow-eyed as upright cadavers. Each held a steaming goblet.

'If you refer to your companion,' the old woman was saying, 'we are still trying to recover her body from the wreckage. You were thrown clear.'

Oh! The wreckage. Cass was still in there. He remembered Cass's face, and how she'd looked at him when she realised what he was. 'She wasn't my companion,' he said.

'She's almost certainly dead. No one could survive that crash.'

'I did!'

'No.'

13

That awful word, so calmly delivered. He fought to let nothing show on his face.

'We restored you to life,' the old woman continued, 'but it is a temporary measure. You have a little under four minutes.

It had always been a rule of the Doctor's never to panic early. If he still had four minutes to fill, it was time to start owning the room. 'Four minutes!' he protested. 'But that's ages! What if I get bored? I need a television, a couple of books, anyone for chess? Bring me knitting.'

'You have so little breath left. Spend it wisely.'

Watch me, he thought. Quick scan. Six women in the room, including the old one. Two exits! One was obviously the cave mouth, the other led deeper into the mountain. Wait, how did he know it was a mountain? Had he been here before? Ah! He'd heard a name earlier. She'd named this planet. And what about this cave? It did look a little familiar. Okay, time to parade his local knowledge, if he could just remember any of it.

'Hang on, is it you? It is, isn't it, it's you.' Of course, he'd got it now. 'Am I back on Karn?' he said, triumphantly. 'You're the Sisterhood of Karn, keepers of the flame of utter boredom!'

The old woman's eyes flashed. 'Eternal life,' she snapped.

'That's the one!' Going by the look on her face, he'd already landed a hit. Good! Time to give it a bit more swagger. He'd clambered to his feet, but as he started to move, he could feel his body shutting down, and the pain of it almost knocked him flat. Buck up, Doctor, he thought. It won't hurt for long.

'Mock us if you will.' said the old woman, 'Our elixir can trigger your regeneration, bring you back.'

Oh, interesting. Were they trying to help him? There had been stories, back on Gallifrey, that the Karn Sisterhood could assist a regeneration in a mortally wounded Time Lord—but why should they care about him? And anyway, did he want to go through it all again? To be torn down and rebuilt into someone else, just to see more of the universe burn. He remembered his old tutor, lecturing at the academy, telling them all about the change they dreaded so much. 'You will walk into a storm,' Borusa had said, 'and a stranger will walk back out. And that stranger will be you.' A stranger to himself, yet again. Why? What was the point any more?

The old woman was gesturing to the goblets held by the others. 'Time Lord science is elevated here. On Karn, the change doesn't have to be random.' She moved among the sisters, pointing to one goblet, then another. 'Fat or thin? Old or young?'

He almost laughed. He was standing in the salesroom of his possible futures!

'Man or woman?' she asked him, pointedly.

Ginger? he wondered, but kept the thought to himself.

Ohila was looking at him, expectant now. He wondered briefly how he suddenly knew her name and realised he'd translated the tiny inscription on her left earring. Good to know some of his skillset was still on-line.

'Why would you do this for me?' he asked.

'You have helped us in the past.'

Had he? A memory surfaced of being tied to a stake in the centre of this chamber, while wood was stacked around him and torches were lit. 'One good burn deserves another?' he decided not to say, then realised he already had. 'The Sisterhood of Karn were never big on gratitude.'

'The war between the Daleks and the Time Lords threatens all reality. You are the only hope left.'

Oh, of course. They were afraid. But why did everyone always expect him to be a soldier?

'It's not my war,' he said. 'I will have no part of it.'

'You can't ignore it forever.'

Ignore it? he thought. No one in the universe could exactly ignore a war that was taking place at every moment in history at once. 'I help where I can. I will not fight.'

'Because you are above such squalid practicalities as the business of warfare?'

Yes, he thought. 'Yes,' he said.

'Because you are the Good Man, as you call yourself?'

'I call myself the Doctor.'

'It's the same thing in your mind.'

'I'd like to think so.'

There was movement behind him, and her eyes flicked to a point over his shoulder. A new look came over her face. Was that cunning, he wondered. Or just cruelty?

'In that case, Doctor,' she said, 'attend your patient.'

Two more of the Sisterhood had entered the cave, and between them they carried what looked like a sack. But then they laid her on the altar stone in the centre of the room, and for a moment he could find no words. She looked so small. Around her chest he noticed a bandolier. It was clearly too old to have been hers originally, and he wondered briefly who had given it to her. Someone she cared about, or who had cared about her. The thought stung him.

He used the screwdriver to scan her for life signs, but he already knew it was pointless.

'You're wasting your time,' Ohila was saying. 'She is beyond even our help.'

I know, he wanted to scream into her face. Instead he just said, 'She wanted to see the universe,' because it was true and it made him ache.

'She didn't miss much. It's very nearly over.'

'I could've saved her. I could have got her off that ship, she wouldn't listen.'

'Then she was wiser than you. She understood there was no escaping the Time War. You are part of this, Doctor—whether you like it or not.'

'I would rather die,' he said, and meant it with both his hearts. *Not a soldier*, he thought. That was the promise. Never cruel, never cowardly, and never, ever a soldier. He knew what was inside him: the anger that could never be given voice. Death first.

'You're dead already,' said Ohila. 'How many more will you let join you?'

He forced his eyes to Cass's face. No accusation there now. No hatred, no fear, nothing. Just another broken child. Just another one, Doctor!

'If she could speak, what would she say?'

'To me? Nothing. I'm a Time Lord. Everything she despised.'

'If she understood the man you are, and the power you could wield, she would beg your help. As we beg your help now. The universe stands on the brink. Will you let it fall?'

There was no scorn in her voice. No cruelty, no cunning. Simple appeal.

How many more, he wondered. How many more children crushed and burnt as he stood apart? He must never be a soldier, he knew that. But it was like a whisper in his ear now. 'How many more will die, Doctor? While you keep your soul pure and your hands clean?' He felt himself gripping on to the stone table, trying to shut out that terrible, forbidden voice.

'What will it take, Doctor?' the whisper continued. 'How many more will suffer and die before you act?' it begged of him.

Ohila was moving among the goblets again. 'Strong or fast,' she was asking. 'Wise or angry? What do you *need* now?'

Blood and rage thundered in the Doctor's ears. To his own surprise, he noticed he was unclipping the bandolier from around Cass's still form. Was he doing that? It didn't feel like him. He was now holding the bandolier in front of his own eyes, as if for his inspection. It was cleaner than the rest of her clothes, and had been repaired many times. Obviously it had been of great value to her and she had worn it to the end. Someone, somewhere would have been happy to know that.

'Warrior,' he heard himself say.

Ohila was staring at him. 'Warrior?'

'I don't suppose anyone needs a doctor any more. Make me a warrior now.' It was his voice, but how could those be his words? It felt like someone else was talking through him.

Ohila was passing him a goblet. 'I took the liberty of preparing this one myself.'

It was warm in his hands, and the smell was bitter one moment and sweet the next. 'Get out!' he said. 'All of you!'

He heard the shuffle of feet. The sisters were moving deeper into the shadows.

'Will it hurt?' he asked.

Ohila's voice seem to come to him from a great distance. 'Yes,' she said.

'Good,' he replied, and raised the goblet. He was alone now, but in that last moment, chose to remember all the times he hadn't been. All the friends who had kept him safe. 'Charley. C'rizz, Lucie, Tamsin, Molly. Fitz. Friends and companions I have known, I salute you.' He looked to the broken child on the altar stone. 'And Cass … I apologise.'

The goblet was almost at his lips now. One last farewell to the man he had been. 'Physician, heal thyself.'

The Doctor drank the poison, and walked into the storm.

The stranger woke. His hands looked different, but he knew that would be the least of it. As he pulled himself to his feet, every nerve and sinew jangled: wrong, wrong, everything all wrong. No, not wrong, he reminded himself. New. Just new. He remembered to breathe, and even that felt strange. He tried to focus on the chamber around him. Oh, the colour balance was wildly different yet again. The reds were a bit greener and the yellows were out of control. He knew he'd get used to it, but it always took a while. Sometimes he missed the monochrome world of his first two incarnations. It had felt like a simpler, cleaner time; so many centuries had passed before he realised he'd just been colour blind. He looked round, testing his focal length, and saw a beautiful woman looking at him.

'Is it done?' asked Ohila.

Is it? he wondered. Is *what* done? Then he saw Cass, dead on the stone, and the sight of her hurt him all over again.

Good, he still had a conscience. But something new flexed under that familiar pain, like the flick of a serpent's eye in the darkness. What was that new feeling? Rage? Vengeance? Was that something to worry about? He ran a hand over his face. Wrong, wrong, wrong!

No, not wrong, new. A new face, for a new man.

There were no mirrors in the cave, but hanging on one of the smoother rock walls, was a highly burnished section of armour plate, some ancient relic of battle. It would do.

The first thing he noticed was that he was now wearing Cass's bandolier round his own chest. When had he put that on? Then he glanced up and met his own eyes.

There is a moment, after regeneration, when the guttering soul of the old man looks out through the eyes of the new. So it was the Doctor who looked into the mirror—but it was me who looked back. And there we stood, the Doctor and I; one man, face to face; an end and a beginning.

My height hadn't changed much, I noticed. My hair was a little shorter, though still dark. Those urgent blue eyes were gone and in their place, a stare like winter. For a moment that stare troubled me. But this was a time of war, and I had been reborn for battle; I was ready to look on a darker world.

I turned my new face one way, then the other. Was I younger? Older? There was something haggard and pained about me now, so it was difficult to tell. Standing before me was a man who had seen horror and no longer chose to hide it. Yes, I thought, this would do. This was right.

I held my own gaze, and spoke. The words came in a cold whisper; a silken rasp; voice like a shiver out loud.

'Doctor no more,' I said.

FEED CONNECTING
FEED CONNECTED
FEED STABLE
PLEASE HOLD THE BOOK STRAIGHT AND TURN OFF YOUR MOBILE PHONE.

Many years later, in circumstances too scandalous to relate, I asked Ohila what had been in the goblet.

'Lemonade and dry ice,' she admitted, as I lit her cigar. 'Or something like that, I was in a hurry and it needed to look dramatic.'

'But the Doctor did become a warrior.'

'The Idiot Child was a warrior his entire life. The universe needed him to be a little more honest on the subject, so I provided a moment of theatre that facilitated his change of hearts.'

'Did he ever suspect you had tricked him?'

'He knew that darkness was always inside him. Allowing him to pretend it came from elsewhere was a mercy of sorts. From that moment on he had quite enough to worry about and I didn't want to add self-loathing to his many burdens.'

'You were being kind.'

'Just practical. The Doctor has been so many different people, self-loathing could take all day.'

'Did you know what was coming?'

'Of course. Of course we did, the Sisterhood always knows. But there was no one else. Simply no one else could do what that man could. He was so special, in so many ways, the Idiot Child.'

Ah, Ohila, always such a beautiful woman, and a thrilling and innovative darts player. She's a little too inclined to lecture me on my sexual politics, but for all that, she makes a lovely cuppa.

Now most of you, as keen students of the Doctor, will also know what was ahead of him at that point in his life. The Warrior formerly known as the Doctor (or the Doctor of War, as people insisted on calling him, despite his protests) went on to wage the bloodiest campaign in the history of the known and unknown and partly known universe. It was said he felt every blow he inflicted, and grieved for every life he took, but that none of this pain ever stopped him or slowed him or diverted him from his purpose. He had become a warrior to end war, and he fought more fiercely in that cause than any soldier known before or since. The wrath of the Doctor of War was the last wonder witnessed by the many billions who stood against him. He took command at the slaughter of Skull Moon; he battled at the fall of Arcadia; he fought to prevent the rise of the Nightmare Child; he witnessed the seven deaths of Davros and he led the final charge up the slopes of the Never Vault.

And as the centuries passed, and he grew old, he realised it was all for nothing. So long as there were Daleks and Time Lords alive in this universe, this war would never end. And now that his own people had become as vengeful as their sworn enemies, he began to see there was only one solution. As is known, he broke into the Time Lord vaults and stole the Moment, a powerful weapon from the ancient times of Gallifrey, and used it to wipe out every last Dalek and every last Time Lord. A single moment of dreadful slaughter, and suddenly there was peace everywhere in the universe—except, of course, in the hearts of that lone traveller who once again called himself the Doctor. He had not expected to survive, and so lived on in the firm belief that his continued existence was punishment, and that his purpose was repentance.

Let it be said, that repentance was sincere. He travelled the galaxies, and brought peace and hope and kindness everywhere his TARDIS landed. In time the peoples of the universe forgot the war, and no one spoke or heard a word of it anywhere—except those brave souls who looked into the eyes of the last of the Time Lords and asked him what was wrong.

This much you all know. But there is so much more. We come now to the second of the Doctor Papers, which can only be described as Chapter Eleven. Yes, I know, but as I have explained, there is no correct sequence in which to tell this story. Timey-wimey, as an idiot once wrote. Before we begin, I wonder how many of you realised that the last document was written by the Doctor himself, even before that fact was made evident? Show of hands, please. No, go ahead, put your hands up. Doesn't matter where you are, I can see you. Oh dear, what a lot of books suddenly got snapped shut. Look, it's hardly my fault if that's where you choose to sit and read.

By the way, all of you reading this at work, you should be ashamed of yourselves. Yes, you. And you. Holding it under the desk doesn't fool anyone, you know. And for heaven's sake, put it down, Chris, you've got far too much to do.

Right then, counting now …

Oh, lots of you figured it out. Well done, many people don't get that. It's an interesting peculiarity of the Doctor's prose style that he almost always refers to himself in the third person. He rarely says 'I', he tends to use 'he'. It's almost never 'me', it's 'the Doctor'.

There are many theories about this. My personal favourite, is that 'the Doctor'—the title he chose, rather than the name he was born with—is more of an idea in his head, than a statement of his identity. The Doctor is the man he aspires to be, not the man he believes he is. What, then, are we to make of his occasional lapses, because there are many times—some purposeful, some seemingly accidental—when 'the Doctor' becomes 'me'. Are these moments, perhaps, of personal weakness or even fear, when he has failed to live up to the standards he long ago set himself?

23

Also, you will notice, he is happy to invent interior monologues for other people, which betrays the arrogance so characteristic of him. In fairness he is blessed with exceptional levels of empathy, and even low-level telepathy, so we should not assume they are entirely fictional.

With all that in mind, I invite you now to identify the author of this next document: The Flight of the Doctor. *Authorship will remain our subject throughout this volume—please don't assume it will always be a simple matter. Pay close attention.*

We shall be rejoining the Doctor many centuries after the end of the Time War, when the memory of it has started to fade, even for him. At this phase of his life he is a happy man, a hero to many, and one who has all but forgotten his dangerous past. He would, perhaps, have been wise to remember that for a time traveller, the past is never truly over.

Chapter 11

The Flight of the Doctor

The Doctor was young—which, he reflected, was a rare pleasure at his time of life. That morning in the TARDIS, over tea and jammy dodgers, he found himself remembering his first proper inspection of the face he was wearing now. It had been a busy day already, he was explaining to Clara, who was listening as rapt as always. He'd just had another massive falling out with the Master, who typically had gone and turned everyone in the world into a copy of himself ('Yes, even you, Clara, shame I missed that'), cleverly saved an old friend from dying of radiation poisoning, started dying of radiation poisoning, said goodbye to all his best friends because he was dying of radiation poisoning, died of radiation poisoning, regenerated, made a mental note to apologise to all his best friends for possibly overstating the situation with the radiation poisoning, destroyed a garden shed which had stupidly collided with his TARDIS during a largely successful emergency landing, met a new friend with orange hair, invented fish custard, had a stern word with some giant flying eyeballs who were mucking about on Earth for no good reason, and put an end to the mysterious plans of Prisoner Zero (plans so mysterious, in fact, that no one ever found out what they were) before finding time to dash back to the TARDIS and spending seven and a half frustrating hours looking for a mirror.

He found one in the three-fingered hand of a mostly dormant robot clown that stood abandoned and ticking in one of the thickly ivied alcoves of the stone deck.

He sat on the stump of a fallen pillar, and there, among the jagged tumble of ivy-throttled masonry, braced himself for the new him. Cheekbones, he thought, staring at his new face. Thin! Ooh, sharp corners! In fact the planes of his face now seemed so steeply angled that he wondered how they joined up at the back. He popped the mirror behind his head to check, then realised he couldn't see his reflection any more. He quickly turned to have a look, but unfortunately so did his reflection.

'Ah,' he thought, with a big smile, 'I'm an idiot this time!' That was good, he'd always liked being an idiot. He decided to give a delighted little clap, missed with both hands, and accidentally hugged himself. 'Possibly a little clumsy,' he noted, picking up the largest shard of the broken mirror, which had somehow gone flying across the room during his attempted clap.

There was a lot of hair now, he noticed. Not ginger, sadly—dark brown. Oh, and thick. He made himself a little dizzy spinning round as he tried to focus on a giant quiff, which was now swaying across his brow. When he checked his reflection again, he noticed the ticking clown passing behind him, as it shambled off into the cloisters. Probably ought to do something about that some day, he thought. He was just on the point of deciding he might be a bit too handsome for comfort, when he turned his face to the side, and saw the chin that adorned the lower half of his face like a diving board. 'Banana-head!' he laughed. 'Face like a boot! I'm Mr Moon!'

Oh, that would do nicely, he decided. Very him, very Doctor. Bit handsome, bit silly, bit like a banana. He did a quick series of calculations in the dust on the floor, and realised this was his eleventh face.

'*No, it isn't,*' breathed a voice in his ear. His hand froze in the dust. Suddenly his hearts seemed very loud in the silence of the cloisters.

'*Would you deny me?*' whispered the voice.

The Doctor took a deep, careful breath, and fought the voice away. Regeneration angst, that was all. 'Eleventh,' he said, aloud and firmly. And eleven, by a lovely coincidence, just happened to be his new favourite number. As he straightened up, he considered another delighted clap, but decided he needed a bit more practice with the arms first.

In truth, over the years, he'd never really got his arms under control, growing convinced that his speech centres had somehow been wired to his hands. He now seemed unable to speak a word without both hands fluttering around him, like two birds trying to escape from a net. He was fairly sure the left one was attempting lip-sync. Sometimes he got so distracted by his own gesticulation that he fell silent, and his hands just froze in the air. This quirk of accidentally surrendering had proven to be a tactical disadvantage on more than one occasion. Why couldn't his hands just stick to straightening his bow tie, like he wanted them to?

Clara was laughing silently. He glanced over at her, and noticed for the first time that she wasn't there. Oh, he'd done it again. He was always chatting away to people without checking if they were there first. He looked sadly at the two cups of tea he'd poured, and remembered that she was at that silly job she insisted on having, even though there was a whole universe of wonders waiting to be explored, and steam engines. He made an attempt at being cross, but ended up sighing. Much as he liked talking to himself, it was more fun with an audience.

And so it was, on the morning of the day that would change every aspect of his life forever, the Doctor, formerly known as the Warrior, also known as the last of the Time Lords, who thought bow ties were cool and that purple tweed was simply the ultimate, decided he was bored.

Moments later, in a field on the outskirts of London, a lone cow looked round in surprise, as a tall blue box appeared out of nowhere. The Doctor popped his head out, and reached for the phone inside the little cupboard on the door. He'd decided, one slow evening, that, since his space-time machine was stuck looking like a phone box, he might as well get the phone working.

'Hello, I'm a perfectly normal bloke, and I wondered if Clara Oswald was coming out to play.'

Mr Armitage, the headmaster of Coal Hill school, rolled his eyes, audibly. 'No, you're the Doctor, and you're an alien from space.'

'Ooh, bit racist. So much for diversity at Coal Hill.'

'She can come out when the school closes.'

'That's not for another 73 years,' he protested. 'Oh, that was a fire.'

'I was referring to today, in fact. There's a staff meeting, she should be free about 5.15. Fire? What do you mean, fire?'

'5.15?? Still ages.'

'You have a time machine!'

'How did you know that?'

'The Governor of this school is an old friend of yours.'

'Is he busy?'

'He and Barbara are leaving on their fourth honeymoon right about now!'

'Tell them to wait, I'm coming along.'

'*No more!*' breathed Mr Armitage.

'No more what?' asked the Doctor.

'I'm sorry?' said Mr Armitage blankly, then added, '*Too long I have stayed my hand, no more!*'

'What are you on about, staying your hand??'

'I didn't say anything about my hand,' sighed Mr Armitage. 'I was saying, if you tell me where you are, I will pass the address on to Miss Oswald, who, I'm sure, will be able to join you later *today you leave me no choice, today this war will end, no more, no more.*'

The Doctor gripped the console to steady it, although it wasn't the console that was shaking. That hadn't been Mr Armitage's voice, not at the end. He knew that voice.

'Doctor?' Mr Armitage was asking.

'*Doctor no more,*' whispered something long dead.

Why now? Why was he hearing that voice now? It was all over and done with, and forgotten, and never to be thought about again. He closed his eyes fiercely, and pictured all his secret days locked away in an old oak chest at the bottom of a deep green sea. It had always worked before, when his past rose up to claim him—but this time the chains round the chest were rusted and broken, and the lid was starting to rise. He snapped his eyes open in fright, and noticed that the console was shaking worse than ever.

'Doctor, are you still there?'

Oh, Mr Armitage! He quickly gave his best guess as to his current address ('There's a field, a road and a cow!') and hung up.

No, he thought, pacing the TARDIS, his feet landing in angry clangs on the floor of the brooding steel chamber. No, no, no! Some things were over and stayed over, and that was it, thank you very much. He grabbed his most boring book, sat on his second favourite staircase, and started to read, angrily. It was a book of complex temporal theory, and he'd already lost several days trying to find Wally. He was starting to think that Wally wasn't actually in every book, but how could anyone be truly sure?

'*You hide yourself in whimsy,*' said the whisper in his ear.

He focused on the boring words, and pretended there was nothing to hear. Those days were gone, that darkness had been spent. Of course he knew that wasn't strictly true. The trouble with living in a space/time ship was that however fast you flew, the past never got any further away; it was always waiting just outside the door. And sometimes, as now, the door knocked.

But no, he thought. He was going to sit here, and read his book, and wait for Clara, and when she arrived they'd fly off and have an adventure, probably with cocktails along the way. The past was the past, the Doctor decided, and in no way, shape or form, did it hold any terrors for me.

Clara Oswald arrived in the TARDIS in a roar and a high wind, swerved the console, and screeched to a halt. He heard her feet clattering on the floor as she dismounted. The Doctor, his eyes still on his book, realised she had probably come on her motorbike. Showing off as usual, he thought, and in retaliation he kept his back to her, and turned a page.

'Draught!' he said, and heard her snap her fingers. The TARDIS doors slammed themselves shut. He'd begun teaching her that trick ages ago, in the confident expectation it would take years to master it, but she'd got the hang of it almost immediately, and could even do it in gloves, which had always eluded him.

'A field and a cow?' said a voice with a Blackpool accent. 'Lucky you put a tracker in this thing.'

'Fancy a trip to ancient Mesopotamia,' he asked, 'followed by Future Mars?'

He looked round. And there she was, taking her helmet off in a swirl of hair, while her motorbike purred into silence behind her. She was giving him one of those looks that made him grateful that big brown eyes and the cheekiest smile in the universe could never have any kind of an effect on a Time Lord such as myself.

'Will there be cocktails?' she asked.

'On the Moon.'

'The Moon will—'

The motorbike narrowly missed her face as it bounced upright and went sideways into a bookcase, the stairs the Doctor was sitting on arced over his head, and the central console was suddenly spinning far above them both as they tumbled round the walls of the control room like socks in a washing machine.

Deep beneath the Tower of London, in an unnumbered room, which appears on no maps or schematics of any kind and is never referred to in any documentation, among a labyrinth of shelves and alcoves and barred doors and sealed chambers, there is a small blue safe, with the word TARDIS on the front. Inside, there are a number of sealed envelopes, one of which shows evidence of having been recently been steamed open and re-closed. The document contained inside is several typed pages and concerns the protocols surrounding 'TARDIS discovery'. It notes that the TARDIS is the most powerful and dangerous piece of alien technology to regularly visit the planet, and warns of the dire consequences if it were to fall into the wrong hands. It goes on to say that the Doctor is in the habit of parking it in random places, and while entry to the machine is all but impossible, the danger of anyone achieving it is too great to be ignored. On a sighting of the TARDIS (various photographs of the police box are appended) by any UNIT personnel, the location must be phoned to Central Command who will immediately dispatch a helicopter to airlift the TARDIS to the nearest secure premises. The Doctor will then be informed of its new location, which doesn't usually create a problem, as he rarely remembers where he left it.

Underneath the typescript, in jagged handwriting suggestive of anger, is a note from the Doctor, which reads:

Could you please, please, PLEASE check if I'm still inside it first???

'Would it kill you to knock?' bellowed the Doctor. The wind was shrieking, the helicopter was thundering and the world was upside down. He was hanging headlong out of the flapping TARDIS doors, phone at his ear, with Clara

31

holding on to his ankles, and the London Thames swaying majestically below him.

He'd guessed what had happened the moment the TARDIS had been lifted off the ground, and he'd dashed straight for the phone when it started to ring. As he threw himself out of the door hundreds of feet above London, he'd reflected, not for the first time, that wiring your principal communications device to the outside of your spaceship was not always practical. He managed to grab the phone, and Clara his ankles.

'I'm so sorry,' said Kate Lethbridge-Stewart, the head of the Unified Intelligence Taskforce. 'We had no idea you were still in there!'

'You phoned me!' screamed the Doctor, hoping Clara would manage to keep hold.

'You've listed this number as your mobile.'

'It's the TARDIS—how much more mobile do you get?'

'He's still in the TARDIS,' he heard her say to someone else. 'Tell the helicopter pilot to take him straight to the site, we'll meet him there.'

'Site, what site?'

'Doctor, I'm sorry, but you are needed.'

'Needed? What do you mean, needed?'

'By Royal command.'

Royal *what??* he was going to ask, but the wind whipped the receiver out of his hand. It whirled in a circle on its cable and cracked him on the back of the head.

When his vision cleared, a pair of blank stone eyes were glowering at him from underneath a giant stone hat and a pigeon was cocking its head at him. Nelson had seen better days, he thought, fuzzily. As the statue drifted upwards past him, followed by the weathered old column on which it stood, he realised he was being lowered, head first, into a cordoned-off section of Trafalgar Square, and that far below him a division of UNIT troops was even now slamming to attention and saluting him.

Dazed, upside down and rotating gently as he descended, the unpaid, unofficial scientific adviser to UNIT attempted to recover some dignity by returning the salute, and hit himself in the face.

Twenty feet below him, Kate Lethbridge-Stewart suppressed a sigh. She knew the men and women around her were getting their first glimpse of a UNIT legend, so kept her face straight. Next to her, Osgood was barely containing her excitement—she was all big round eyes behind big round spectacles, and now and then she even remembered to breathe. 'Inhaler,' Kate said, and Osgood took a puff, without taking her eyes from above. You wait, thought Kate, he's not what you're expecting.

'He's an idiot,' Kate's father had explained, long ago. They were in the UNIT Research Institute and at the far end of a sprawling laboratory, a tall man with a mass of curly hair and a booming voice was protesting that he was caught in some kind of force field, while a dark-haired young woman patiently disentangled his scarf from a pair of double doors. Kate found herself staring at the scarf. It was stupidly long and multi-coloured. Who would wear a scarf like that? Although she was only seven, she had already guessed that this was the scary, funny man who worked with her father, and who sometimes kept the whole world safe.

'The Doctor?'

'Yes, the Doctor,' said her father, who always seemed a bit cross when he talked about his old friend. His moustache was twitching as if separately irritated.

'I thought you said he was a genius?'

'He is, of course he is. The most extraordinary genius anyone has ever met.'

The Doctor was booming away again. 'Yes, Sarah, yes,' he was saying, 'but there might have been a force field *as well*!'

'Then he's not a genius all the time?' asked Kate.

'No, it's all the time,' said her father, with funereal regret.

'So when is he an idiot?'

'All the time.'

'That doesn't really make any sense,' said Kate, after a moment's consideration.

'Yes, that's about the size of it,' he replied. The Doctor was striding towards them now, and as always her father straightened his shoulders and put some effort into a smile. Many years later, Kate found herself doing the same.

'Doctor,' she said. 'May I extend the official apologies of UNIT.'

'Kate Lethbridge-Stewart, a word to the wise!' said a very different version of the same man, who was now scrambling to his feet. 'As I'm sure your father would have told you,' he continued, 'I don't like being picked up.'

'That probably sounded better in his head,' said a pretty young woman, appearing next to him. She'd just emerged from the TARDIS, which had now come to rest in the square. Ah, yes, Kate thought, Clara Oswald, the schoolteacher. Where does he find them all?

'I was acting on orders direct from the throne,' said Kate and nodded to Osgood—who, she noticed in sudden horror, was wearing a stupidly long, multi-coloured scarf. Dear God, this was no time to be fangirling.

Osgood had passed the thick, ancient envelope to the Doctor, who was now inspecting the wax seal with what looked like alarm. Kate frowned: alarm, she thought, or could that that be guilt? Out loud she said: 'Sealed orders from Her Majesty Queen Elizabeth the First.'

'The Queen?' asked Clara, whose eyes had somehow got even wider. 'The *First*? Sorry, Queen Elizabeth the *First*??'

'Queen Elizabeth the *only*,' snapped the Doctor, who suddenly didn't look like a buffoon any more. 'She didn't like being numbered, and I sympathise entirely.' He looked dubiously at the envelope, as if he didn't want to open it, didn't

34

even want to hold it. So much for his famous curiosity. 'How do we know this is genuine?'

'Her credentials are inside,' she replied.

With visible reluctance, the Doctor started to break the seal but Kate laid a hand on his arm. 'No,' she said. 'Inside.' And she gestured to the huge ornate building behind her.

'Inside the National Gallery?' asked Clara. 'What kind of credentials do you keep in a gallery?'

'Nice scarf,' said the Doctor to Osgood, and left her fumbling for her inhaler as he strode toward the steps. Clara was already running to catch up.

Kate watched them go, and kept the frown off her face. The change of mood was quite striking. 'Sometimes you get the clown,' her father had said, in his final illness, 'sometimes you get the ancient beast.' Then he'd started to laugh which had set him off coughing again, and she'd had to sit him up and get him some water. When he'd recovered, he corrected himself. 'Actually, I think you always get both.' And he'd given her that smile which had always comforted her as a child, but now just made him look frail and old. They'd sat in silence with only the clock ticking and the rain at the windows.

'God, I miss that man,' he had said at last.

'Maybe he'll visit tomorrow,' she had said, her hand tight on his.

'Maybe tomorrow,' he had smiled, closing his eyes.

She could never decide, over the years, if those were the best or the saddest last words.

The Doctor and Clara were striding in step through the evacuated gallery, when Kate caught up with them.

'Did you know her? Elizabeth the First?' Clara was asking.

'Unified Intelligence Taskforce,' the Doctor replied.

'I'm sorry?'

35

'This lot,' he said, waving a hand at the various soldiers standing guard around the building. 'UNIT. They investigate alien stuff, anything alien.'

'What, like you?'

'I work for them.'

'You have a job?'

'Why shouldn't I have a job? People have jobs. I'd be brilliant at having a job.'

'You never have a job.'

'Yes, I do. This is it. This is my job.'

'What kind of job could you have?'

'This one. This one I'm doing right now, in front of you.' The Doctor threw an eye-roll over his shoulder at Kate.

It took an effort, but Kate managed not to slap him. Had he really never mentioned any of it? Clara was obviously, at the very least, his friend. Had he never told her he'd spent years, trapped on Earth, in her father's protection, working with him? They'd stood guard on a world together, they'd been friends. Best friends, she'd thought. She fought down the memory of the dying old soldier in the hospice. Maybe tomorrow.

I'm sorry, said a voice in her head, and it almost froze her. She'd been briefed about the Doctor's occasional telepathy: low level, they'd said, and rarely used. *I miss him too.*

Not now, she thought back at him, we've got work to do. She felt her cheeks flush and her jaw tighten: he should have the damn decency to stay out her head!

As you wish, said the Doctor, and stepped politely away. But as I returned to my own thoughts, I took an image of Kate's dying father with me, and filed it for later: Alistair waiting for me. 'One should live with one's sins,' I'd told a young man once, though I couldn't remember who or why. Clara was glancing at me, so I kept striding and smiling, as she expected. Clown and ancient beast—was that really what Alistair had thought? Was that what Clara thought too? I resisted having a look inside her head. In front of us, a pair of doors were being opened, and I forced my mind back to the present. Work to do! I squared my shoulders, straightened my bow tie, and the Doctor stepped through the doors.

At the far end of a long, darkened room, two soldiers were standing on guard, either side of a large painting mounted on an easel. The painting itself was draped in cloth, like it was something forbidden. Or maybe they were just keeping the dust off—why did he always think it had to be something sinister? He resisted the part of his mind that was now listing all the reasons in chronological order.

Kate had stepped ahead of him now, and given a nod to the soldiers. The drape was pulled back and an oil painting lit up the room like a fireplace.

A shattered city below a black and orange sky; plunging battleships suspended over a burning skyline; an intricate lattice of stabbing energy beams; running people, frozen in their screams.

The Doctor could feel the double slamming inside his chest. He wondered if everyone could hear his hearts.

Kate's voice now, from so far away. 'Elizabeth's credentials,' she was saying. 'She left an account of where to find this painting, and its significance to you.'

The Doctor couldn't find his voice. His eyes were locked on the painting. He felt himself taking Clara's hand, although it wasn't Clara who was afraid.

'This isn't why you were called here today. This is just proof that the message in your hand is from Elizabeth herself. Obviously, over this amount of time, forgery is a possibility.'

He tried to make sense of her words over the roar of the painting, but surely no one could. Surely everyone could hear those screams? And then, from deep inside him, from another place and another life, he found himself saying: 'No more.'

'That's the title!' said Kate, evidently surprised.

'I know the title,' snapped the Doctor, and reached for Clara's hand, before remembering he was already holding it. She was shaking, but dimly he realised it might not be her.

'Also known as—'

Don't say it, don't say it, *don't say it!*

'—*Gallifrey Falls*,' finished Kate.

The Doctor didn't reply for a moment. He noticed Clara's grip was very tight, then worried he might be hurting her and released her hand. He willed himself to speak. 'It's the fall of Arcadia,' he said. 'Gallifrey's second city.' Say it, say it, *just say it.* 'The last day of the Time War.'

The last day. The floor tremored at his feet. Were there shockwaves coming out of the painting?

The last day. He was back on Karn, so many faces ago, and he was drinking the poison, ready to walk into the storm.

The last day. The desert was hot beneath his boots, and a tiny barn shimmered on the horizon.

The last day. Elizabeth of England tilted back her face to be kissed, but it wasn't really her.

The last day. He was trapped in a cell with two old men who hated him, but the shadows hid their faces.

The last day. He was standing in a gallery, and Clara was asking him if he was okay.

The last day of the Time War. That was wrong, he suddenly realised. Because somehow all those different days, spread across his life, were also the last day. Somehow the last day had become millions of days, each of them, impossibly, the last. *No such thing as last*, something screamed in his mind, laughing at him.

And understanding arrived, like sickness: a truth he had been running from for centuries. A long time ago, he had taken a decision to become a warrior, and many years later he'd thought he could walk away from it. How stupid. Of course not! He'd drunk the poison, and walked into the storm, and never found his way out. He had forsaken his name, gone

38

to war, and in one terrible moment of unparalleled savagery, slaughtered them all, Time Lords and Daleks alike. Everyone had screamed, and then everything had stopped.

The murderer who stood alone and alive, in that awful silence, told himself what he'd done was justified; that peace was worth any price; that the war, at last, was over.

He was wrong of course. The Time War wasn't over. Not for me.

FEED CONNECTING
FEED CONNECTED
FEED STABLE
PLEASE KEEP THE PSYCHIC PAPER OUT OF DIRECT SUNLIGHT AT ALL TIMES TO AVOID FATALITY.

Whatever these modern authors might say on the subject, there comes a point in every story when it has to begin. So, at last, we proceed to Chapter One, The War of the Doctor. If the last day of the Time War is ever to be understood, then what follows is the first step on that journey. Or in the case of this book, the third. That's the thing about writing live, it's already too late when you realise you have contradicted yourself. Anyway, authorship is again central to our studies—so you might want to take the gum out of your mouth. It's hard enough writing all this, without you squelching away. Yes, you. Spit it out please, now, you're holding up the book up for everyone.

Right, good, thank you!

Now authorship. The last chapter was—as I'm sure you realised—written by the Doctor himself. If I may be candid now, almost all the Doctor Papers *are written by the Doctor himself, at least where we can be certain of authorship. Chapter Nine, The Truth of the Doctor, is the only one where the provenance is uncertain (for reasons that will be evident when we get to it) but still the majority of scholars remain convinced it is again from the Doctor's hand.*

Ah! I sense some of you keen to skip ahead to Chapter Nine. Please do not, it complicates the live stream no end. Additionally, it is the most dangerous chapter in this book (it's not even listed on the contents page for that reason) and a proper briefing before reading will be required—

Oh, stop it, come back here. No, not you lot. I mean, you lot. Reading this book out of sequence is highly ill-advised—it's ALREADY out of sequence. Oh, if you insist. But if you do read it now (don't, spoilers, enormous) come straight back here and rejoin us at the top of the next paragraph.

Right then! Here we all are. Chapter One is ready to roll. And I can now reveal to you, at last, that this chapter, unlike the previous one, is not written by the Doctor.

Your close attention is advised. Emotional engagement should be minimised. Because this is the day the Doctor killed them all.

Chapter 1

The War of the Doctor

She wasn't listening and I didn't think she ever would.

'He's here,' I said, keeping tight rein on the panic levels in my voice. 'I can hear him, moving about. He's in Time Vault Zero. The Doctor is in Time Vault Zero.'

There was nothing but static for a moment. Even this far below the surface, the pounding from the sky was growing louder by the minute. Grit and live-fibre was pouring down on me from the cracked ceiling, and the last of the emergency lights had started to flicker. The Daleks were raining everything they had on the very heart of Gallifrey; it could only be a final assault. The end couldn't be far away. The comm-link sputtered again, and I slammed it with my fist. In truth, it was a wonder that any of links were still working.

Her voice came like a miracle. 'The Doctor is currently located in Arcadia, he was sighted there this morning—'

'He was there this morning,' I shouted at her. 'He blew up a lot of Daleks, and wrote, *No More* on the side of a building, with a fusion blaster! I know where he was this morning, everybody does. But that was *hours* ago …'

'We have no reason to suppose he's in the Capitol.'

You've got *me*, I wanted to scream, but I kept my voice calm. 'Yesterday he was on Skaro. He blew most up most of the Emperor's fleet, stole a gunship, and burned a message over

43

half their city. Do you know what it said? *No More!* Do you see? He's saying it to *both sides!*'

There was more crackling. When she spoke again, she was clearly terrified, and her words sounded rehearsed. 'The Doctor, while rogue, and often alarming and unpredictable in his behaviour, is nevertheless on our side.'

'He hasn't been the Doctor for centuries, and he's not on anyone's side any more. He's just declared war on the Daleks, and the Time Lords, and now he's in Time Vault Zero. Do you know what's inside Time Vault Zero??'

Of course she knew. Everybody knew, although no one was supposed to. 'There is no breach indicated for the Time Vaults.'

'And I'm standing outside the doors, and they're still sealed, but *I know he's in there.*'

'The doors can only be opened from here.'

'I know that, of course I know, don't you think I know. I also know *he's in there!*'

'How?' she asked, her voice so low and fearful I could barely hear her.

'I feel him. I sense him. We grew up together, we've been psychically linked all our lives. Please believe me when I say I know that man, I know that he's in the Vault, and I know what he's going to do.'

I could tell by her silence she didn't believe me. Whoever she was, she wasn't stupid. 'Have you talked to him?' she said, at last.

'We don't need to talk to him, we need to kill him,' I screamed at her. 'I'll help, I'm good at killing him, it won't be my first time. Please just tell the General he's in there!'

A silence. Then: 'Just a moment.'

I leaned against the wall and felt the city shudder. I pictured the scene, far above, in the war room. She'd be pulling the General aside, and at first he'd be irritated, and then he'd be frowning. Time Vault Zero, he'd be thinking. The final resting place of the Moment, also known as the Galaxy Eater: a weapon so powerful, so independently intelligent, it had been sealed in the deepest vault for eons untold, and had remained untouched and unused even during this war. Legend had it that the Moment had grown so powerful, the Interface had evolved its own conscience. Who would dare to use a weapon of such colossal power, when it could, if it chose, stand in judgement over you? Right about now, the General would be realising there was only one ego in the universe big enough to even try. There would be panic in his eyes, as he started to think what might happen if the Moment felt into the hands of a madman.

The comm-link fizzed. 'The General and the elite guard are on their way down to you. Please remain on site.'

'Where would I be likely to go?' I snapped.

'I am commencing the door-opening sequence, so please stand clear.'

Behind me, the two tall, iron doors shivered and whined, as mechanisms deep within them spun back to life.

'The General's not here yet,' I protested. 'Don't open them now.'

'The Vault has been sealed for a very long time; we're not sure how long it will take to unseal it. We don't have time to waste!'

'But I'm alone down here,' I shouted. 'You can't leave me down here, with *him*.'

'You should probably take cover.'

'Are you listening to me? It's him! *It's him* and he's got the deadliest weapon in the history of the universe—where exactly do you suggest I take cover?'

'I'm sorry,' she breathed, and the comm-link pinged into silence. I imagined her sitting there, traumatised, caught between the Daleks above, and the devil below. Her fear wouldn't last long, of course: she would be dead very soon.

As it happened, she was wrong: the doors didn't take long to open. In fact, they were grinding open already, and the heat of ages past stung my face.

The chamber was walled in dripping black rock, and the far end was lost in steam and shadow. At the centre stood a plinth, seemingly fashioned from a lattice of blades, and resting on the blades was an ornate wooden cube, about a foot square. It looked like an antique puzzle box, but when my eyes came to rest on it, it stopped my breath.

The Moment. The Galaxy Eater.

I willed my hands to stop shaking, lifted the box from its glittering nest, and placed it carefully inside my sack. Before I left, I scratched the words *No More* in the stone of the ancient floor.

The desert was hot beneath my boots, and a tiny barn shimmered on the horizon. Somewhere far behind me, in the burning city, the General would be screaming orders and even as Gallifrey fell, the Time Lords would be calling for the head of the Doctor. Why did they still call me that? The man the Doctor had been was long dead, and at my hand. Everything the posturing, prancing fool had stood for had burned on Karn, and I was what had walked out of the fire. Did it comfort them to think that pity could still slow my hand? If so, today they would learn better.

I'd stopped walking and forced myself to start again—I was nearly home.

About now, a voice would start echoing round every building still standing on Gallifrey; round ever Dalek habitation in the known universe; it would ring in the ears of every Time Lord and Dalek still fighting, anywhere in space and time. And the voice would be mine. It had given me no pleasure, but immense satisfaction, to record my final message to them all.

'Time Lords of Gallifrey, Daleks of Skaro, today I serve notice on you all. Too long I have stayed my hand. No more. Today you leave me no choice. Today this war will end. No more. No more.'

I wondered briefly how they would react, but I was too tired even to think about it. No, not tired, old. As old as I would ever get. One more act, and I was done. No more.

46

They might try and track my TARDIS, of course, but they wouldn't find me—I'd walked for miles, and the wind would have scattered my tracks in the sand. Of course, if any of them, on either side, had the slightest grasp of emotion, or how a life is lived, they would have known exactly where I was going. I was, as any warrior must, returning to the beginning. Only at the beginning can one find the courage to make one's end. I had walked the circle of my life, and here was where the circle would close.

The barn was right in front of me now. Older, but as I'd remembered it. A boy had slept in fear here, every night, but I wasn't afraid now. No more fear. No more me. I wondered if any of the others were still around, and whether they'd recognise the battle-weary old man who'd just walked out of the desert. Probably not. Somewhere a wolf howled, and I suppose it should have worried me, as I scraped open the door, that there had never been any wolves in this desert.

Inside was brighter and smaller than I'd remembered. Flies buzzed, ancient machinery rusted under rotting canvas, and blades of yellow sunshine slanted through the gaps in the wall to rest in bright spots on the earthen floor.

I pulled open the sack, and released the box from inside it. It stood there in the straw and dirt, and clicked and ticked and gleamed. 'How do you work?' I said aloud, running my hands over it. Each face was different, inlaid in patterns of gold and shining black and another substance, which was warm to the touch, and pink, like the flesh of a baby. It was as if something alive had been compressed inside, and its skin was leaking through the cracks. It seemed to me that this fleshiness hadn't been there before, but I fought the thought away—this was no time to be fanciful. I looked for a control panel, or any kind of interface, but there was nothing. 'Why is there never a big red button?' I asked of no one in particular. The howling came again, like a reply, closer this time. I returned quickly to the door, but when I looked out there was only the beating heat and lunar silence.

47

'Hello,' I found myself calling. 'Is someone there, hello?'

'It's nothing,' said a voice behind me.

I turned, and a young woman was sitting on top of the box. 'Just a wolf.'

'Don't sit on that!' I shouted, louder than I intended.

'Why not?' she cocked her head at me, and blonde hair tumbled round strange, black eyes. 'Pretty,' noted a voice in my head. I slammed a door on the thought and reminded myself I'd be killing her in a very few minutes.

I strode over to her, grabbed her arm, and started pulling her to the door. 'Because it's not a chair,' I snarled. 'It's the most dangerous weapon in the universe.'

As I pushed her outside, she turned to look at me, but I still managed to slam the door in her face.

'Why can't it be both?' she asked, from behind me. I turned. She was back sitting on the box, as if she'd never moved.

'How did you do that?' I asked. She was quick, I was telling myself, though I already knew it had to be more than that.

'Why did you park so far away? You walked for miles. Didn't you want her to see?' She looked at me, as confident of an answer as a child. It was a small barn, and there was no one else here, so it was going to be hard work avoiding those eyes.

'Want who to see?'

'The TARDIS,' she breathed, her eyes excited, like she was uttering the most thrilling word in the universe.

I'm on Gallifrey, I told myself. People know about TARDISes, even in the drylands. This was nothing more than a perfectly reasonable guess.

'Doesn't she approve?' she asked. 'Are you hiding from her, are you ashamed?' Suddenly she was at the door—so fast I didn't see her move—and she was looking out over the desert. 'You walked for miles,' she said, 'miles and miles and miles.'

'I was thinking,' I told her, even though I never told anyone anything.

'I heard you,' she said, and winked.

'You heard what?'

'Your thoughts,' she said, patiently, as if talking to an idiot.

I was on a planet of natural telepaths, but I had learned, over centuries, to shield my mind, and no one could—

'No more!' she said, and something cold turned over inside me. 'No! More!' she said again, now stamping a foot on each word, like a child stamping through puddles. 'No! More! No! More! No! More!' Now she was marching all round the barn— 'No! More! No! More!'—as if everything I'd done had been nothing more than a joke. She was mocking me.

I hadn't realised how angry I'd been, for how many centuries, till it broke inside me in that moment. 'Stop it, stop it, *stop that!*' I screamed, and made to grab her arm. Instead, her hand was suddenly stroking my face. 'No more,' she said, and the thunder died in my ears.

She held me there a moment, and cocked her head again, contemplating my face, detail by detail. It was neither pity, nor judgement—it was an eye down a microscope. How old was I now, I wondered. How ravaged was the flesh under her hand?

A ticking from behind me. I pulled away from her, and looked at the wooden cube. I could hear gears whirring and turning and panels were sliding and folding across the surfaces. The Moment was coming to life, and whoever this strange girl was, she was no longer my problem.

'It's activating,' I told her. 'Go now, get out of here!'

I knelt at the box. What was I supposed to do? I touched the gold inlay. My fingers burned and I snatched my hand away.

'What's wrong?' she asked. She had ignored my instruction to leave, of course.

'The interface is hot,' I told her.

'Well, I do my best,' she replied. For a moment I wasn't really listening, because I'd noticed the fleshy sections of the box had disappeared, almost as if something inside had—

49

What did she say?

I turned. I looked at her. I stood. Finally I spoke. 'I said the interface was hot ...'

'You did.'

'And you said you did your best.'

'As indeed I do.'

I stared at her. The only explanation was as preposterous as it was inescapable.

She was blonde, 151 cm tall, 121 pounds, her eyes were brown (not black as they had seemed to me) and she wore a simple dress, which—I ransacked my vocabulary and discovered I had no further words to describe dresses. There were no fractal repetitions or compression artefacts as she moved, and the dust particles arranged themselves around her in the correct dynamics for the air density, so I was inclined to discount any kind of hologram. I had felt her hand on my face, so she was physically substantial. Or at any rate, seemed to be; I couldn't rule out a psychic projection. But no, I *felt* her presence, with none of the ghosting that comes with sensory manipulation. By those billions of receptors that process the world around us and alert us when another living thing is close by, I *knew* there was a woman standing in front of me. They said the Moment was powerful. Powerful enough to do anything? To *be* anyone?

I looked at her. She was real, she was here.

'Nice smile,' came that unbidden voice again, and I quashed it. She was staring at me now, expectant, and I realised I had been silent too long.

'So,' I said at last. 'You're the interface.'

The physically manifested AI of the deadliest weapon in the history of the universe shrugged girlishly. 'They must have told you the Moment had a conscience.' She gave me a little wave. 'Hello! I'm the officiating conscience of the weapon of universal destruction known to you as the Moment, known to most others as the Galaxy Eater.' She let the truth of that land for a moment. Whatever look she saw on my face must have satisfied her. She laughed, and with a toss of her hair, asked: 'So, my dear, who will we be slaughtering today?'

I had so many questions I found myself saying nothing at all, which made her laugh again.

'Oh, look at you. Stuck between a girl and a box. Story of your life, eh, Doctor?'

She knew me? I didn't think I'd spoken aloud, but she replied anyway. 'I know you,' she said. 'I *hear* you. All of you, jangling away in that dusty old head. I chose this face and form especially for you—do you like it? It's from your past. Or possibly your future—I always get those two mixed up.'

She wasn't from my past, I was certain I'd have remembered her. But the alternative was impossible. 'I don't have a future,' I snapped.

'I think I'm called Rose Tyler,' she said. I searched my memory for the name but there was nothing. She was frowning now. 'No, hang on. Oh, that's interesting. Bit confusing! In this form, I'm called …' Her eyes seemed to glow, and somewhere I heard that howling again. 'Bad Wolf,' she said. 'Are you afraid of the big bad wolf, Doctor?'

'I have absolutely no idea what you're talking about, but please stop calling me Doctor.'

'It's the name in your head.'

'It shouldn't be. I've been fighting this war for a very long time, I am not the Doctor any more.'

'Then what do people call you now?'

I thought of Cass Fermazzi, how she'd snatched her hand from mine. 'Nothing. I travel alone.'

She frowned like a petulant child. 'Not today,' she informed me, primly. 'Today you're traveling with me. The question is, why? What does the Doctor want with a little old galaxy eater like moi?'

'I'm not the Doctor!' I told her, but she wasn't listening. Not to me, at any rate. She'd cocked her head, and there was a look of faint concentration on her face, as if she was trying to tune into something right at the edge of hearing. 'Ooh, Daleks,' she said. 'Is that what they call themselves? Noisy, aren't they? Ever so cross. Look at that one—those colours are awful. Didn't have Daleks in my day. Can't say I like them much.' She narrowed her eyes, concentrating. 'Millions of them, massing round the planet. Yes, well, if you asked very nicely, and you had a very good reason, I dare say I could blow them up for you.' She was coquetting now, batting her eyelids, a parody of flirtation. 'But you realise that if I did, I'd blow up all your little Time Lord friends too?'

I said nothing. Her eyes lit up, as if I'd told her something thrilling. She laughed and clapped her hands. 'Oh, that's the idea, isn't it? Oh, that's *naughty*! You're very keen on killing for someone who calls himself the Doctor.'

'I don't call myself the Doctor!' I said. 'I haven't called myself the Doctor in a very, very long time.'

'Ooh, what's this feeling I'm getting now,' she said. 'You saying that gave me a feeling, but I'm a bit rusty on the names.' Her eyes widened, 'Sadness. I'm feeling sad.' Suddenly she was standing far too close to me. Whoever this Rose Tyler was, I was certain I hadn't met her yet. Those were not eyes I would forget.

'Why does the man who used to be the Doctor want to kill so many people?' she asked.

'The war is destroying all reality. Everything is at risk.'

She looked a little incredulous. 'And you're the one to save us all?'

'Yes,' I said, wishing there was another answer.

'If I ever develop an ego, you've got the job.' she said, laughing. 'Ooh, I've got sarcasm now. Rose Tyler's fun, isn't she?'

'If you've been inside my head, then you know what I've seen. The suffering. Every moment in time and space is burning. It must end! And I'm going to end it, the only way I can.'

'And you're expecting me to do that for you, are you? One big boom and peace for all?'

A voice rose inside me, protesting, but I throttled it. 'It's the only way,' I said. The only way, *the only way*.

'Kill, kill, kill, then happy, happy, happy. You living things have a touching faith in that idea, don't you. Makes me wonder why you're so keen on life in the first place, when you spend most of your time trying to stamp it out.'

'It's the only way,' I repeated.

'Oh, I can do it,' she said. 'I'd love doing it, it's the way I'm made. Slaughter is my favourite high, I'm a slave to my endorphins. That's why I decided to grow a conscience—I was worried I'd started to binge kill and, if I didn't watch out, I'd run out of lives to end. You need to keep something in the larder, don't you? But, you see, a conscience is a bit tricky when you're the hard-wired psychotic AI of the most powerful weapon of universal destruction in the history of space and time, both directions. I think you could say I had conflicts. I'm afraid I took to sulking in a basement.'

'You have been locked up, in the deepest time vault, for billions of years,' I told her.

'Locked up?' she laughed, 'Oh sweet-pea, what could possibly ever lock *me* up?'

She had a point, so I ignored it. 'Will you do as I request?' I asked.

'Oh, probably! Mass murder is my preferred start to the day. But, you know what consciences are like. Can't live with 'em, can't live without 'em, am I right? There have to be checks and balances, it's just the way I'm wired.' Her look held mine, and her eyes weren't brown, they were definitely black. 'I'll give you all the slaughter you want—but there will be consequences for you. Do you understand that? Do you understand consequences, Doctor?'

Still that name? Why did everyone still insist on calling me that? 'The Doctor is gone,' I said. 'I'm what took his place. And I have no desire to survive this day.'

For a moment, I thought she hadn't heard me. There was only her black-eyed stare and the flies fizzing inside the sunbeams. Then came a slow smile and the air turned cold around me.

'Then that is your punishment,' she said, at last.

'Punishment?'

'If you do this—if you use me to kill them all, Daleks and Time Lords alike—then I have in mind a very special consequence for you.' Not a smile now, a grin. A grin like a wolf. I found myself stepping back a pace. 'The perfect punishment for the warrior formerly known as the Doctor. You, old man,' she said, moving closer, taking my hand. 'You, ancient warrior … will *live*.'

Her words seemed ridiculous. Preposterous. I couldn't arrange them into sense in my head.

She was walking round me now, close, her hands tracing patterns on my shoulders, her breath warm in my ear. 'Gallifrey,' she whispered, like a seduction. 'You're going to burn it, and all the Daleks with it—but all those children too. Doesn't it give you shivers, just thinking about the little ones?' Her hand was running through my hair. 'How many children on Gallifrey right now?'

No! No, I thought, you can't ask me that. 'I don't know,' I said. 'Not hard to work out,' said that voice inside me, but I slammed that door again, angrier this time. *Shut up, Doctor!*

'One day you will count them. One terrible night. Do you want to see what that will turn you into?'

No. No, I didn't.

'Oh come on!' she laughed, as if she was daring me; as if this was no more to her than a childish game. 'Aren't you curious?'

All she did was flick her eyes. The first thing I noticed was the wind. When I turned to look, the back wall of the barn was gone. In its place, there was a silent swirl of light and clouds; a slow, soundless whirlpool, like a spiral of smoke suspended in water. The absolute quiet of it was electric. It drummed through my feet and crackled on my skin, like a storm waiting in the air. 'What is it?' I heard myself ask. 'What is that?'

54

I knew, of course. With a barely a glance, this girl had reached between the planes of reality, plucked a piece of the time vortex from the void, and hung it on the wall of a barn. No, not *girl*, I reminded myself—*weapon*. The most powerful weapon in the universe.

'I am opening windows on your future,' she was saying. 'A tangle in time through the days to come, to the man today will make of you. I am summoning the future of the Warrior formerly known as the Doctor!'

There was a deep, hollow droning, a wolf-howl, and something was flying towards me out of the vortex. Instinctively, I ducked, but it flopped harmlessly at my feet. I stared at it. I tried to make sense of it. I failed.

'Okay,' said the most powerful weapon in the universe, 'I wasn't expecting that.'

Lying in the dirt and straw, smoking gently after an impossible journey from a future I'd never intended to see, was a hat. It was red and battered, and of the type usually known as a fez.

FEED CONNECTING
FEED CONNECTED
FEED STABLE
***IF YOU EXPERIENCE ANY SPLIT INFINITIVES,
PLEASE DON'T PANIC, IT'S A STUPID RULE ANYWAY.***

Oh dear, I suppose I was a little bit naughty there, telling you that the previous chapter wasn't written by the Doctor. But, you see, it wasn't—at that time his life, he had abandoned both the name and the philosophies and ideals he had come to associate with it. Of course, everyone largely ignored his decision. In some ways you could say he ignored it himself, but we'll come to that in later—or earlier—chapters.

On the subject of chapters, I've been receiving a lot of complaints about the content of Chapter Nine. Look, I did warn you about the dangers of reading an out-of-sequence book, recounting out-of-sequence events, out of sequence, so you really only have yourselves to blame. Please remain calm and remember that this is the simple story of one adventure that happened to one man, several times, in the wrong order. Oops, that sentence got away from me. Never mind, best to hold tight and do as you're told. And stay away from Chapter Nine until you are specifically told otherwise. To repeat: there is a reason why Chapter Nine is not listed on the contents page.

So with that in mind, let us now proceed to Chapter Ten, where we will rejoin the Doctor at another, very different, point in his complex life. Here we find him long after the Time War, but considerably before his summons to the National Gallery. Authorship remains your challenge, but let me clarify one thing from the very outset: this chapter is again written by the Doctor, in his usual third-person style. However, as you all know, the Doctor is not one person, but through the miracle of regeneration, many very different people. So the question is not 'Who wrote this?' but 'Which Doctor wrote this?'

These next few pages cover much material that is contentious, and even salacious, so it won't come as a surprise to any of you to know that the title is: The Love of the Doctor.

Chapter 10

The Love of the Doctor

The Doctor shrugged, as best he could in the circumstances. 'I should have come to you first,' he admitted, 'but Professor Candy knew all about the hives, and I'd managed to translate the migration protocols anyway, and well … Look, I'm never quite sure, with you, whether you're going to … you know … stick to the subject. The matter in hand. Not get all distracted.'

'Well I hope I've managed to settle your mind on that point,' said River Song from the other end of the bath.

'Not entirely,' admitted the Doctor.

'Is the water warm enough, by the way?'

'Yeah, lovely and warm, thanks.'

'Oh good! Maybe you could slip off your suit then?'

'No, no, I'm fine.'

'Or even your shoes.'

'I can't, my toes prune.'

'How about your coat?'

'I'm always worried I'll leave it behind somewhere.'

'One lives in hope,' said River sweetly, and the Doctor wondered if she was teasing him again, in that way he always missed at the time. 'We could get rid of those awful plimsolls while we're at it.'

'So,' he persisted, 'Zygons. There's a whole nest out there on the run, and I've lost track of them …'

'Shape-shifters are always tricky. You should try dating them.'

'Have you?'

'Jealous?'

'Well, no, I've never wanted to be a shape-shifter.'

'Says the man with all the faces.'

The Doctor frowned. How many of his faces had she seen? He'd only met her fairly recently, but she had known so many future versions of him. They were conducting their—what?—friendship?—in reverse order to each other: she'd known him for many years, but from his point of view, they had barely met. It was the hazard of a relationship between time travellers. Who was he to her? Who would she become to him? She already knew it all and he was making his slow way to discovering what she had already lived through. But he did so freighted with a memory that grew darker and heavier behind him, till its shadow now spilled over the road ahead: the first time they'd met, in a long-abandoned library, battling the Vashta Nerada, he had watched her burn and die.[1] At the time it had been the death of a stranger, and he could hardly mourn the loss of someone he had barely met. But since then he had bumped into younger versions of her a couple of times. Inevitably they'd grown closer—now, here they were, sitting in a bath together—and the memory of her death was hurting more than it had in the moment. How much more would it hurt, as he made his way into a future that was already her past? No more, he thought. He should avoid her from now on. The future wasn't written yet, not for him. Maybe, by avoiding her, he could divert her from the deadly path she didn't know she was taking.

'You really mustn't frown,' she was saying. 'You simply have no idea where those eyebrows are going.'

---

[1] See *Doctor Who and the Silence in The Library*, available in all good alternate realities.

'I am interested in Zygons,' he said, as sternly as anyone could, fully dressed in a bath with a beautiful archaeologist. 'In particular, the missing hive, of the Under Wave. I know you've tracked Zygons before, you're even an expert on the subject—'

'They're on Earth, as you suspected,' she said. 'A time eddy knocked them back a few centuries, but that's where you'll find them.'

'Big planet, long history, I'll need a bit more—'

'All the information you need is already in the TARDIS databank.'

'No, it isn't!'

'Yes, it is, I uploaded it myself before I got in the bath.'

'Well, why didn't you tell me?'

'I suppose I was hoping you might take your coat off.'

He was already climbing out of the water. 'Thanks, River, I owe you,' he said. And in return, he thought, I'll make sure I never see you again, so maybe there's a chance you'll live happily ever after. And then he frowned, because there was a bottle of champagne rattling in an ice bucket, which definitely hadn't been sitting on the side of the bath a moment ago.

'I was hoping,' said River, reaching for the bottle, 'that you might stay just a little longer.' There was a sound like a pistol shot, and a cork shaved past his ear. He sighed, partly because she always did that, but also because River Song always insisted on looking so alive.

It had been dark and cold that deep beneath The Library, and it should've been the Doctor not River, who died to save them all. But she'd got the better of him, and taken his place, and then had burned to death, screaming, right in front him. He couldn't stop seeing it, and the pain got fiercer every time she smiled. It was, he reflected, as she poured the champagne, quite a smile. How many more smiles would there be? How much more painful would it get? Time can be rewritten, he reminded himself. Perhaps her future could be avoided, her death averted, if he just stayed away. And anyway, there were rogue Zygons to chase, a planet to save. He was still the Doctor after all—he had taken back the name, and it came with responsibilities. It was difficult, with that smile filling the room, but he reached a decision, and he knew she could see it in his face. He smiled back at her, and leaned in to give her a peck on the cheek, before leaving as quickly as he was able to, a little under seven hours later.

The note she'd left on the TARDIS console directed him to England 1562, and the Royal Court. Zygons always made a beeline for the nearest power structure, she explained, as it was where their shape-shifting abilities had the most immediate advantage. She recommended he infiltrate the court—'*As a noble, please, you're utterly hopeless at being a servant. Except when you're with me, obviously*'—and try to work out if anyone had been replaced by a Zygon. '*Normally you can tell by their breath, but they'll be well camouflaged in that century—honestly, it's like living inside cheese. So you'll need to build some sort of detector, I would think. One of your lovely gadgets will do the trick. Try not to get carried away with the apps, you don't need to download comics from the future, or anything.*' She ended by apologising for not coming with him. '*Don't be cross, I have a date. Well, not a date, a job. The Felman Lux Corporation want me to go and unseal some giant library somewhere. "Get a Kindle," I told them, but they kept asking and it might be fun. I'll buzz you on the psychic paper if anything kicks off. Unless that's all already happened for you. Spoilers!*' she signed off, and he imagined her saying it. Then he sat on the TARDIS floor, leaning his back against the console and spent an hour resisting the brandy in the cabinet. He'd meet her again, of course. And again, and again, and the shadow of the past would lengthen over him. He had to avoid her, it was as simple as that; resist every invitation, ignore every summons, turn and walk away every time he saw her across a room; rewrite her future, without him in it, for her sake. He was on his feet now, slamming the controls, harder than he needed to. Because they all died, he knew that, if he knew anything. Died in fire, like Cass, or in sickness like Reinette. Or in a single act of unforgivable violence, like all those millions of children on Gallifrey when he had allowed himself to believe there was any such thing as the greater good. The shadow behind him wasn't just River, he knew; it wasn't just anyone; it was *all* of them. All the screaming the Doctor could never outrun. 'All those children,' he thought. How many more would he have to save, before he could convince himself he'd been justified?

He remembered the night he'd rampaged round the TARDIS, destroying every mirror he could find. Whatever face he happened to be wearing, he'd been absolutely sure he never wanted to look at it again. One face later, he hadn't changed his mind.

He spun the TARDIS into the time vortex, and he stared into the scalding light of the central column. He had to stop thinking before it tore him apart! What he needed, right now, was trouble.

Several weeks later, Elizabeth tilted back her head, as if to be kissed, and asked, 'Why am I wasting my time on you, Doctor? I have wars to plan.'

'You have a picnic to eat,' he replied, and popped a grape in her mouth to divert her from any other ideas. The day was beautiful, the picnic was sumptuous and, apart from Alison, tethered to a tree a few feet behind them, he was alone with the Queen at last. The bees were humming, the sky was blue, and even the sway of the grass in the light breeze seemed unusually tranquil—in fact, if it hadn't been for the Zygon detector buzzing silently in his pocket, he might have forgotten that he was about to unmask an alien mastermind and would-be conqueror of the Earth.

'Wars don't happen by themselves,' she was saying. 'You could help me.'

'I'm helping you eat the picnic.'

'But you have a stomach for war.' Her face was still tilted back below his, as they reclined together on the rug, and now her hand was on his cheek. 'This face has seen conflict,' she said, studying him with a tender frown. 'It's clear as day.'

'I've seen conflict like you wouldn't believe,' he told her. 'But it wasn't this face.' And there it was, he thought, exultant. Nothing! No reaction at all, not even a flicker. He was right!

'Did you win?' she asked him.

'No,' he replied. 'I lived.' Enough! he thought. Time to get to work! He scrambled to his feet. 'But never mind that, your Majesty,' he said, grabbing her hand to pull her up with him. 'On your feet!'

'I'm sorry?' she said, clearly intending to express affront, but only achieving something between a squeal and a giggle.

'Get up!' he ordered. 'Stand! Now, please!'

'I'm the Queen of England,' she reminded him, very nearly without laughing.

'I'm not English,' he said.

She made a show of reluctance, as she clambered to her feet, but it wasn't very convincing. As soon as she was standing, he dropped to one knee, and took her hand reverently in his.

'Elizabeth,' he said, 'will you marry me?'

She looked down at him, in genuine shock, and for a moment the future of all humanity hung in the balance.

Inveigling himself into the Royal Court had been easy. He hadn't even bothered dressing the part (tight suit and Converse, unimprovable!), and he'd adopted an alias which changed slightly every day, because he could never quite remember it. The first principles of going undercover, he'd always said, were fitting in as badly as possible, and drawing as much attention to yourself as you could, because those were exactly the things that spies never did. No one was ever stupid enough to suspect an attention-seeking clown of espionage. It also helped to throw around blatant anachronisms every few seconds, since the only people who could recognise them as such weren't supposed to be there either, and those were probably the ones you were looking for. 'There's no such thing as average,' he'd once explained to a female wrestler on a foggy London night, 'so anyone who *seems* average is almost certainly acting, which is why I can spot a spy the moment they walk in the room.' Sadly the wrestler had turned out to be a spy, and he'd spent the rest of the night handcuffed to a streetlamp in East Cheam, but he felt the general point remained sound. And anyway, she was basically nice, and had even posted his sonic screwdriver back to him the next day, along with his trousers.

Contact with the Queen herself had taken longer, but not much. That she was a remarkable woman was obvious immediately. She ruled her court, and her land, with diamond-sharp efficiency, and a ruthlessness that put the High Council of Gallifrey in the shade, but it was in her personal relations that her true power became apparent. At a distance, she blazed. Up close she twinkled. The first day he'd seen her, sweeping through the halls, surrounded by a fluster of courtiers, he'd mistaken her for tall and imperious, but when his antics at court drew her attention, and he found himself summoned to her presence, the woman patting the cushion next to her was smaller than he expected, bubbling with mischief and laughter, and there wasn't a hint of reserve or calculation in her merry eyes as she took his hand and explained that he was obviously a spy and she intended to have him tortured for information and executed. 'Well, better get it in the right order then,' he said, and they shared their first laugh together, as the Duke of Norfolk beat him to the ground.

She was his only regular visitor during the months of his incarceration, and though she always arrived trying to look stern, she was quickly reduced to squeals and giggles by his stories, and increasingly, so was the torturer. 'Stop it, *stop it!*' he'd say, leaning against the crank handle and wiping his eyes through his hood.

'*Me* stop it? *Me?*' said the Doctor, his eyes wide with comedy outrage, and they all grew so helpless with laughter, the team from the next torture chamber started popping their heads round the door in puzzlement, which only set them off again.

Sometimes, he was able to use his big sad eyes (his best pair yet, and his first brown ones) to good effect, and she started opening up to him, recounting tales of her childhood, and all the loves she had forsaken in the name of duty. Once she was telling him a story of such intimacy and evident truth, that the torturer had asked if they wanted to be alone. 'No, no,' she'd flustered, embarrassed, 'you carry on.'

He found himself looking forward to their sessions together, despite the constant screaming.

She was often busy, of course, and sometimes weeks would go by with no visits, and given the Zygon situation, he couldn't help worrying. So after a gap of several months, he was relieved to see her, pink and happy and waving at him, as he mounted the scaffold.

'I stand tall among you today,' he said to the crowd, on being granted some final words. 'Taller, I think, than I have ever stood. People don't tell you that about the rack!' The crowd roared, and he managed to keep them laughing for an hour. In the end, he found he'd talked himself hoarse. 'Sorry, just have to clear my throat,' he said. 'And here's the man to do it,' he added, throwing an arm round the Axeman. 'Milk it,' he whispered to him, as the crowd cheered and laughed.

Kneeling at the block, he wondered if he'd done enough. If he hadn't, he wasn't entirely sure how regeneration worked in the event of decapitation. It would be fatal, certainly, but would both severed parts attempt to change? If they did, would they still match? That might cause some confusion when they loaded him into that long box he'd been avoiding looking at since arriving on the scaffold.

The boards creaked as the Axeman moved into position, and the crowd fell into a thrilled silence. There was a grunt of effort and the shadow of the axe swept across the floor. Cold air lay in a line across his bared neck and breathing was suddenly an enormous thing, now that he knew each breath could be the last.

One breath. Come on, Elizabeth.

Two breaths. She liked him, he made her laugh.

Three breaths. He'd smiled through all the pain, he'd joked, he'd listened.

Four breaths. Please, please, Elizabeth!

Five breaths. Were they just making him wait, out of cruelty?

Six breaths. At least it was okay to be afraid now, because kneeling at the block, no one could see my face.

Seven—

Footsteps ascending to the scaffold!

A murmur among the crowd.

Elizabeth? Please let it be Elizabeth. There was a swirl of golden fabric, then two merry eyes were looking into his. 'You think your jokes and clever tongue have saved you, don't you, Doctor?' He forced a quizzical look onto his face, and hoped no one could hear the thudding of his hearts. 'Well, sorry my dear, but your humour is the disguise of your intelligence, and your charm is the mask of your nature, and we are still quite resolved to take your head. However, I'm sure you would not deny your Queen a last kiss, while you're still in one piece.'

She kissed him gently on the lips and was gone in another swirl of gold. He found himself staring into the basket again. The bottom of it was bloodied from many impacts, and he wondered if he'd be able to feel it when it smacked against his face.

Realising he was now, beyond all doubt, about to die, the Doctor rose up inside himself, steadied his hearts, and chose his final thought with care.

The children. The children of Gallifrey.

'However,' Elizabeth was saying, as he heard her feet trotting down the steps, 'while taking your head remains a necessity, we are moderately inclined to think that it is slightly more entertaining while still attached to the rest of you.'

Silence pounded in the Doctor's ears. *What? What did she say?* It took him a moment to understand that the steely clatter behind him was an axe being laid aside, and that the gentle exhalation from all around was the disappointment of a large crowd.

'We grant you a day's pardon, for you to arrange a picnic,' Elizabeth continued, now standing below, and looking up at him with twinkling eyes. 'It will be for the two of us only, tomorrow afternoon. Please understand that we have villainously high standards when it comes to picnics, and can be volatile when disappointed. Remember to bring your head, and we'll decide over dessert which of us takes it home.'

Oh Elizabeth! He'd have leapt down from the scaffold and kissed her, if he hadn't known she was a Zygon.

'Will you marry me?' he repeated because Elizabeth was still just staring at him, one hand pressed against her chest, as if trying to contain a storm within. It was, he conceded, a reasonable impersonation of strong emotion for an upright squid.

'But I tortured you!' she said.

'Was there torture?' he laughed, gaily. 'I only noticed you.'

'Yesterday, I nearly cut your head cut off.'

'Oh, let's not dwell on the past. Elizabeth, of England, I'm asking you again—for the *third* time, in fact—will you marry me?'

And the words burst from her. 'Oh, my dear, sweet love, of course I will.'

He leapt to his feet, triumphant. 'Gotcha!' he shouted.

'My love?

'Oh, forget the play acting, I'm on to you. Sorry, dear, but the performance just isn't good enough. Even Alison saw through it!'

'Alison?'

'My horse.'

'My dear, that horse is male.'

'Yeah, and he's called Alison. Don't box him in, he's very easily triggered. I was going to call him Trigger, actually, that escalated quickly. He didn't want to carry us both out here, but I told him it was going to be an Earth defence picnic and that's the only reason he let us both on.'

'Your words make no sense, my love!'

'Then let's break it down, nice and simply. One! The real Elizabeth would never have accepted my marriage proposal. Two! The real Elizabeth would notice when I just casually mention having a different face. But then the real Elizabeth isn't an alien shape-shifter from outer space! And—*ding!*

He'd pulled his Zygon detector from his pocket, and thrust his wire-trailing but strangely magnificent lash-up of clock-and-smartphone in front of her face, managing to keep the bit made from coat-hangers to the back. She stared at it with what must have been shock and awe, but somehow came out looking a bit like pity.

'What is that?'

'It's a machine that goes ding! Made it myself—it lights up in the presence of shape-shifter DNA! Also it can microwave frozen dinners from up to twenty feet and download comics from the future—I never know when to stop. Didn't work properly at the Court. Too many people, all that cheese-breath. But since we rode out here, it's been going non-stop!'

'My love, I do not understand.'

'I'm not your love, and yes you do! You're a Zygon!'

'A Zygon.'

'Oh, stop it, it's over. A Zygon, yes. Big red rubbery thing, covered in suckers. Surprisingly good kisser. Do you think the real Queen of England would just decide to share the throne with any old handsome bloke in a tight suit, just cos he's got amazing hair and a nice horse?'

He glanced over at Alison as he spoke, but there was only a discarded saddle and tether under the tree, and where his horse had stood a moment before, a mass of something red and glistening was thrashing on the grass. For a moment the Doctor wondered if his horse had exploded, or somehow burst itself inside out, but then a pair of tiny eyes blinked open among the jumble of organs, and an obscene foetus-like head started to rise up, as if forming itself out of the boiling viscera. Bones cracked into new places, nerves and sinews slithered and snapped around them, and in moments, a jerking, pitiful meat-thing, as ravaged and skeletal as a dissected rat but taller than a man, was struggling upright on stick legs. Flesh stretched and popped and bloated around it and suckers starting forming out all over its crimson skin. What now stood there, like a humanoid squid, with a giant baby head and a tiny chimp face, was a fully formed Zygon.

Understanding bore down on the Doctor, like a grand piano from a high window. The horse, *the horse.* His detector hadn't been detecting Elizabeth at all, it was the horse. His own horse had been the Zygon all along. Not the Queen, the horse. 'Oh!' was all he managed aloud, followed by another 'Oh!' when he realised that the woman now gripping his arm was not only the real Elizabeth, but also his fiancée. *I'm going to be King*, he thought, as he grabbed her hand and started to run.

Directly ahead there was a crumbled old folly (no, not a folly, wrong period, a real ruin) and a thick forest swept away to the right. The trees would be decent cover, but scattering wildlife would provide an easy means of tracking them, while the ruin was both less predictable and the counterintuitive choice. Following the instincts of a lifetime, he made straight for the thing that looked like a folly.

'I don't understand,' Elizabeth was protesting. 'What was that creature, what's happening?'

'We're being attacked by a shape-shifting alien from outer space, formerly disguised as my horse.'

'What does that mean?'

'It means we're going to need a new horse.'

He threw her ahead of him, into the shadows of the ruin. Quick scan: there were two other exits, one climbable wall, and a useable vantage point with a nearby pile of throwable rocks. She was smart, Elizabeth, she could make something out of this. 'I'll hold it off, you run, or hide, or do a clever thing—but stay alive, your people need you!'

He was turning to go but she grabbed him back. 'And I need you alive for our wedding night!' The kiss was wet, noisy and engulfing, and he found himself thinking of the forming Zygon.

'I will return with help,' she called over her shoulder, as she dashed off through the ruin. He didn't doubt that for a second. In fact, he thought, frowning, she wouldn't normally run away for any reason—certainly not because he'd suggested it—and the only times he'd ever seen her kiss anyone it was to stop them thinking straight. He wondered briefly what it said about him that on meeting a Queen with a steel-trap mind and gold-plated leadership skills, he had immediately assumed she was a squid from space—at which point he decided he'd be more comfortable being attacked by an alien. But when he turned to face the approaching Zygon, the meadow was deserted. A flock of rabbits raced across the grass, but there was no other movement anywhere.

'Never break eye contact with a shape-shifter,' Borusa had droned at the Academy, 'because that's the last time you'll see it. Or more accurately, you'll see it everywhere you look, and never be able trust anyone again.'

The Doctor noticed he was running, and wondered why. Oh, of course the rabbits! As usual, his legs had figured it out first. Zygons were multi-nucleate, and there were plenty of accounts of them transforming into flocks of birds, so why not a flock of rabbits? Provided the scattered nuclei remained within reasonable distance, the psychic link would stay viable, and the Zygon could sustain its consciousness as a network, rather than an individual. The tactical advantages to a Zygon alone in the field were clear, even if it risked losing part of itself to a pie. And blimey, rabbits couldn't half run!

The flock was sweeping round a hill, and the Doctor sped up—he needed to keep them in view.

One of the rabbits had peeled off. It was sniffing round a patch of greener grass as the others disappeared from sight. The Doctor slowed. What was this? The swarm leader? Was he being invited to parlay?

The rabbit raised its head from chewing the grass, and eyed him innocently. He came to a halt and held its gaze for a long moment. Finally, in his gravest tones, he said: 'Hello, Alison.'

To its credit, the rabbit kept its calm. Okay, thought the Doctor, if that's how you want to play it!

'Whatever you've got planned,' he said, 'forget it. I'm the Doctor. I'm 900 hundred years old. I'm from the planet Gallifrey in the constellation of Kasterborous. I'm the oncoming storm, the bringer of darkness …'

He broke off, because the rabbit was chewing the grass again, and there was a terrible possibility at the back of his mind which was trying to get his attention. He sighed. 'You're basically just a rabbit, aren't you?'

The rabbit glanced briefly at him, and hopped off after the others.

If he'd had something to kick, he'd have kicked it halfway round the planet. How could he be so stupid? Why was he getting everything so wrong?? The Queen! The horse! The rabbit! What was the matter with him? Was the shadow of the past so deep now, he couldn't find his feet?

And then, almost before he knew it, he was running again, faster this time, back the way he'd come. Elizabeth! *Damn her!*

The ruin where he'd left her, was coming into view. He prayed to everything he'd never believed in that it hadn't become her tomb, and tried to stop his mind from racing.

The kiss! She'd kissed him the same way she kissed everyone: to put him off his game. Just as she'd pretended to accept his proposal, to make him feel special.

The ruin was empty, but when he scrambled up the wall to scan the area, he couldn't see her. Okay, she must have headed to the trees.

She didn't want him for a husband, she wanted him for her war cabinet, and she'd played him perfectly. Just like all the other love-sick hopefuls at court, bouncing around her like corgis.

Into the trees now! Thick and dark, but look, see everything! Broken twig, wisp of gold on branch—keep running, *keep noticing!*

And of course, she hadn't run away. She'd realised that she, not he, was the Zygon's target, and she was leading it away from him, not the other way round. And it wasn't because she liked him, it was because she was the Queen and it was her duty.

Single footprint, scattered pile of leaves, two birds returning to a tree after a recent disturbance—*everything, Doctor, see it all, and run, run, run.* It was much easier to save them, he thought, when they weren't so much cleverer than him.

Through the trees ahead, a horizontal slash of gold. He threw himself towards it, tearing his way through the branches. She lay in the centre of a glade, unmoving, one thrown arm lying limp, red hair tangled with the bracken. As he reached to check her pulse, he saw that she was breathing. 'Your Majesty?'

Her eyes flickered open.

'My Doctor?'

There was no time to lose, so he was already pulling her to her feet. He could check her for injuries once they were safely away from here. 'That thing,' she gasped, 'it attacked me. What is it, what does it want?'

'That's what I'm trying to find out. Probably just your planet.'

'Doctor?' she said, and he frowned in puzzlement, because this time her lips hadn't moved and the voice seemed to be coming from behind him. He looked round.

73

Another flash of gold, and Elizabeth was stepping through the trees, her eyes fastened on the woman beside him. 'Step away from her, Doctor. That is not me. That is the creature!'

He looked between the two of them. Elizabeth and Elizabeth. Both perfect in every detail.

The Elizabeth at his side was staring in astonishment at the new arrival. 'How is that possible?' she asked. 'She's me. Doctor, she's me!'

'I am, indeed, me,' replied Elizabeth, staring into her own eyes. 'A compliment that cannot be extended to yourself.'

'Extraordinary,' said Elizabeth. 'The creature has caught my exact likeness—this is exceptional.'

They were both ignoring him now, circling each other, with the evil fascination of cats.

'Exceptional? A Queen would call it impertinent,' replied Elizabeth.

'A Queen would feel compelled to admire the skill of the execution—before arranging one,' replied Elizabeth.

'You have captured my wit but not my speed.'

'I was about to say the same.'

'But just a little later.'

Two of them, thought the Doctor. What if they worked in shifts—he'd never get a day off. Then he remembered the equipment in his hand. 'Sorry, ladies, if you could both just stay still for a tiny moment, this is a routine Queen check.' He twisted the dials, but nothing happened. He banged it against a tree trunk. 'It's not working,' he said. He looked up into four identical blue eyes now levelled at him like a firing squad. 'Could I have a minute to change the bulb?'

'One might surmise that the creature would learn quickly to protect itself from any simple means of detection,' remarked Elizabeth.

'Clearly you understand the creature better than I. But then, you have the advantage,' retorted Elizabeth.

'Indeed,' smiled Elizabeth. 'I have ridden its back.'

'Oh, a distinct touch!'

'A simple truth!'

'It is no easy thing to match wits with a being of unearthly attainment.'

'So you are to be congratulated!' they both said, and laughed.

No, thought the Doctor, they can't be bonding, that won't work! One's a megalomaniac from space and one's from Greenwich.

When the wind hit his face, he knew he'd felt it before, but for the moment he couldn't remember where. It was a warm wind, too warm for England, and smelled of old wood baking in the sun. He looked up. Hanging impossibly among the trees, was a slowly turning spiral of clouds and light, beautiful, eerie and silent. He knew in an instant he was looking into a slice of the time vortex—and what seemed even more impossible was that it felt familiar. As if he'd looked into that exact slice of vortex before. But how? When, where?

The Elizabeths were demanding to know what was going on, but now he was barely listening to them. Whatever was happening, it was more important than Queens and Zygons.

'Back, both of you, now!'

'What is that thing?' asked Elizabeth, and he didn't bother to check which one.

'It's a rupture in space and time, and I'll tell you something else—I think I've seen it before.'

'Where could you possibly have seen that?'

Where indeed? This was something from his past, he felt certain. But the trouble with the past, when you travelled in time as much as he did, was that a lot of it was still going on. Sometimes, as now, his memories felt more like a live feed. He found himself thinking of a barn. *That* barn. *That* day. The box at his feet, all those people about to die by his hand, all those children. But someone else was there too. Someone stood in the barn at his side. That wasn't right! He'd gone there alone, too ashamed to be witnessed. So who was this woman now laughing in his memories? She was sitting on the box, then she was stamping round the floor, mocking him. For a brief moment, as she laughed, her face turned clear of her hair, and *no, no, it couldn't be.* He hadn't known her then, that was before they'd even met. But then she laughed again, and yes, it was her. Impossible though it seemed, there she stood, in his memory, smiling at him from the last day of the Time War—Rose Tyler.

Elizabeth was pushing past him now, approaching the vortex. 'But how does it hang there?' she asked. 'It appears completely miraculous!'

The Doctor grabbed her away from it, pushed her round behind him. No time for ceremony.

'Sorry, your Majesty. Just stay away from it. That's a timeline fissure, it's not supposed to be here.'

'Your words are meaningless,' said one of them.

'You will explain, forthwith, what that thing is,' demanded the other.

'I can't, it's difficult. It's something from a long time ago. It's my past.'

Rose! How could Rose Tyler have been there?

'What about your past?' one of them was asking.

'I think it's playing up,' he said.

And then something came tumbling through the vortex. It landed just in front of him, a soft thump on the earth. His stomach turned over. For a moment, he didn't look down at what had arrived, because he didn't need to. This had all happened before, and now, somehow, it was happening again. No—it was *still* happening. It had never *stopped* happening. The air roared in his ears, the world turned at his feet, and shadows rose around him. Suddenly he understood, and the impact of understanding stopped his breath. He'd come so far, he'd saved so many, he'd made his penance, over and over—but not one day of it had been real. He had been living a fantasy—the hope-driven delusion of a repenting murderer. He had walked away from the slaughter of billions and dreamed an impossible redemption, and now he was waking to discover that none of it had happened. He was still in the barn. This was still the last day. The Time War had never ended.

It would take a moment to find the strength to look down, but of course he already knew what he'd see. Lying at his feet, there would be a battered old red hat of the type generally known as a—

There was a thunderous crack, followed by a tremendous crash and everywhere birds went clattering up from the trees. Something much larger had arrived from the vortex above, and had just hit the forest floor with a whirl of arms and legs and a loud 'Oof!'

The Doctor stared in astonishment. Struggling to his feet in front of him was a strange flail of a man—a jangle of limbs in purple tweed, a startled face under a swaying quiff, and a pair of nervous hands fluttering either side of a bow tie as if disagreeing about how to straighten it.

'Who is this?' demanded an Elizabeth.

The man was staring at the Doctor, thunderstruck. Then he laughed and clapped and all but twirled on the spot. The smile on his face was pleased and silly but there was a look of presumption about his eyes that annoyed the Doctor intensely, so he sent what he hoped was a very similar look right back.

'Doctor, who is this man, and what is he doing here?' demanded the other Elizabeth.

'Just what I was wondering,' said the Doctor, stepping towards the man, as the man, in mirror image, stepped towards him.

FEED CONNECTING
FEED CONNECTED
FEED STABLE
IF YOU ENCOUNTER ANY TYPOS, CONTINUITY
ERRORS OR PLOT HOLES, PLEASE CLOSE AND
RE-OPEN THE BOOK.

We are about to return to the Doctor in the National Gallery, who (if you can remember that far back in the future) had been called out by the military intelligence organisation known as UNIT, on the sealed orders of Her Majesty Elizabeth I—a woman we now realise was more intimately acquainted with the Doctor than history generally records. But you know what history is like, it's so easily embarrassed.

Now I can see a few of you looking uncomfortable, and one of you has just thrown the book across the room. Please give warning when you're feeling inclined to do that, I nearly dropped the pen. I suspect you worry about the vulgar light in which this book is presenting a cherished historical icon, renowned as the most famous virgin who ever lived, but I would remind you that the popular assumption of complete chastity and purity is almost certainly ill founded—after all, he had a granddaughter.

Now! To the gallery! The Doctor is standing in front of a painting of the Time War, with the sealed orders of his former—

oh, what shall we call her?—playmate?—in his hand. Those of you who want to pop back and refresh your memories, please do so now. Oh, there they all go, dashing off. Stampeding like a comfort break. Please be careful, flicking the pages like that, I'm getting a draught in here. And stay away from Chapter Nine, if you happen across it. All in good time, as the old fool himself would probably say.

Ah, here you all are, back again. Splendid.

One last warning before we resume. As you will have seen, at the end of the last chapter, we are now entering the area of the narrative where more than one iteration of the Doctor is active simultaneously. Now it is common among students such as yourselves to refer to the Doctors by number—the seventh Doctor, say, or the third Doctor—but of course he never does this himself. The Doctor thinks of himself only as the Doctor, whatever face he's wearing, so these papers can only refer to him that way—even when there is more than one Doctor present in a given sequence. To clarify: you are about to read material where multiple participants have the same name and are the same person, and it will be up to you to work out which one is talking or being talked about from the contextual evidence.

So please pay close attention, as we proceed to the next of the Doctor Papers, *Chapter Twelve,* The Leap of the Doctor.

Chapter 12

The Leap of the Doctor

'That's impossible,' Clara Oswald was saying. 'How's it doing that?' She had stepped forward to the painting, and now raised a hand to touch its surface. 'It's an oil painting,' she continued, 'in 3D!'

I pulled myself together to answer her. 'Time Lord art,' said the Doctor, straightening his bow tie. 'Bigger on the inside, a slice of real time, frozen.'

She was rocking from side to side in front of the picture, watching the buildings turn against the glowering sky. It was like looking down on a burning city, through a window—but the flames were frozen, and the window stood on an easel in the middle of a room. 'You don't even need those funny glasses,' she marvelled.

'He was there,' said the Doctor.

'Who was there?'

'Me.'

Clara looked at him. 'Doctor?'

'The other me. The one I don't talk about.'

'I don't understand,' said Clara, and glanced at Kate.

'You're not being clear, Doctor,' said Kate. 'Are you referring to yourself or someone else?'

Yeah, easy question, if you're a tiny little human with a ten-minute life span and one face. He felt himself recoil from his own anger. Where had that come from him? He'd closed the

81

door on all that rage a very long time ago. Keep it calm and clear, Doctor!

'I've had many faces,' he explained, 'many lives.'

Kate nodded. 'Yes, I know, we all know that. Regeneration. You have had a number of forms and faces.'

'Lives,' he insisted. 'But I don't admit to all of them. There's one life, one face, I've tried very hard to forget.'

There was a squeak from the side of the room. He glanced round. The girl in the long scarf was staring at him in what looked like panic.

'Yes, well, my colleague here is the expert on your faces,' said Kate. 'She's become quite obsessed about numbering them, so if you're about to pop a new one in, I think she'd have preferred to know *before* she got the tattoos.'

The girl went as red as a Zygon, and she looked so quickly at the floor the Doctor wondered if the rush of blood to her face had toppled her head forwards.

Zygons? Why was he thinking about Zygons?

'Okay,' Clara was saying, the brisk schoolteacher again. 'So this is a painting of the Time War, and you were there with a different face—you've told me the story, I know what you did—but it was ages ago. Why's this coming up now? Why have we been brought here to look at a painting?'

Ages ago! despaired the Doctor. Oh, Clara! When you're a time traveller, *nothing* is ever ages ago.

'We didn't,' Kate was replying. 'The painting serves only as Elizabeth's credentials. Proof that the letter is indeed from her. It's not why you're here.'

The Doctor had almost forgotten the envelope in his hand. He looked at it—the stiff, dusty paper, the ancient wax seal. Elizabeth! How had he left it with her? He had a vague sense that he hadn't behaved well, and that she was probably cross with him. He had bumped into her much older self at the Globe Theatre once, and she'd attempted to have him killed. But then that wasn't a first for her, and in truth a lot of his old friends did that when he called round. Winston Churchill had personally dug a pit for him, but then he loved a bit of gardening.

He ripped open the envelope, and unfolded the letter. Her handwriting was as clear and firm as the level blue gaze in his memory.

By order of HM Queen Elizabeth.

My dearest love, I hope the painting known as Gallifrey Falls *will serve as proof that it is your Elizabeth who writes to you now. You will recall that you pledged yourself to me as a protector of my Kingdom. It is in this capacity that I have appointed you as Curator of the Under Gallery, where deadly danger to England is locked away. Should any disturbance occur within its walls, it is my wish that you be summoned. God speed, gentle husband.*

He quickly folded the letter away before Clara could read the last word. Husband? He'd always had a vague sense that he'd probably married Elizabeth at some point, but it had been a busy life, and he was bit unsure as to why or when. He wondered if it was a happy marriage, but then realised the chances were slim, given that he hadn't seen her for several centuries, and she was dead.

He looked to Kate. 'What's happened?'

'Easier to show you,' she said. She nodded to the soldiers standing guard on the painting, and started to lead the way out of the room. Clara was already following her, and as the Doctor turned to do the same, he noticed another of the UNIT personnel—a scientist, going by the white coat—frowning in puzzlement at the screen of his mobile phone. Clearly he'd just answered it, and now seemed to be staring in disbelief at the caller ID. The Doctor would barely have registered this, if the scientist hadn't then looked up directly into his face, stared at him for a moment in seeming shock, before turning quickly away. As the Doctor headed after the others, he heard the scientist talking into his phone. His voice was low and urgent, with a faint Irish accent, but it carried down the long, cavernous corridor: 'But that's not possible, sir,' came the scientist's voice. 'He's right here.'

'I'm a schoolteacher,' said Clara, suddenly crashing across his thoughts, as usual.

'I know. I know that. Did I know that? I'm sure I knew that.'

'I'm good at reading handwriting. Even upside down.'

'Good, great, I'm glad you shared that. So long as we're discussing rare skill sets, when it comes to the pogo stick—'

'Husband!' said Clara.

Oh! thought the Doctor. They walked along in silence for a moment, but he knew she wouldn't let it lie.

'Husband,' she repeated. 'Queen Elizabeth the First called you husband.'

'Yeah, she did, didn't she? I think that's probably just a term of affection sometimes.'

'No, it absolutely never is. Not even in marriages. Are you married?'

'I may have been. I've been around a bit, Clara, I'm probably married to lots of people, it happens,' he said, and made a dismissive hand gesture, to suggest that the occasional marriage was really no more than a parking ticket, and a moment later heard a vase smash behind him. He really had to get his peripheral movements under control.

'But to her, though?'

'Oh, to her, to him, to who-knows. Sometimes the conversation just gets out of control. I think I'm even married to Jack Harkness, but there were a lot of people in the room at the time, it was hard to keep track.'

'Jack who?'

'He'll get around to you.'

Ahead of them, Kate was opening a pair of doors and, as she stood aside to wave them in, the Doctor found himself coming to a halt. Whatever he had expected to see in the room, it hadn't been this.

The eyes were as lethal and blue as ever, the hair still a tangle of red, and she hadn't aged a day. The smile he'd known so well wasn't there, but looked as though it might arrive any second, and as usual, she wasn't giving anything away. He straightened his bow tie, sent a silent message to his quiff to behave itself, and took a moment to shine his shoes on the backs of his trouser legs, as he had always done when entering the presence of his wife, Elizabeth I of England.

'Is that her?' Clara was asking. Usually she had no sense of occasion, but this time she had the decency to whisper. He contained himself to a brisk little nod. 'Who's the skinny bloke?'

In the shadows behind Elizabeth, stood a youngish, sharply featured man who seemed somehow familiar. There was a look of presumption about his eyes that annoyed the Doctor intensely, so he sent what he hoped was a very similar look right back.

Kate had stepped forward. She now reached across the Queen, clicked something behind the frame, and Elizabeth and the skinny stranger swung out of sight as the whole painting hinged open like a door.

Cold air and the smell of damp stone spilled from behind the painting, and the room seemed to darken, as if the light was being drained into the open doorway that was now revealed. Just visible was the beginning of a stone staircase leading sharply down, into the distant glimmer of torchlight.

'Welcome,' Kate said, 'to the Under Gallery.'

'The what?' Clara asked.

'In the reign of Elizabeth the First, certain artworks were deemed too dangerous for public display.'

'Nothing changes,' said Clara. 'People always lock up art.'

Kate had passed them both electric torches, and now clicked on one of her own. 'In the case of this particular gallery, they had a reason,' she said, stepping into the dark. 'They had to stop it getting out.'

'The universe was born alive,' said the Doctor, answering Clara's question, as they crunched down the second flight of stone steps, 'but it could only become aware of itself by developing sensors across its surface, known as life forms—that's us—each of which suffers a temporary delusion of separate identity during data collection—that's what we call consciousness—but in reality has no more individual existence than the hairs on your forearm when they tell you there's a draught—'

'I was asking,' said Clara, as they descended yet more steps, 'about you and Elizabeth.'

'You said begin at the beginning.'

'Not the beginning of the universe.'

'You didn't specify.'

'You're just trying to waste time. You're avoiding the subject.'

'Ah, that's exactly where you're wrong,' he said. 'You can't waste time, because the passage of time is an illusion caused by the permanent discrepancy between your memory and your circumstances across all the simultaneously experienced moments of your life. Is that noise bothering anyone else?'

'What noise?' Kate asked, turning from in front of them. But the Doctor just frowned and shook his head, and they began crunching down the steps to the next level.

Each deeper layer of the Under Gallery seemed darker and colder than the one before. As they descended, it became clear that the purpose of this place was not display but containment. All the statues were bound and sheeted—the muffled shapes of reaching hands and straining faces looming in their torch beams—and the paintings were all hung face to the wall, some with warnings printed on the back. One of them read, DO NOT TURN WHILE ALONE. Everywhere there were glass-fronted cabinets, tall as wardrobes, with bars and padlocks. Clara had shone her torch in a few of them. In one she saw racks of green daggers whose blades seemed to reflect her eyes back at her whatever angle she was looking from. In another there were rows of skulls that looked human but each with only one central eye socket above the grinning teeth. There were shelves of thick, bulging books bound shut with twine, a few with nails driven into the spines and dark stains crusting round the punctures. She looked in a mirror that only showed the back of her head, and as she turned away from it, sensed her own face in the glass turning to watch her go. Suddenly in her torch beam, there was a cabinet crammed to bursting with mummified rats, their claws and teeth splayed against the glass doors. As she recoiled a step, the rat mass seemed to twitch.

They descended another staircase, and she noticed more and more of the cabinets stood open and empty, as if they'd been ransacked.

'Some of the stuff has been moved elsewhere,' explained Kate.

'Where?' asked Clara, flashing her torch across a few of them. There was a letter B chalked on the door of every emptied cabinet.

'And by whose authority?' added the Doctor.

'The Curator.'

'I thought I was the Curator.'

'It's complicated. You're never here, the job had to be split.'

'Among whom?'

'It's complicated.'

'Really,' protested the Doctor, 'is that noise not bothering anyone else?'

'Well perhaps if you told us *what* noise?' said Clara. 'Or alternatively, what you were up to with Elizabeth the First, and why she calls you husband.'

He came to a halt, looked at them impatiently for a moment, then started walking on the spot. Crunch, crunch, crunch. 'The crunching. The crunchy crunch-crunching. Can't anyone else hear crunching?' He directed his torch beam at the floor. 'Forgive an enquiring mind,' he said, 'but what have we been walking in?'

In the light of their torches, they saw that the floor was covered with what looked grit or sand. Kate sighed. 'Well I'm terribly sorry if our housekeeping isn't up to your standards, Doctor ...'

'That's the thing about being a curator, you can't turn your back for a minute.' The Doctor was kneeling on the floor now, running a handful of grit, through his fingers. 'Dust,' he mused. 'Dust made of stone.'

'You mean sand,' said Clara.

'Stone dust. Dust, or powder, composed entirely of tiny particles of different varieties of rock.'

'Yeah, sand.'

'*Sand!*' declared the Doctor, as if he'd just invented the word.

'Do you think it's important?' Kate asked.

'Dunno. But in twelve hundred years, I've never stepped in anything that wasn't.' He licked a little of the grit from his finger, sloshed it round his mouth, then tried a little more.

'Can you tell something from the taste?' asked Clara.

'No, just peckish.' He straightened up, flashed his torch beam behind him. The girl in the long scarf startled back from the light. 'You,' he said. 'Are you sciencey or soldiery?'

Self-consciously, she straightened her white coat. 'Yes,' she husked, and the Doctor thought if her eyes got any wider, they would fill the lenses of her spectacles.

'She's science,' said Kate from behind him. 'And she's brilliant.'

'Good, science and brilliant are my favourite words. Do you have a name?' he asked.

'Yes.'

'Great, I've always wanted to meet someone called Yes, that's also my favourite word. If your name is already Yes, it's going to save a lot of time when I make suggestions.'

'Her name is Osgood, her IQ is through the roof, and if you patronise her again I will cut you off at the bow tie,' said Kate.

'Osgood is now my new favourite word. Osgood, could you get this stone dust analysed. Tell me what it's made of, tell me everything.'

'Yes!' she said, before adding, 'Yes!' and then, 'Yes!'

'I can see why they call you that.'

'Doctor!' warned Kate, then turned to Osgood. 'Get a team here, fast as you can, analyse the stone dust, sand, whatever it is.'

'Yes,' said Osgood, still staring at the Doctor. She was taking big whooping breaths, which bounced the spectacles on her nose, and the Doctor found himself pleasantly reminded of the TARDIS engines.

'Inhaler!' snapped Kate.

Osgood jammed her inhaler in her mouth, and hurried off, back the way she'd come.

The Doctor watched her disappear into the shadows, wondering why he made her so nervous, and if there was anything he could say to relax her. 'Great to meet you, Osgood!' he called after her, in his most reassuring voice. 'I'd love to see your tattoos some time!'

There was a squeak from the darkness, and the crash of a collision.

'This way,' said Kate, with the determined calm of a woman who had successfully not punched someone. 'We're nearly there.'

'Nearly where?' asked the Doctor as he and Clara followed.

'This is the deepest level. Most of the stuff above was added later. Some of it is nonsense—fairground hoaxes, a lot of it, and some frankly lunatic attempts at censorship.' They had rounded a corner, and Kate was now shining her torch on what looked like a bank vault door, which stood slightly ajar, slicing a wedge of yellow light across the floor. 'But down here is the original purpose of Elizabeth's Under Gallery.'

'Hence the updated security?' asked Clara.

'Quite so. The maintenance of the seal on this door, in all its incarnations down the centuries, is the longest-standing executive order in England. It was guarded throughout the London Blitz by an entire platoon of soldiers, permanently stationed here.'

Clara frowned. 'So why's it open?'

'That's what we were wondering.'

'So it wasn't you who opened it then?'

'It was found this way.'

'Was anything taken?' The Doctor spoke from a few feet behind them. Kate looked round, to see him bent over at a cabinet, peering inside with his torch.

'Nothing is missing. Only damaged.'

'What, someone broke in and just vandalised?' asked Clara.

'Essentially.'

'Vandalised what?' said the Doctor. As he spoke, he'd buzzed his screwdriver at the cabinet doors. They swung open and he pulled something from inside.

'Doctor,' sighed Clara. 'You don't need another fez.'

The Doctor ignored her. He turned the battered old hat over and over in his hands, his face troubled, as if haunted by a memory.

'Why would you lock up a hat?' he asked.

'I told you, there's an awful lot of nonsense down here, it's probably nothing.'

'Nothing ...' repeated the Doctor, thoughtfully. Then he caught Clara's worried stare, grinned, and popped the fez on his head. 'What do you think?'

'You don't need another one, you've got four in the TARDIS.'

'I can't wear those, they're presents from Tommy. How do I look?'

'Like an idiot.'

'Ker-ching!'

'If I can drag you back to the current moment,' Kate said, 'and the reason you're actually here.' She gestured to the vault door. 'You wanted to know what had been vandalised?' She led the way inside.

In contrast to the rest of the Under Gallery, the room was white, well lit, and almost empty. A modest selection of paintings hung on the walls, these ones facing out in the normal way. They were perfectly ordinary landscapes for the most part, and only two things made them unusual in any respect. One was that in every case, the glass in the frames had been smashed, and lay in fragments on the floor. The other, Clara didn't notice until she stepped forward.

'They're 3D,' she said. 'Like the one upstairs.'

'Time Lord art,' confirmed the Doctor. 'Or at rate, art made by the same technology, though these seem to be Earth landscapes. Elizabethan period, probably. Part of the same collection as *Gallifrey Falls*?' he asked Kate.

She shook her head. '*Gallifrey Falls* is the personal property of the Curator.'

'You mean me?'

'It's complicated. These are from the private collection of Elizabeth the First. No information on how they came into her possession. On her personal order, they were stored first underneath Richmond Palace, then moved here for greater security, in 1826. By Royal command, they are to be stored under lock and key as long as England exists, and shown to no one. They can't even be mentioned in written material. The paintings you are looking at have officially not existed since 1562.'

'And now someone's broken in and just smashed the glass?' said Clara.

'No,' said the Doctor. 'I'm afraid that's not what happened at all.' He looked at Kate. 'Is it?'

'It doesn't seem that way no.'

'Look at the glass, Clara. I think you'll find it's interesting.'

Clara frowned, bent to the look at the fragments on the floor. 'Why? Because it's broken?'

'No. Because of where it's broken *from*. Look at the shatter pattern. The glass on all these paintings was broken from the *inside*.'

'How's that possible?'

'Lots of ways, none of them good. Is there a theory, Kate?'

'Not a theory, exactly, but there's an anomaly. As you can see, all the paintings are landscapes—no figures of any kind.'

'Okay, yes. So?'

'There used to be.' Kate had pulled her phone from her pocket. On the screen, she showed them photographs of the paintings they could see on the wall. Although they were the same landscapes, in the photographs, there were distant figures scattered across them.

Clara's eyes went to the glass on the floor. 'Something came out of the paintings,' she said.

'A lot of somethings,' said the Doctor. He stepped to the vault door and buzzed it with his screwdriver. 'This door was forced from the inside. From in here.'

'Yes, that's what we thought too.'

'This wasn't a break-in. It was a break-*out*.' He turned his frown on Kate. 'I presume you've searched this place?'

'There's nothing here that shouldn't be. And nothing has got out of the building—that would set off every alarm in UNIT HQ.'

The Doctor's eyes found Clara's and it was one of those moments where the air seemed to crackle. 'So whatever came out of the paintings is still down here. In the dark. With us.'

'We've done a complete sweep, there are no hostiles present.'

'There's an awful lot of sand.'

'Are you suggesting the sand is hostile?'

'No, it's sand. It's inert, in no way alive, just rock particles.' He was pacing up and down now, drumming his fingers on the top of his fez. 'But it's everywhere, everywhere, *everywhere*! You're missing the point, Kate!'

'What point?'

'No idea, I'm missing it too. Clara, what's the point?'

'Don't know.'

'Great, now Clara's missing the point. Could everybody *stop missing points all the time!*'

The first thing he noticed was the fez flying from his head and tumbling across the floor. The second was the sand in the corridor outside whipping into the air. He bounded out of the room, and straight into a wind that now battered and buffeted through the gallery. At first it smelled of old wood in a desert, but a moment later it was an English forest in spring.

He turned towards its source, already knowing what he would see. He was aware of Kate and Clara coming to join him. They were probably staring too, but he didn't turn to check.

'What is it?' Clara was asking.

Not now, thought the Doctor. Please don't come for me now, I'm *busy!*

'Doctor, are you going to tell us what that is?' asked Kate. 'Or don't you know?'

Clara was stepping forward, curious. The Doctor took hold of her arm and stepped her back from the swirling vortex of light and clouds now filling the other end of the corridor. It was just hanging there, turning in silence, as it had in the barn a long time ago, and then later above him in the forest.

'Doctor?' Clara was saying. But memories were flashing through his head, blotting out the present. Rose Tyler in the barn. But that wasn't right, she'd never been on Gallifrey. Two Elizabeths in a forest. But why were there two of her? He didn't remember that. And now a man was crashing down out of the sky, right at his feet. Who was this banana-faced idiot, laughing at him?

'*Doctor!*' Clara's voice.

'Sorry,' he said, trying to force himself to concentrate. 'It's just ... my past, I think.'

'Your past?'

'Yes. It's playing up.' Hang on, he'd said that before. He'd said those exact words before, in a very similar conversation. When, though, *when, when?*

93

Kate was talking now, her voice rising. 'Doctor, can at you least theorise on what this is—I am responsible for all UNIT personnel on site. Is it do with the paintings?'

'No,' he replied, 'this is something else.' Fragments of memory were surfacing now. Details, glimpses. Not everything, but enough to know that whatever was about to happen, it was huge.

'Clara, fetch me that fez,' he said, before becoming aware of the look he was receiving and fetching it himself. He stood in front of the vortex, as if hypnotised by it. It seemed to him that the other two might still be talking, but it was so hard to focus now. He wondered how he ever managed to hear anyone with all these memories banging away in his head.

'Doctor!' Oh, that was Clara again. 'Doctor, are you okay?'

'Excuse me, both,' he replied, smiling. 'This is where I come in.' And he wound back his arm, and threw the fez as hard as he could. It spun down the vortex and was sucked out of existence, with an electric crack and a whiff of ozone. But where had it landed? The past, certainly, but which past? The barn? The forest? Both perhaps, but how? Clara and Kate were still talking, but they sounded miles behind him now; the silent vortex drowned out everything, buzzing in his hair, humming in his blood. This vortex had been following him for hundreds of years. He couldn't exactly remember why, or how it had all started, but he knew, with absolute certainty, he was looking down the tunnel of his own life; a tangle of days, leading back to the man he had once been. All the paths he had chosen to reach the place he stood now had opened at his feet again; all the mistakes and regrets and wrong turnings. No second chances, he had told someone once. Was that true? It was time, he decided, for a leap of faith.

'Geronimo,' shouted the Doctor, and leapt into history.

He'd thought perhaps he'd tumble down a void for a moment, but it was simpler than that. The Under Gallery just disappeared, there was a rush of wind and sunshine, and suddenly trees were spinning round his head. He'd just started to wonder how he could be flying through the air, when the ground slammed into him. He didn't recognise any of the stars now whirling round his head, but some of the little tweeting birds seemed familiar. He tried to focus on the forest floor, which had somehow risen up to stand vertical, and was pressing into the side of his face. It would probably sort itself out in a minute, if he just leaned against it and had a bit of a rest. He winked at one of the funny birds, and it winked back.

'Who is this?' demanded a voice he almost recognised. Give us a moment, love, just got here.

'Doctor, who is this man, and what is he doing here?' The same woman. Honestly, settle down, there's birds and stars and the ground is all leaning against me.

'Just what I was wondering,' said a man's voice he didn't recognise at all. He made an effort to focus. Four Queen Elizabeths stood staring at him. He shook his head, cleared it, and noticed with relief that there were only two. *Two?* When had there been two? He thought hazily of that birthday when River had cloned herself, then remembered just in time to delete that incident from any written account of his adventures. Also staring at him, he noticed, was a pair of Converse. He looked up. Frowning down at him, from a few feet away, was a man he thought he should recognise. He looked vital and wiry, in a tight suit and tie. The big dark eyes would have seemed tearful if the face hadn't been so cheeky. He stood like he was posing for an album cover, feet planted wide on the ground, fists balled at his sides, head angled for maximum glare; as skinny and sharp and clever as Mum's favourite in a boy band. That was odd, thought the Doctor—he could remember describing someone else that way. Who had that been? It seemed to him that he'd been looking into a mirror at the time, and the man he'd been describing was—

Himself. It was him. The man in the forest, staring down at him from one face ago, was *him*. The Doctor scrambled to his feet and stared in fascination at his younger self. 'Skinny!' was all he could find to say. 'That is proper skinny! I've never seen it from the outside. Matchstick man!'

The Doctor was now stepping towards him, and he found himself doing the same. Although those big brown eyes were now clouded in puzzlement, he noticed an air of presumption about them, that irritated him intensely, so he shot an even more presumptuous look back, until he was rewarded with a confused frown.

'You're not …' said the Doctor, as if finally understanding who this new arrival was. 'You can't be …' The eyes now looked pained, as they flashed to the Doctor's bow tie. The Doctor returned the pained look with a smile. You'll get there, mate, he thought, bow ties are cool, and reached under his coat. He paused a moment, as he saw that the Doctor had reached under his jacket in exactly the same way, and had now also paused. They stood there like mirror images for a second, eyeing each other, then they smiled and produced their sonic screwdrivers. They held them up, like badges of office.

The Doctor noticed that his new screwdriver was substantially larger than the old version in the Doctor's hand, and found himself smiling. The Doctor returned his smile with a look of disdain, and asked, 'Compensating?'

'For what?' asked the Doctor.

'Regeneration,' replied the Doctor. 'It's a lottery.' He stuffed his teeny-tiny, ickle-wickle screwdriver back in his jacket. 'Now look,' he said, trying to make his voice all deep, 'what's going on? What are you doing here, in my time zone?' He glanced at the Elizabeths. 'I'm busy!'

His time zone?? What did he mean, *his* time zone. For a moment the Doctor wondered just who the Doctor thought he was, then followed his look to the two Elizabeths, who were staring in confusion at them both. 'Oh, busy, is that what we're calling it?' He gave his best elaborate bow. 'Hello, ladies!'

'Just don't,' warned the Doctor, from behind him.

'Private little outing, is it? Couples only? Just the three of you? Well, four of us now. Ooh, complicated. Double dating for two!'

'Don't start. I'm in the middle of something.'

'Oh, I can see that, you're right in there,' the Doctor laughed. 'But look, fair play, whatever you get up to in the privacy of your own regeneration is your business.'

'One of them's a Zygon.'

'Well, I'm not judging you.'

'Are you listening to me? One of these two is an alien hostile, intent on the conquest of this planet!'

'Well in that case, mate, I don't think much of yours.'

There was a humming, sizzling noise from above. The Doctor spun round—the vortex from which he'd just emerged was flexing in the air, stretching and twisting. 'What's wrong with it?' the Doctor asked him.

'I don't know,' he replied.

'Well what's it doing here then?'

'I don't know that either.'

'Well, you're the one who fell out of it.'

'You're the one I nearly fell on,' the Doctor snapped back, and turned to the Elizabeths. 'Listen, you two. That thing up there— possibly very dangerous. You both need to get out of here.'

Rather to the Doctor's annoyance, they both looked straight past him to the Doctor. 'But what about the creature?' they asked in unison. The Doctor took a step towards them, making frankly unfair use of the big brown eyes. 'Whichever of you is the real Elizabeth,' he said, 'turn and run in the opposite direction to the other Elizabeth.' Clever, thought the Doctor, as he listened, and wondered if he was being immodest. The Elizabeths looked at each other, and then each in turn stepped right past the Doctor and planted a long and noisy kiss on the Doctor. As each kiss went on and on and on, the Doctor found himself standing next to the other Elizabeth, shrugging apologies, while she observed in horror the activities of his younger self. In the catalogue of his personal humiliations, the Doctor decided this was a new low.

'One of those was a Zygon,' the Doctor reminded himself, as the Elizabeths tore off in opposite directions.

'I know,' said the Doctor, discreetly wiping his mouth on his sleeve.

'Big red rubbery thing. Covered in suckers. Venom sacs in the tongue.'

'Yes, I'm getting the point, thank you.'

'I think I'm still getting rid of the taste.'

'Oh, you think you're so funny!'

'From you, that's a compliment.'

There was another crackle from the vortex above, and this time a voice. 'Doctor? Is that you?'

Clara! It was Clara's voice, no question. 'Clara? Hello? Can you hear us?'

'Yeah, we can hear you. Are you okay?'

'I'm fine, yes. Are you still in the Under Gallery?'

'Course, yeah. Where are you?'

The Doctor realised he didn't know, and glanced at the Doctor, who called out, 'England, 1562.'

'Who's that?' called Clara. 'Who are you talking to?'

The Doctors looked at each other, and grinned. 'Myself,' they said in unison.

Now it was Kate's voice. 'The portal, or whatever it is, seems to be becoming unstable.'

'Possibly, yes,' replied the Doctor. 'This end too.'

'Then you should come back through, immediately,' said Kate, sounding more like her father than he thought possible. 'In case it closes.'

She had a point. The Doctor looked around, and then grabbed his fez off the ground. 'Where are they talking from?'

the Doctor asked him. 'Who are those people?' The Doctor ignored him, and shouted into the vortex again:

'Physical passage may not be possible in both directions,' he explained. 'Let me just try something first. Fez incoming.' He threw his fez up into the vortex. He watched as it was sucked out of existence, and waited. Silence. 'Did you get it?' he asked. 'Is it there?'

'Is what here?' asked Kate.

'The fez! I threw the fez back through.'

'Nothing came through here.'

He was vaguely aware of the Doctor, now grinning cheekily right at his ear. 'Looks like we're down one fez. Go on, try the bow tie next.'

The Doctor wasn't listening. His hand had gone to his head, and he could almost feel the connections snapping together inside. He understood now. He knew exactly where the fez had gone. It had disappeared into the vortex, whirled backwards through time and landed slap bang in the middle his memories. If he was right, it was now lying at his own feet, on the floor of a barn, a very long time ago.

The Doctor interrupted his thoughts. 'Okay, you used to be me, this is your second go. What happens now?'

'I don't remember,' he replied.

'How could you forget this?'

'It's not my fault. You're obviously not paying enough attention!' It wasn't strictly true, he realised. However hard the Doctor concentrated, two of them standing together played havoc with the timelines and made it all but impossible to form lasting memories. He had a sudden image of himself, pacing in a cold room, explaining that the timelines were tied in a knot and his memory was all over the place. Where had that been? He dismissed the thought and raised his screwdriver.

'What are you doing?' asked the Doctor.

'Reversing the polarity.'

'Is that all we ever do?' said the Doctor, raising his very much smaller, teeny-weeny screwdriver. 'Isn't there anything new in the future?'

The smaller screwdriver buzzed alongside his, as they both aimed into the vortex. 'It's not working,' he said, after the moment.

'We're *both* reversing the polarity!' said the Doctor.

'I know!'

'There's two of us—I'm reversing it and you're reversing it back again! We're standing here, cancelling each other.'

'Well stop then.'

'*You* stop!'

'No, *you* stop!'

He reached for the Doctor's screwdriver and in the same moment the Doctor tried to grab his. Their momentary tussle was interrupted by a tremendous crash from a few feet away. They stared at one another, neither wanting to turn and look. Something else had dropped through the vortex, and hit the forest floor. There had been no cry of pain on impact, but now they heard a few grunts of effort and the crack of an old man's knees. Someone had just climbed to their feet.

The forest was still. Birds twittered, bees droned, wind rustled. Still they didn't look.

'Anyone lose a fez?' said a voice like a silken rasp.

The flesh of his face hung like the leather of his jacket and his smoke-slitted eyes glittered like blades.

FEED CONNECTING
FEED CONNECTED
FEED STABLE
PLEASE REMEMBER THAT THE PAGE NUMBERING IS ENTIRELY PSYCHIC AND MAY VARY AT TIMES AS A COMMENT ON YOUR READING SPEED.

Now look, this is getting out of hand. Too many of you are complaining about Chapter Nine, and the publishers are now forcing me to take action. Look, I did warn you all, it's really not my fault.

While I'm dealing with this, please proceed to Chapter Two, The Children of the Doctor.

Chapter 2

The Children of the Doctor

Whatever I had expected it wasn't this. The trees around me suggested Earth, and it was a brisk, beautiful day though not quite summer; the sunlight was golden, but the air still held that refreshing chill. The glade I found myself in was almost entirely deserted and as I looked around I could see no sign of a TARDIS, or any possible iteration of myself. Had something gone wrong?

She had stood, smiling, by the vortex and told me my future lay on the other side. I had stepped through, if not in hope, in curiosity. But here I stood, alone. Well, almost alone. I glanced again at the two identical twelve-year-old boys who stood a few feet from me, apparently having a little squabble. This time I noticed they were dressed slightly differently, perhaps so people could tell them apart; one of them wore a big coat with a bow tie, and the other one had clearly stolen a suit from Daddy's wardrobe, though he'd only been able to find a pair of tennis shoes to go with it. Obviously they were playing dress-up. Boy wizards, perhaps, cavorting around a forest, looking for demons to battle. In my previous life, as the Doctor, I'd rather enjoyed those books, and there had a been a time, long ago, when I might even have joined in their games. Perhaps created a little magic for them, with the sonic screwdriver.

But today I had work to do.

I cleared my throat and, realising my sudden appearance among the trees might alarm them, I spoke softly. 'Anyone lose a fez?' I held up the battered, red hat which must have been thrown from this very spot.

They looked at me in obvious terror. I was used to that. Time and warfare had not been kind to my appearance.

'You,' squeaked one of the boys. 'How can you be here?'

'More to the point, why are you here?' squeaked the other.

I looked into their wide, tearful eyes, and wondered why the Interface would have chosen this place, and these two, for my vision of the future.

'Good afternoon,' I said, as gently as I could, 'I'm looking for the Doctor.'

'Well you've certainly come to the right place,' said Daddy's Suit.

'Good, right,' I said. So they knew my future self, that would speed things along. And wherever Future Me was, he was calling himself the Doctor again, which was interesting. 'Well, who are you boys, then?' I asked, trying to sound jovial. 'His companions?' I added, with a laugh.

'His *companions*?' squeaked Bow Tie. He sounded a little indignant and, looking at their hurt faces, I realised that I had been too amused at the idea of either of them being likely TARDIS crewmembers.

'Goodness me,' I said, giving them my warmest smile. 'They get younger all the time! Well if you could just point me in the general direction of the Doctor ...'

They looked at me, defiant. They each held a magic wand in their hand and now proffered them for my inspection. I fought down a sigh and tried to look impressed. I even smiled, approving, but still the wands were being held out. As they awaited some further reaction, I started to notice a hint of presumption in their eyes, which I found intensely irritating, but given their youth, I resisted an impulse to give them a very similar look back. Then, as I turned my attention back to their magic wands, I noticed something. They weren't magic wands at all! In fact, I was looking at a pair of sonic screwdrivers. The implications of that took a few seconds to unravel in my brain.

It is fair to say that in those seconds, for the first time in a very long and often difficult life, I understood why people carried hip flasks.

I stared into their faces again. They weren't twelve years old, now that I looked properly. Indeed, they were taller than me. The one with the tennis shoes was probably shaving. A terrible possibility was now circling in my head but I wasn't quite ready to let it land. 'Really?' I heard myself say.

'Yes!' said one, and 'Really!' said the other.

'You …' I said, and my voice failed me. 'You are …' but again I couldn't complete the thought. I scanned their faces for any trace of dignity, of wisdom, or any of those qualities I flattered myself I had displayed throughout my lives. Nothing stared back at me, except perfectly modulated vacuity. It was like watching television! I steeled myself, and spoke the necessary, yet preposterous, words. 'You … are *me*?'

'Yes!' they both declared at a pitch of outrage that must have alerted dogs for miles around.

'*Both* of you.'

'Both of us!'

I pointed at the one with the bow tie and asked, 'Even *that* one?'

'Yes!'

Try as I might, I couldn't assemble the thought in my mind. 'You …' My voice faltered again, but I braced myself for the final assault. 'You … are my future selves?'

'Yes!'

I fought for words. Those two smooth faces, barely used, unmarked by character or history; all that hair, clearly attended to and even styled; the affectation of the tennis shoes; the desperation of the bow tie—the Interface had shown me my future, and here it stood in front of me, ready to present *Blue Peter*.

'Am I having a midlife crisis?' I snapped, and then realised I might have spoken too abruptly. Certainly they both stepped back, in seeming alarm, and swished their magic wands towards me. No, not wands, I forced myself to remember. Sonic screwdrivers. 'Why are you pointing your screwdrivers like that?' I demanded. 'They're scientific instruments, not water pistols!' Only then it occurred to me that the screwdrivers were not aimed at me at all, but a point just over my shoulder. I now heard a voice crying out from behind.

'Surround them, take them now!'

I cursed myself. For the longest-standing veteran of the Time War to be so easily surprised was shaming indeed. I spun round, and to my relief saw nothing more dangerous than a large number of armed soldiers. They came pouring through the trees, surrounding the three of us. Elizabethan, I noted, probably early 1560s going by the scabbard length, 32 of them, average height 172 cm, swords and dogs only. In normal circumstances, I wouldn't have laid aside a sandwich, but today I was encumbered. I glanced round and sure enough, there they were, prancing all over the place, randomly pointing their screwdrivers at the new arrivals, as if that would accomplish anything. 'Will you stop pointing those things,' I thundered at them. 'They're screwdrivers! What are you going to do, assemble a cabinet at them?'

'You are encircled,' declared a young man, with a face so forgettable I couldn't retain it while still looking. 'Which of you is the Doctor?' he demanded.

'You mean you're not?' I replied. 'That makes a refreshing change.'

'I would have the Doctor's head,' he declared.

'Well, take your pick,' I replied. 'This has all the makings of your lucky day. What has the Doctor's head been up to, if I may ask?'

'The Queen of England is bewitched.'

'Ah, Elizabeth the First, splendid. Remarkable woman, though I have not yet had the pleasure of a personal encounter.' I thought I heard a snigger from behind me, but I ignored it. 'In what way is she bewitched?'

'She placed the Doctor on the scaffold, then spared his life and took him as her lover. There must be witchcraft in this.'

I roared with laughter. Lover indeed! 'I assure you, sir, the Doctor is an old—let's say, friend of mine—and while he might be inclined to interfere with history, he rather draws the line at interfering with—' I broke off, because I had glanced behind to see that one of the Harry Potters was looking decidedly shifty.

The other one gave me a little shrug and an apologetic look. 'In fairness to him,' he said, 'it might have been the squid. It's 50–50.'

'What is that?' The shout of alarm came from the forgettable young man. (I assume it was the same one, but there was no real way of telling.)

The soldiers were now looking up at the vortex above them. It had started to buzz and shimmer, and so drawn their attention. I wondered if the dimensional anchors were working loose. I wouldn't have long, if I wanted to return that way.

'What witchcraft is this?' cried out the young man. (Again, probably the same one.)

'Yes, that is witchcraft, in fact,' said a voice, ringing with authority. I looked round in surprise. Bow Tie was now striding into the centre of the ring of soldiers, suddenly demonstrating a calm and a command, that I would not have judged him to possess. 'Ooh, witchetty witch-o witchcraft,' he went on, completely destroying the effect, with what I can only describe as a moment of boogie. He now moved towards the vortex and shouted into it. 'Hello?' he called. 'Hello, in there? Excuse me, hello! Am I talking to the wicked witch of the well?'

There was, of course, silence. What did the fool think he could possibly accomplish by—

'Hello?' came a voice from the vortex. 'Sorry, what were you saying?' It was a young woman speaking, but it certainly wasn't the voice of the weapon interface, which had not, thus far, carried even a hint of Blackpool. But how was this possible? There had been no one else in the barn. Unless, of course, this dimensional opening gave onto multiple locations, which was, I judged, entirely feasible.

'Trying to talk to the wicked witch, actually,' Bow Tie told the vortex.

'Why do I have to be a wicked witch?'

'Ah, there you are, wicked witch. Would you mind telling these prattling mortals to get themselves begone?'

The vortex buzzed again, and shimmered. I gave a silent prayer that it would hold firm.

'What he said,' came the girl's voice, at last.

'Tiny bit more colour,' insisted Bow Tie.

Even across the dimensional divide it was possible to detect a sigh. Then she resumed in a high, commanding voice: 'Right, prattling mortals, off you pop, or I'll turn you all into frogs.' She sounded like a schoolteacher.

'Frogs, nice. You heard her.' The boys were now wagging their fingers at the surrounding soldiers who somehow managed to look impressed. Not an elite division, then.

'Doctor, what's going on. How can you be in 1562?' called the voice.

'Oh, it's nothing, never mind,' replied Bow Tie, waving a hand and coming within a dangerous inch of slapping me. 'Just a timey-wimey thing.'

'A what? A timey-*what*?' I said.

There was a touch on my arm, and Daddy's Suit was giving me a sympathetic look. 'I have no idea where he picks up that stuff.'

'The Queen!' cried one of the forgettables, and for a moment I was puzzled to see all the soldiers drop to their knees. Then, from among the trees behind us, came a voice, clear as a bell and of exquisite refinement.

'You don't seem to be kneeling. How tremendously brave of you.'

I turned. She was not as tall as I had expected, nor as imperious in her demeanour, but beneath the merriment of her eyes, I sensed strength and resolve at a level I rarely encountered. This would be an ally indeed, I thought, as Queen Elizabeth of England stepped into the glade. I was about to introduce myself, and make the appropriate obeisance, when Daddy's Suit went prancing in front of me.

'Which one are you?' he demanded in his squeaky-voiced way.

'I am Elizabeth,' she replied.

Bow Tie was flapping around her now. 'What happened to the other one?'

'Indisposed.'

'What does that mean?' snapped one or other of them. (I was losing the will to distinguish.) I saw a smile on Elizabeth's face that made me fear for any who crossed this woman.

'Long live the Queen,' she said.

'Long live the Queen!' chorused the kneeling soldiers.

'Arrest these men,' said Elizabeth, sweeping her hand at the three of us. 'Take them to the Tower.'

Daddy's Suit whirled round to the soldiers as they started to rise. He pointed at Elizabeth and struck a pose of such studied drama I wondered if he was expecting a wind machine. 'That is not the Queen of England—that is an alien duplicate!'

'And you can take it from him,' added his playmate, 'cos he's really checked.'

'Oh shut up!'

'Venom sacs in the tongue—all I'm saying.'

'Just cut it out, okay?'

'No, hang on, wait!' Bow Tie was now flapping about the place, as if his hands were having two separate fits. 'The Tower, you said the Tower! Brilliant, love the Tower. I demand to be incarcerated in the Tower with the rest of my boy band. Yeah, I know what you're thinking, but this one scrubs up a treat,' he said, thumping my arm. 'Straight away, thank you. Chop, chop, if you'll pardon the expression. We'll have breakfast at eight please, is there Wi-Fi?' He made an attempt to mime the concept of Wi-Fi, and two of the soldiers were forced to duck.

'Are you capable of talking without flapping your hands about?' I asked.

'Yes,' he said, as one of his hands narrowly missed his nose. 'No,' he added, a little despondent.

'Silence,' commanded the Queen, rather to my relief. 'The Tower is not to be taken lightly. Unless you are in a hurry to lose your head.'

'Oh, what's in a head?' laughed Bow Tie. 'What's in a tower? Just another day at the office.' And it seemed to me that as he said the word 'office', he winked at the vortex still revolving above us.

The soldiers were now grabbing hold of each of us. I saw no profit in resisting for now, so allowed myself to be manhandled with the other two. As they began marching us from the glade, I heard another sizzle and hum from the vortex. It was sounding more discordant now, almost brittle. I looked back to see it flex, and darken, then twist itself into nothing with the gentlest of sighs. The vortex had closed. My one escape route was gone.

As we made our way through the trees, my thoughts were sombre. I was trapped in this place now, and almost certainly about to be beheaded. Worse than that, I reminded myself, I was about to be beheaded three times. Having begun the day in the absolutely certainty of my own death, it was a surprise to me how quickly the situation had deteriorated.

FEED CONNECTING
FEED CONNECTED
FEED STABLE
IF YOU ARE READING A BORROWED COPY OF THIS
BOOK, INFORM YOUR FAMILY YOU MAY BE PRONE
TO VIOLENT PSYCHOTIC EPISODES AND STEALING.

At the request of the publisher, Chapter Nine has had to be rescheduled. No, don't all flap at once! I didn't say cancelled, I said rescheduled. In fact, brace yourselves, we're going in right now.

A word of warning. By reading this book you have confirmed yourself to be a serious student of the Doctor and his adventures. You may have formed very strong views on the many controversies surrounding him: the precise reason why the TARDIS exploded during the Pandorica incident; the exact dating of his exile to Earth during the late twentieth century; why on a planet like Gallifrey his granddaughter had a name like Susan; the rumours about whether he is half human. These controversies are at an end, as they will all be resolved in this, Chapter Nine. Be aware: you will have to concentrate as what you're about to read involves an encounter with the mysterious order sometimes known as the Priests of Silencio. These creatures have evolved a form of concealment known as memory proofing: they are able to induce complete amnesia about themselves in any life forms they encounter. They are also known, more popularly, as the

FEED CONNECTING
FEED CONNECTED
FEED STABLE
IF ANY ASPECT OF THIS BOOK IS MAKING YOU
ANGRY, PLEASE KNOCK YOUR HEAD LIGHTLY
AGAINST A WALL TO RESTORE PERSPECTIVE.

And at last we come to Chapter Three, considered by many to be the most challenging of the Doctor Papers. *Please remember our general topics: who wrote this about the Doctor and which Doctor did they write it about. The moments when the Doctor chooses to use, or not use, his preferred title, are, as always, revealing.*

Depending on your point of view, the Doctor was locked in a dungeon for two hours, or four hundred years. He was without friend, or TARDIS, and while to all outward appearances there were three of them there, in fact he was alone.

Consider then, the Doctor alone.

(NB We are still receiving complaints about Chapter Nine, which you have all read. No, we didn't forget to publish it—you forgot to heed the warning. If you doubt me, try again.)

Chapter 3

400 Years of the Doctor

The dungeon was dark and square and cold, and has stayed in my memory, like a trap. Every door I have stepped through since, every corner I have turned, I still expect the walls of that chamber to close around me again. If that seems fanciful, think about this: from the moment I arrived there, I knew I was destined to return. My future stood in front of me, twice over. Even if, somehow, I managed to escape, if I found my way to the TARDIS and tore across the galaxies, if I ran to the limits of the universe and hid in the darkest void, in time my path would take me back to this spot, and to these men I was destined to become. I knew this place would be my prison, not just today, but in time, and time again.

I am writing this account so that perhaps, finally, I can leave it behind.

I made that journey from Richmond to the Tower three times. Or rather I made it once, and saw it through three different pairs of eyes. The first time, thrown in the back of the cart, sitting opposite my two future selves, I found it all but intolerable. Had my hands not been tied, I might have taken my own life—by throttling the pair of them.

At first Bow Tie was mercifully quiet; just sitting there, with a big smile that on most faces would have suggested a light concussion—or at any rate, would have encouraged one from anyone with a free hand—while Tweedle-dumber shot glance after glance at him, before finally saying: 'You're very quiet.'

'They tied his hands,' I explained to him, and to my surprise he laughed.

'Bad habit,' said Bow Tie, 'laughing at your own jokes,' before laughing at his own joke.

'I saw the wink,' said Daddy's Suit. 'You winked at the vortex. What was that?'

'Non-verbal communication,' replied Bow Tie. 'You should try it.'

One could only agree.

'It was a wink, an actual wink. I know what a wink means, especially when it's me winking. Except I don't know what it means, what did that wink mean? Do you have a plan?'

'Yeah, might have a plan.'

There followed a rapid-fire, twenty-minute conversation covering the merits of plans, the dangers of revealing your plans too early, the option of pretending to have a plan and hoping that something will come up that you can pretend was your plan all along, the need for this particular plan to be clarified as soon as possible, a reminder that just possibly the driver of the cart might overhear the plan, and a request from the driver to keep it down a bit.

'Look, I like plans,' hissed Daddy's Suit in an only slightly lower voice. 'Love a plan, me, I'm *made* of plans. But I'd really like to know what this plan *is*, because in case you haven't noticed, *we're all about to get our heads cut off!*'

'At which point,' I said, 'is there the slightest chance either of you will stop talking?' They looked affronted at me. 'Because I'm putting in a request,' I continued, 'not to be on the next spike.'

Within two hours, we had arrived at the tower and been marched to a dungeon deep beneath it. Once inside, Thomson and Thompson lost no time in wasting it. Daddy's Suit started running round the walls, in what looked like an entirely pointless attempt at parkour, while Bow Tie scrabbled around on the floor for a while, before finding a rusty old nail, which he showed to me with all the delight and pride of a small child who had found a dead mouse in a milk bottle.

I turned and hammered on the door. 'You can't lock me up with these two!' I heard myself yelling, 'I'll take the beheading straight away—tell them I'm ready now, I'll have the whole thing off!' I was hardly surprised at the lack of an answer.

There was now a scraping from behind me. I turned to see that Bow Tie was busy scratching away at the wall with the nail he'd found. The other one stood at his shoulder, cocking his head in puzzlement. 'What are you doing?' he asked.

'It's the plan.'

'What plan?'

'The *office* plan,' said Bow Tie.

There was a look of dawning understanding on the other one's face. 'Oh, that's clever! Wish I'd thought of that.'

'You will think of that!' and the two of them started laughing together. I turned back to the door, and took refuge in analysing it with my screwdriver. Daddy's Suit was at my side in a moment.

'Sonic won't work on that,' he said. 'Too primitive.'

'Maybe we should ask for a more sophisticated lock, so we can break out,' piped up Bow Tie.

'I am investigating alternatives,' I said, 'to listening to you two. Apparently there aren't any.'

'Okay, let's sum up, shall we?' I could hear those ridiculous tennis shoes now pacing the floor. 'The Queen of England is now a Zygon, but that's not what interests me. You know what interests me? You!' I didn't look round, but I could sense his eyes on me. 'You, Grandad.'

I continued working at the door. I could guess what was coming. He was pacing again.

'So here's the thing. This is where I'm supposed to be. Tracking Zygons in Elizabethan England, this is my part of the timeline, my patch. Then that vortexy thing opens up and basically my past and my future get dumped on my head. Very *Christmas Carol*. But why?'

I started a deep-level scan of the door, mostly so I had a reason not to look at him.

'I'm asking you why, Grandad?'

The scraping had stopped. I sensed both pairs of eyes on my back but I didn't turn. 'Why don't you ask your little playmate. He's not supposed to be here either,' I said.

'Nah. Me and Chinny, we were surprised. But you showed up already looking for us. You knew it was going to happen. Who told you?'

'Don't you remember?'

'Oi!' came a plaintive voice. 'Chinny?'

'Course I don't remember. Our timeline is tied in a knot in this room, our memories are all over the place. You know how this works. Selective amnesia. You meet yourself, you don't retain any memories till the trigger event repeats.'

'*Chinny?*' repeated Bow Tie.

'Mate, you do have a chin on you.'

'Well, that's something to look forward to.'

'I'm booking the extra shaving time.'

'This door,' I said. 'There's a way through it, you know.'

'Don't change the subject, I'm trying to ask you a question.'

'I'm trying to get through a door. Three of us contained in one space over time could cause some very nasty anomalies.' I turned to them, braced for their stares. 'I could trigger an isolated sonic shift among the molecules—in theory, the door would disintegrate.'

'You'd have to calculate the exact harmonic resonance of the entire door at a sub-atomic level,' said Bow Tie, and it struck me that he didn't seem quite so young any more. 'Even with the sonic, it would take years.'

'No,' I corrected him, 'it would take centuries.' I activated the screwdriver. 'Might as well get started. It might help to pass the timey-wimey.'

They exchanged glances, then Bow Tie returned to his work, whatever it was, and Daddy's Suit resumed his endless prowling round the room.

In my hand, the screwdriver buzzed—the calculations were beginning. Centuries, I thought! Hopeless! I sighed and watched the other two for a moment. 'Timey-wimey,' I repeated. 'Do you have to talk like children? What is it that makes you so ashamed of being a grown-up?'

Daddy's Suit stopped pacing. Bow Tie stopped scraping. Two pair of eyes turned on me, and the look they gave me, across the room, across the hundreds of years that stood between us, left me in no doubt as to their answer: me. I was the source of their shame.

'The way you both look at me,' I said. 'What is that? I'm trying to think of a better word than dread.'

Their expressions didn't change, and in the silence that followed, and lengthened, I started to wonder about the look they were seeing on my face. What did these troubled young men see, as I looked back at them? How was my face answering the fear in theirs? How could I be so terrifying?

Many years would pass before I would understand.

That look of dread stayed clear in my mind, in the years following my first visit to the dungeon. My memory of the conversation fluctuated over time (I have greater clarity now) but the image of those two angry young men, staring at me, hating me from my own future, never dimmed. Sometimes that dread-filled stare would find me again, but only when I was unwise enough to stand in front of a mirror. Even regeneration, and a new face, didn't lessen the judgement in my eyes. One night I smashed every mirror in the TARDIS, trying to escape the accusation in my own gaze, but, as any time traveller knows, the past is never over. The tangle of the timelines had erased much of my memory, but the important details stood clear. I had left that dungeon, I had returned to the barn, and standing there alone, I had murdered them all. And as my world screamed and died, I had walked out of the fire, impossibly alive. It didn't matter how many mirrors I broke, that dungeon stood waiting in my future, and one day I would have to face my own judgement again.

I flew round space and time, like a maniac. I smiled and laughed and whirled, and hoped no one would see through my disguise. I helped where I could, I fought where it counted and I made peace happen wherever I walked. I saved life after life, and I knew I was trying to make up for every one I'd taken. More than anything, I was trying not to count how many children had been on Gallifrey that day.

There were times when I thought I was obsessed. Once, I rode the TARDIS through a supernova to save a robot clown, and then spent a week trying to restore its higher brain functions. All it ever did was sit there intoning 'How do I look?' over and over again.

'Better than I do, mate,' I said. I set it loose in the corridors of the TARDIS, and went looking for someone else to rescue. I knew that everything I did was in penance for the crimes I had committed, but I also knew that nothing would ever be enough.

My memories of the dungeon grew fainter over time—for a while I could barely remember how I'd got there, or how I'd left—but I never lost sight of a single, unalterable fact: one day, I'd be going back.

My second journey to the Tower, felt very different from the first. This time I sat on the other side of the cart, and studied myself, sitting opposite—I didn't look like someone to inspire dread, not in that moment anyway. I looked old and tired; a battle-weary soldier, I thought, in the twilight of his war. But then his fierce old eyes met mine, and I turned quickly away.

'You're very quiet,' I said to Future Boy, sitting next to me, smiling away in his bow tie.

'They tied his hands,' snapped the old soldier. As he said those words, I remembered sitting there saying them, and then I remembered being surprised by a laugh from my future self, who had been sitting exactly where I was sitting now, and I laughed because, some days, time travel just doesn't know how to behave itself, and the old soldier looked at me, surprised by my laughter.

Boy Wonder looked offended, and we began a stupid argument about plans. I didn't really listen to what either of us were saying—I'd have another chance, after all—instead I found myself studying this future version of me. When I'd sat on the other side of the cart, I'd thought he was a bumbling oaf. Up close, he was still a clown, but not all the time. When he frowned he was a petulant nine-year-old, but when he smiled you noticed his eyes. It was as if he found the universe infinitely cruel, but was too gentle to mention it. Sitting there next to him, I wondered how I looked through those sad old eyes, and how long it would be before I found out.

The moment the dungeon door closed on us, I began an inspection of the walls. I told myself I was assessing the stone density through a controlled series of light impacts, but really I was just keeping moving, suppressing my terror at finding myself back here—the prison of past and future; the dungeon of time and again. I had forgotten the sharp stale smell, the scuttling rats, the sound of constant dripping.

Boy Wonder was now snuffling about the floor, looking for something, and the old man was yelling at the door, about having his beheading rescheduled. Had that happened last time? Yes, I remembered it now. Fragments of the past were surfacing, but never till their time came: when the conversation began it was as if each word spoken, each glance exchanged, lit up in my memory, but only as it came round again, so that every passing instant became ancient the second it arrived. When the question was finally spoken, I felt like I'd been waiting a lifetime.

'The way you both look at me,' came my own voice from long ago. 'What is that? I'm trying to think of a better word than dread.' Finally, so many years later, I saw myself standing there: I was small and frail, and afraid. I'd expected a stone-faced general, not this. And yet, looking back at myself, I still felt all the dread I remembered seeing on my face, and I was starting to understand why.

'It must be really recent for you,' I said, to break the silence.

'Recent?' he asked.

I frowned at him, my memory flickering. Dimly, I knew he'd come here from the barn, from the last day of the Time War ... but when exactly? Was this the forgotten aftermath of the explosion I had somehow survived?

'The Time War,' said Boy Wonder from behind me. 'The last day. The day you killed them all.'

I shot the kid a look. 'The day *we* killed them all.'

'Same thing,' he replied.

'It is not the same thing,' I told him. My words kept bouncing round the walls, and I realised I'd shouted. Boy Wonder was looking at me oddly. I wondered what he was feeling, and how long it would be before I felt it too. 'How recent?' I said, turning back to the old man. 'The last day, the end of the Time War. I'm asking how recent that was for you.'

'I don't talk about it,' he said.

'You're not talking about it,' I pointed out. 'There's no one else here.'

He fell silent and looked at the floor, so I left him to it. The kid had nearly finished scratching the string of numerals into the wall. It was a good plan, I'd give him that.

'Did you ever count?' The old man had found a bench at the side of the room, and he was sitting now. His gaze rested on the floor and his voice was low.

'Count what?' asked Boy Wonder.

'The children.' The dungeon must have been cold from the moment we arrived, but this was the first time I'd felt it. 'Did you ever count how many children were on Gallifrey that day?'

There was a silence. And as it grew in the room, I had a faint memory what I was about to say. Dimly, I remembered rage and shouting—my own face, staring in disbelief. But which face?

The silence dripped and scuttled and paced.

I was an old man, sitting, staring at the floor, waiting for an answer I never wanted to hear.

I was pacing the same floor, many years later, willing myself to speak, and failing.

Far in the future, I stood frozen at a wall, with an old nail in my hand, and numerals scratched into the stone in front of me.

Still I didn't speak. I knew I was about to answer, and after that a storm would break—but how could I bring myself to say those words?

'Did you ever count?' asked River Song, a few years later, as we picnicked with the old Gods. I was doing a magic trick with a chicken leg, just to irritate Thor.

'Long story,' I said, 'Have you hidden my Converse?'

'No, but seriously, did you ever count them?' she asked again, a few years after that, in the Underwell of Jim the Fish.

'What have you done with all my bow ties?' I demanded.

'Sweetie, please just tell me,' she asked for the twentieth time in over a hundred years. 'Did you ever count?' We were in the TARDIS workshop, for an evening of basic maintenance and kebabs. She was assisting me by doing all the work, and prodding me with a stick when she needed something passed to her.

'Does it matter?'

'Obviously.'

'Why obviously?'

'Because you don't talk about it.'

'Ow!'

'Zeus Plugs.'

'I already gave them to you.'

'Those are castanets.'

'I had to adapt them for an emergency party with Madame de Pompadour. How's he doing?'

The robot clown's hands were twitching, as he lay on the bench, but the lights hadn't come on in his eyes.

'There are no higher brain functions to restore,' she said. 'I think it's a very basic children's therapy bot.'

'Ow!'

'Madame de Pompadour?'

'Jealous?'

'Of course I'm jealous. Keep your hands off her.'

'Okay, so a children's therapy bot ...'

'Popular on the outer colonies, for a while. Children would tell them stories they were too afraid to tell adults.'

'And what would the bots do?'

'Take the pain away, according to the manual.'

'But it just wanders about, asking how it looks.'

'Yeah, it's got locked in its last therapy session. I'm trying to release it from a looping subroutine.'

'Who gets their therapy from a bot?'

'People who aren't as lucky as you.' She gave me the usual stare. 'People who don't have someone like me. Any bad memories you want to share, sweetie?'

'I found two of my bow ties cut in half.'

She gave me another in her selection of looks, and resumed working on the bot. Only River could rewire neural interfaces crossly.

'What we will we do with it when you've fixed it?' I asked, after a few minutes' silence.

'Drop it off somewhere it might be needed, I suppose.'

'Good idea.'

'Tell you what else is a good idea.' She carried on soldering, didn't look up. 'Don't. Don't ever count how many children were on Gallifrey that day. And if you've already counted, do your very best to forget about it.'

'Why?'

'Because you live in a time machine. All of history is still happening outside those doors. On a good night that means everyone you ever met is still alive and you can't wait to see them again. On a bad night, it means everyone's dead, and you want to charge around the universe, pretending you can do something about that.' She looked up at me. 'I know which version of you I prefer.'

And there she was, so alive again. I remembered her, twisted, burnt and dead, in the depths of The Library. 'What if there are people who died because of me?' I asked. 'What if there are people I should have saved?'

'People die. All people, everywhere. We grieve and we move on. That is how we respect the dead. That is how we forgive ourselves in their presence and their absence.'

She'd bent to her work again, and I was very glad she couldn't see my face.

I knew she'd come back to the children of Gallifrey, again and again. But there was only one conversation I would ever have about that. The timelines had choked off my memory as before, but I knew there was a silence in a dungeon, waiting to be broken. Whatever I was going to say, when I returned there, it was going to bring rage.

The third time I made the journey from Richmond to the Tower was the strangest, perhaps because I knew it was the last. The other two prattled away, and every time they spoke, their words popped up in my memory, twice, at different distances. I joined in, when I was supposed to, my lines arriving in my head as I said them. I was as mechanical as the robot clown. It would be different in the dungeon, I knew. There would be silence, and then there would be anger, and try as I might, I couldn't remember why. As the Tower came into view, along the river, I felt more afraid than I ever had before. It was time for the third and final part of my sentence.

This time I remembered the stale, sharp smell, and the scuttle of the rats. Old fella was battering on the door and shouting away, and Captain Swagger was larging it round the dungeon walls, pretending he was assessing rock density, or whatever I'd told myself at the time. I played my part, and searched the floor for the nail; I'd known for hundreds of years that this was how I'd get a message to Clara and Kate. I started scratching the numerals on the wall, and let the other two get on with it, joining in when my own voice surfaced in my memory. Still, I couldn't remember how the silence was broken, and which of us had got so angry.

'Do you have to talk like children?' the old boy was saying. 'What is it that makes you so ashamed of being a grown-up?'

It was time to turn and stare at him: to tell him the truth with a look. *You. You're why we're ashamed.*

Again, that puzzled face in response. 'The way you both look at me,' I was saying, hundreds of years ago. 'What is that? I'm trying to think of a better word than dread.'

Hundreds of years later, I looked back at myself. He was so ordinary. Broken, and humble. Even desperate. Those eyes weren't blades, they were wounds. I'd expected the face of a murderer. In a way, that's what I'd wanted. It would have been so much easier to see him as the slaughterer of the billions; to stand in judgement on the forgotten, hated part of myself that I'd cut out and left in the past. But the old man standing there wasn't that; he was kind, and brave, and hurt. On Karn they said they'd make me a warrior, but whatever this man believed himself to be, and whatever he'd done in the name of that belief, he'd never been a warrior in his hearts. Had the Sisterhood lied to me? What had been in that goblet? One day, if I survived, I would ask Ohila.

But for now I understood the dread on my own face; this man was me. Not some other mutation or strange alternative— just the Doctor. The man who'd turned on his own kind, and slaughtered the children of an entire world, was, and always had been, me. Simply me. The dread on my face was the lifetime I'd spend living with that.

I turned back to the wall. I was on the final numeral, but now my hand was shaking.

Captain Swagger was asking how recent it was, but the old fella didn't understand. 'The Time War,' I explained, not wanting to look at him. 'The last day. The day you killed them all.'

'The day *we* killed them all,' snapped the Swagger. I know, I want to shout. *I know.*

'Same thing,' I said, because my memory said I had to.

'*It is not the same thing!*' he screamed back at me.

I returned to scratching the last numeral into place—and I waited for the question.

'Did you ever count?' That low wearied, voice. How long since I'd asked that?

'Count what?' I forced myself to say, though I knew the answer perfectly well.

'The children. Did you ever count how many children were on Gallifrey that day?'

We didn't answer. The old boy sat, waiting, and the silence grew like thunder. I kept scraping. Swagger kept pacing. He wasn't ready to speak yet, which didn't surprise me, because several hundred years later, I still wasn't. I sighed. If you want something done, do it yourself, I thought—though, in this dungeon, there was little alternative.

I took the nail from the wall. Now. Say it now. I turned and faced him. 'I have absolutely no idea,' I told him.

I heard the pacing stop, but I kept my eyes on the old boy. He was staring at me, fascinated. Maybe even appalled.

'How old are you?' he asked, finally.

I shrugged. 'I dunno, I lose track.' I turned back to scraping on the wall. 'Twelve hundred and something, I think. Unless I'm lying. I can't remember if I'm lying about my age, that's how old I am.'

'Four hundred years older than me. And you've never wondered how many there were. Never once counted?'

I completed the final numeral, shrugged again. 'What would be the point?' I felt his eyes on me, so I glanced at him. He wouldn't release my gaze.

'One should live with one's sins,' he said.

'2.47 billion,' said a voice, very close to me.

I froze. I didn't want to look round.

'You *did* count,' said the old man, sounding a very long way away.

'2.47 billion,' said the voice, sounding very close indeed.

How could he know that? When did I—

A hand reached in front of me, grabbed hold of my shirt, and yanked me round. Now his big brown eyes didn't look sweet at all; they looked more angry than I could ever remember being. '2.47 billion!' My coat lapels were in his fists, and he wasn't Mum's favourite any more. '*2.47 billion children!*' He was screaming now, right into my face. 'Of course I counted them. How could I *not* count them?? Of course I did! And *you forgot??*' he roared into my face. '*How do you forget that??*' And then I have a feeling he might have thrown me across the room. Anyway, a wall got suddenly in my way, and at the same time all the lights started to flicker. As I slid to the floor, it occurred to me that there weren't any lights in the dungeon.

The darkness wasn't a problem for long, because it was sunny outside the TARDIS, and River was laughing as she clung to my arm. We were watching the robot clown march across the fields, towards a little farming settlement.

'Clever, how they work,' she was saying. 'You tell it your worst story, and it edits the nasty bits out of your memory.' She smiled, that way she did when she'd done something she shouldn't have—which, in fairness, was the only way she ever smiled.

Then, somehow, an old man seemed to be bending over me, looking concerned, and suddenly I wasn't sure exactly where I was …

'I always tell the young men in my command not to beat themselves up when the day goes badly,' said the old boy, as he helped me to my feet. 'I'd be grateful if I could follow my own advice.'

Swagger was pacing up and down the other side of the dungeon, still shouting away. He never hit people, he was yelling. Hitting people was against his principles. But 2.47 billion children! He launched himself at me again, but the old boy intercepted with surprising speed.

'I moved on!' I was yelling. 'There's no choice, you have to.'

'How do you move on from that?' he was screaming, over and over.

We were circling each other now, with the old boy in the middle, holding up his hands. 'Gentlemen, this is pointless,' he kept saying. 'This is unworthy.'

And then Swagger was pushing past him, and suddenly I was in a headlock. He was shouting, 'How could you forget? *How could you forget?*'

I don't know how long it went on for, but when it finally ended, I was too dazed to understand why. They were stepping back from me, staring. Swagger was disgusted but the old boy was just puzzled. Something wrong with my face? I wondered. I checked if my bow tie was straight.

'Is something funny?' asked Swagger. 'Did I miss a funny thing?'

Only then did I realise I was laughing—laughing so hard I had to use the wall to get to my feet.

'What's funny?' he demanded again. '*Tell me!*'

'Look at us,' I said. 'Go on, look! You're trying to tear me apart, he's trying to pull us off each other, and now I've got the giggles.'

'Why the hell is any of that funny?' he thundered, but his face was so hurt and confused I almost wanted to hug him.

'Because,' I told him, 'this is what I'm like when I'm alone.'

It took a long time for us all to stop laughing. When we did, we sat in a row on the little bench at the side of the dungeon, and wondered what we could talk about. In truth, between the things we all knew anyway, and the things the other two weren't supposed to know yet, there wasn't a lot we could say. So we talked about the old days on Gallifrey, and why we left, and what must have happened to the others. Several hours had passed, when my screwdriver buzzed.

'Did you get a text?' asked the old boy, with a caustic look.

I stared at the screwdriver. It had buzzed like that, once before, long ago. But when?

'It did that before,' said Swagger, as puzzled I was. 'I remember that.'

I looked to the old boy. 'The door,' I said. 'You were going to calculate the harmonic resonance of the door at the sub-atomic level.'

'In theory, we could disintegrate it. But the calculation would take centuries.'

'Did you start it? The calculation?'

'Yes, I did,' he replied, checking his screwdriver.

I looked at the screwdriver in my own hand. The case was new, but the main drives and the software were the same as the old boy's. In fact, they'd been the same for hundreds of years. Many thoughts were now jumping up and down in my head, and some of them were cheering. 'How long have we been here?' I asked.

'About a day,' I think.

'No,' I said. 'No, we haven't.' I stood up. Despite my best efforts, a stupid grin was muscling its way all over my face. 'We've had a good chat, haven't we?' I said. 'Ups and downs, but good from time to time, right? It might interest you to know,' I continued, 'that from my point of view, we've been chatting for about 400 years.' I held up my screwdriver. It buzzed again, reminding me it was now ready. 'Or to put it another way— 400 years later, calculation complete! Pack your bags, ladies, it's moving day.'

Captain Swagger and Captain Old stared at me. They rose to their feet.

'You know we've had our differences,' I said, as I readied the screwdriver to disintegrate the door, 'which is surprising under the circumstances. But when it comes right down to it, whatever anyone says about me, we are getting out of this cell because we are three awesomely clever Time Lords.'

To underline the point, I spun round on the spot and with a big flourish (yeah, I can do it too, Captain Swagger!) I aimed the screwdriver right at Clara Oswald.

I think I probably just stood and stared for a moment. There seemed to be tyres screeching to a halt somewhere, but it might have been the sound in my own head as I processed what was right in front of me.

Clara Oswald.

Standing in the dungeon doorway.

With the door open.

Obviously I wanted to know how she'd got here, and how she'd found her way to this cell, but in that moment, the thing I was most confused about was the dungeon key. Specifically, the fact that she didn't appear to have one.

'How did you open the door?' I asked her.

I have four centuries of memories about that dungeon; the time I spent inside it, and the many years I travelled in its shadow. But I think the most vivid one of all—and the most important because it felt like the final lesson of those four hundred years of my life—was Clara Oswald looking at me puzzled, and saying: 'It wasn't locked.'

FEED CONNECTING
FEED CONNECTED
FEED STABLE
***PLEASE KEEP THIS BOOK DRY AT ALL TIMES OR
YOU MIGHT MAKE THE PAGES ALL SOGGY.***

A word, then, about UNIT—

No, sorry, we've moved on from Chapter Nine. I'm sure you all did your best, it's a tricky one for the smartest of us. Try again, if you really must, but human brains are not equipped for this sort of thing. Stick to texting and soaps—I do.

Now then: UNIT has strict protocols concerning—

No, really, pipe down. You've all read Chapter Nine, every last one of you. I've got the records right here, look. Oh, you can't see, I haven't turned on the webcam. Well, sorry, I don't want to use that till later, it's murder on the bandwidth.

Oh, hang on—just had an email from the publishers. (Well, I say 'just'. As I explained, I'm writing from ten years in the future so, really, I'm catching up on my messages a decade late, which is pretty good for me.) Ah, now, this is interesting. Owing to you lot whinging so much, they're adding an extra bit to the book. At the very end, you will find an additional blank page (the cover price will reflect this, I'm afraid). Next time you read Chapter Nine, turn to page 232 and make a mark. That way you can assure yourself, whatever the state of your memory, you have read the chapter in question. Satisfied? Good, good.

Now. UNIT has some very strict protocols regarding written material covering any aspect of their various missions—the silly old whelks. Nothing can ever be held on computer, or any form of digital storage. No, the only accounts you will ever find of UNIT activity are handwritten by one or more of the participants. It is their belief, bless them, that handwriting cannot be hacked (hee hee!) or corrupted (oh, my aching sides, stop it!).

Once, during one of my many visits, I asked old Alistair (Lethbridge-Stewart, do keep up!) what was the most important quality in a UNIT commander. He thought for a moment, in his usual grave way, and said, 'Good handwriting!'

Oh, we laughed. But we always laughed, he and I, right up to the end. The mischief we got up to! But look, you're not reading this book to hear about two old boys, chortling away together in a hospice, I do realise that—the fact is, I just don't care. He was a good friend, the bravest of soldiers, and a devil with the ladies till his last day. Gracious me, that man could tango—but as soon as a pretty girl came in, I was shoved straight out of the way.

Kate was the apple of his eye, of course. She could do no wrong by him. Though when she came to see him at the hospice, he'd tell her she was his only visitor, just so she'd come round more often. The old dog! Sometimes I was right there, hiding under the bed.

Now Kate's handwriting, it must be said, is exceptionally good (ah, see how I slalom back into relevance) as you are about to see for yourselves. Or rather, you aren't, since this will be a printed version. Now I've already told you that the existence of anything other than handwritten accounts of UNIT operations is forbidden by law, but there are pretty good reasons for this exception, and I have a high degree of confidence that many of you won't be arrested for owning this book. You will recall that the Doctor, in one of his aspects, was deep beneath the National Gallery investigating the mystery of the oil paintings with the missing figures, before he jumped into a mysterious time vortex and got involved in the

Elizabethan Zygon shenanigans (what a delightful way to be able to describe one's day).

Fortunately, an account of how events unfolded in his absence, has become available to us in the impeccable handwriting of two of UNIT's finest. You may wonder, as you read, why and when and even how this account came to be written. All will become clear in due time. Or it won't, if I forget to explain it. It's a rollercoaster, isn't it?

Here then is Chapter Four, the aptly titled, In the Absence of the Doctor.

Chapter 4

In the Absence of the Doctor

LOG 34445986++8U
EXCERPT ONLY
STATUS: VERIFIED
CONTENT: RESTRICTED
AUTHOR: KLS2

EXCERPT BEGINS

My earliest memory is of a bird standing on one leg, on a beach.

My saddest memory is of my father, sitting by a fireside, clutching a whisky. There were tears in his eyes, and my mother was snatching me away.

My vision swam and I focused. My name is Kate Lethbridge-Stewart.

...I dropped the sheet back into place and steadied myself on the wall. I could feel the sweat on the palm of my hand against the cold of the stone. Why those particular memories, I wondered, and why here and now? I made an effort of concentration and forced myself back into the present: I was in the lower levels of the Under Gallery, eighty feet below the London streets. Seven storeys of forbidden historical artefacts were stacked between me and the sunlight. Was there something here, possibly alien, that could affect a human brain? I noted, without surprise, that

I'd just referred to myself as a human brain—alien contact, over time, often results in dissociative cognitive processes. I decided to action a psyche evaluation for myself at the first opportunity. I found a handkerchief and carefully dabbed the sweat from my face and hands. I had a UNIT response team under my command, the Under Gallery had been breached, and the Doctor had just gone missing—I needed to maintain appearances.

'We're not supposed to touch them,' came a voice from immediately behind me.

Petronella Osgood. I remembered a note on her file, and had to suppress a smile: *Petronella has a talent for being under your feet before you even know she's in the room.* She was also, in the absence of the Doctor, UNIT's number one tactical asset.

'The statues—we're not supposed to approach or touch them,' she said. Her eyes flicked to the handkerchief I was slipping in my pocket, then back to the sheeted figure behind me. She must have seen me adjusting the covering as she arrived.

'It's just a statue,' I said, shrugging. 'Take a look.'

'We're not allowed to—'

'We have an incursion, normal protocols are lifted. Examine the statues, examine anything you like—but it's the stone dust on the floor the Doctor wanted you to focus on. Did you get a team?'

'There's a few more heading over from Tower Base—McGillop's already helping me, but he's being a bit thing.'

'A bit what?'

'I don't want to say.'

'Well, you sort of did say.'

'I stopped before the adjective, I'm improving. Where is the Doctor? Is he still downstairs?'

I debated what to tell her. Although she had an IQ so high Geneva Base had rejected the test results three times, her temperament could be unpredictable. I had a memory of saying she was so uptight it was a wonder her feet managed to reach the ground. I considered how best to explain to her that just one floor below us a time portal had opened up, leading to Elizabethan England, and the Doctor had jumped through it, apparently with no means of returning.

'He's off site,' I summarised. 'Get back to work.'

'How could he get off site, he was downstairs, and the only exit is—'

'Off site,' I repeated. 'Stone dust, off you go. No, no, wait a moment!' I remembered Clara listening to the Doctor talking on the other side of the portal. 'I think there's three of them now,' she'd said, and then looked a little stunned to be told there was a precedent for that.

'Actually, I was looking for you,' I went on. 'Am I right in saying, there's a precedent for three incarnations of the Doctor being present in the same time zone?'

'Yes, we've got records of that. The Cromer Files. But it only happens in the direst emergencies.' She said 'direst emergencies' with a dramatic widening of her eyes, as if she practised in the mirror every night. On her personnel file someone had added 'fangirl' to her list of qualifications. 'You know, when the danger is so terrible, even the Doctor cannot stand alone.'

'Inhaler.'

'Yes, sorry.'

'Send me any information you have on the strategic advantages of three Doctors in play, simultaneously.' I said. 'Then get that stone dust analysed. I'd better get back down there.'

'Is Clara alone, then? Because you said the Doctor was off site—'

'Back to work!'

I hurried down the stairs. If the active presence of three Doctors indicated a bigger emergency than normal, then possibly it was time for us to take aggressive action.

Clara was still standing at the portal, listening, and I could hear the Doctor's voice, prattling away. 'No, hang on, wait! The

Tower, you said the Tower! Brilliant, love the Tower. I demand to be incarcerated in the Tower with the rest of my boy band.'

Clara noticed my arrival. 'He's talking rubbish. That means he's got a plan.'

I filed the insight. 'Has he made any attempt to come back through?'

'The fez didn't make it. I guess he can't either.'

'Not easy, finding time travel in Elizabethan England.'

A woman's voice from beyond the portal was saying something about the Doctor not taking the Tower lightly, unless he was in a hurry to lose his head.

'Oh, what's in a head?' came the Doctor's laughing voice. 'What's in a tower? Just another day at the office.'

Clara looked at me, frowning. 'I think he just winked at me. When he said "office", he winked.'

'You can't see him,' I said.

'His voice does a thing when he winks.'

'He winks *audibly*?'

'He really does.'

I searched my memory for any possible cypher in the word 'office'. There were a list of known code words used by the Doctor, which distracted me for a moment, before the obvious occurred. 'Dear God, that man is clever,' I said. 'Come on!'

I sprinted for the stairs. Behind me, I heard Clara shouting: 'No, Kate, wait! I think the portal is closing.'

'We don't need the portal,' I shouted back. 'Come with me!'

'Where are we going?'

'My office,' I said, 'otherwise known as the Tower of London.'

'UNIT HQ is housed in the Tower of London,' I explained, in the back of the car.

'Which is where they just took the Doctor,' replied Clara. She was frowning now, trying to piece it all together. I remembered how quick and clever she'd been on her last visit.

'Nearly five hundred years ago, yes.'

'Well, I know he's got a big old life span—but he gets cranky if he sleeps in.'

'As I'm sure you realise, we can do better than just leave him there for hundreds of years.' I clicked a switch and a glass screen rose, sealing us away from the driver. 'Clara Oswald, I need to inform you that the Unified Intelligence Taskforce does not know of, condone, or have access to any means of time travel.'

'Why?'

'Because we do, and I'm lying. Excuse me.'

Ignoring her look of bewilderment, I got on the phone and gave the necessary orders. The dungeons in the Tower were all to be searched. Numbers, I told them—a string of numerals, scratched into a wall or a floor. As soon as they were found, they needed to be sent directly to my phone. I was careful not to tell them of my current location, or that I'd left the Under Gallery. The operation had entered a critical phase, and all information was now tactically weighted.

By the time I had briefed them all, we had arrived at the Tower. We walked through the Jewel House door, and entered the maze of corridors. I was using my Zero Pass so that my arrival wouldn't be flagged. Avoiding the operations room, and the security cameras, I led Clara by the most circuitous route to the Black Entrance. She frowned at what looked like a pair of cupboard doors, then stared as I opened them. Fifty feet of corridor stretched in front of us, as tall and thin as a canyon. Dust hung in the dim light like a swarm and yellow circles pooled the floor below green-shaded lamps. At the far end was an iron door, and a man with a shadowed face, and a white shirt. He was sitting at a desk and remained as still as a mannequin as we started towards him.

'What do you think?' I asked Clara.

'Bit World War Two,' she said.

'That was the last refurb, yeah. Just before it, actually. Where do you think we are?'

'Should I know?'

'I think you're probably figuring it out. I can hear cogs whirring.'

Clara shrugged. 'In the Under Gallery, those empty cabinets—all the stuff you moved to more secure premises.'

'Yes?'

'There was a letter B next to all those cabinets. Whatever this place is called, I'm guessing it starts with a B, and it's where you put all the stuff you think is dangerous.'

Smart, I thought, and doesn't mind who knows it—which is to say: clever, but not wise.

'The Black Archive. Highest security rating on the planet. The entire staff have their memories wiped at the end of every shift.' I pointed to the lights. 'Automated memory filters in the light fittings.'

We had arrived at the desk. Atkins looked up at us. His eyes were as watery and panicked as I could remember seeing them, and he looked thinner and more ravaged than ever. Repeated memory wipes, on a daily basis had their consequences; it may have seemed necessary to someone once, but face to face with the living result it just seemed barbaric.

'Access, please,' I said.

Atkins nodded at each of us in turn, carefully: 'Ma'am. Ma'am.' Concentrating hard, like a child remembering instructions, he moved to the iron door behind him, the key already in his hand.

'Atkins, isn't it?'

'Yes, ma'am, Atkins. It's my first day here.'

'How are you feeling?'

'Still getting used to this place, ma'am. First day here,' he repeated, oblivious.

I looked at Clara. 'Been here ten years,' I whispered, and nodded at the lights. She looked shocked, and I didn't blame her.

'He's a volunteer,' I said, 'Not that he knows that any more.'

142

There was a cool draught from the opened door, and Atkins moved aside to allow us through.

'Thank you, Atkins.'

'No problem, ma'am. It's my first day here.' He gave us both a puzzled look, as if trying to remember something. He would be doing that for the rest of his life.

I stepped Clara through into the warehouse. It was a huge black cube of a room, and the walls gleamed like polished granite. I looked around. I hadn't stood on this spot for a very long time. It was now crammed with shelves and packing cases and a few of the Under Gallery cabinets. Other than seeming taller and more spacious than the building around it would allow (the advantage of stolen technology), it could have been any storage hangar anywhere. Until, of course, you looked more closely at what was on the shelves, or placed your hand on the smooth, shining walls, and felt their heat. Decades of alien contact had left UNIT with an extraordinary amount of extraterrestrial technology on its hands. Given that most of it had been harvested during attempted alien invasions, a high percentage of the technology was some kind weaponry. The Doctor had wanted to destroy it all, or take it off world, but UNIT had been too quick for him. Now, as a matter of procedure, it was all stored here, in the one place on the planet the Doctor's TARDIS could never go. Whoever had control of this room had effective control of planet Earth. Which could, I reflected, prove to be the key strategic error of the entire human race.

Clara looked around, and I could tell she was determined not to be impressed. She was easy to read, in some ways, and I wondered if she knew how dangerous that could be.

'The largest repository of abandoned and redeployed alien technology anywhere on the planet,' I told her.

'And it's all just under lock and key—bit basic, isn't it?'

I followed her look to the still open door. Through it, I could see Atkins reaching for the phone on his desk. His movements were slow and nervous.

'Can't afford electronic security down here, we've got to keep the Doctor out,' I said. 'The whole of the Tower is TARDIS-proofed. He really wouldn't approve of the collection.'

'But you're letting me in?'

Atkins had lifted the phone now. It was one of the old dial telephones, probably here since the Second World War, and he seemed momentarily confused about what to do with it.

'You have a top-level security rating from your last visit,' I told her, and nodded towards some photographs on the wall. She glanced at them—and then stared, visibly rocked. She could see herself in a number of the photographs, standing on the same spot, in the same room she thought she had just entered for the first time. 'Memory filters,' I apologised. I glanced over at Atkins again—he was still hesitating, phone in hand. Now, confused, he hung up again. His hand shook as he withdrew it. The poor man was a dreadful mess.

'But why was I here?' Clara was asking.

'We have to screen and interview all the Doctor's known associates—we can't have information about the Doctor and the TARDIS falling into the wrong hands. Public knowledge about him can have disastrous consequences.' I pointed to the two movie posters on the wall, and saw her eyes widen.

'Peter Cushing played the Doctor? The guy from *Star Wars*?'

'Oh, yes. Twice. We did try to suppress the films, but they kept showing up on bank holidays.'

'Has the Doctor seen them?'

'Seen them? He loves them. He loaned Peter Cushing a waistcoat for the second one, they were great friends. Though we only realised that when Cushing starting showing up in movies made long after his death.'

'What's that doing here?' she asked. I didn't realise what she was talking about till I followed her look. The *Gallifrey Falls* painting—the one shown to the Doctor when he had arrived—was leaning against the wall, as if someone had just left it there.

'I don't know. That's odd, I didn't give any order for it to be moved.'

'Does it matter?'

We're in the middle of an invasion, I wanted to shout, *everything matters!* 'I don't know, I'll check what's going in a moment. This way.' I led her to the centre of the room, where there was a small steel chamber—a tiny cube within the larger cube of the Archive. There was a door, which could only be opened by my retinal scan. I activated the lock, and led Clara inside. She found herself staring at what appeared to be a leather wrist strap mounted on a stand. She managed to remain as unimpressed as ever.

'A vortex manipulator,' I said. 'Bequeathed to the UNIT archives by Captain Jack Harkness, on the occasion of his death. Well, one of them.'

'What is it?'

'Time travel. One-man time travel, basically. Pop the strap on your wrist, and off you go. Top security rating of any item here—no one can know we have this, not even our allies.'

'Why not?'

'Are you serious? Americans with the ability to rewrite history? You've seen their news coverage.'

'Okay—so this is how we're going to rescue the Doctor?'

'We can't. I doubt there's enough power in it for a two-way trip. And anyway, we don't know the activation code. The Doctor knows we have this, so he's always kept the code from us. If he wants us to help him, he's going to have to change his mind.'

Finally, Clara understood. 'And he's in the same building as us, five hundred years ago.' She grinned. 'He's going to leave us a message.'

'Carved into a wall, I assume. I've got my team looking for a string of numerals, in the old dungeons. They'll send me what they find.' I plugged my phone into the contact node on the wall—the only way a call could be received within the Black

Archive. Perhaps because my mind was on the phone, I heard the turning of the dial, even across the room.

'Excuse me,' I said to Clara, 'I have to talk to Atkins.'

Atkins was still dialling, when I got to his desk. As gently as I could, I removed the receiver from his hand and put it back in the cradle. 'Please don't report my presence here,' I said.

'It's protocol, it's procedure.'

'It became procedure because I made it procedure. What I'm telling you now is that it's not procedure for today.'

'It's my first day. It's procedure. I'm sorry. It's my first day.'

I looked at him for a moment. What had been done to this man, in the name of security, was beyond cruelty. UNIT had a lot to answer for. 'Listen. We are in a state of emergency. At times like this, information about my whereabouts becomes of such strategic value, it is withheld from everyone. For the safety of the entire planet. Do you understand?'

He tried to. I could see it in his face. But his eyes clouded again. 'It's my first day.'

My jaw tightened. After many years of service, I still felt the same anger when I witnessed the indignities so often visited on the brave. 'Come here,' I said.

'Sorry, ma'am?'

'Stand up and come here, please.'

He did as he was told, of course, and stood, terrified, in front of me. I could feel him shaking as I wrapped my arms around him. 'Ma'am. What are you doing?'

'I'm hugging you, Atkins, is that all right?'

He hesitated. 'It's my first day.'

'What has been done to you is unacceptable, and insofar as it is my place, I apologise on behalf of the people who did it to you. Do you understand?'

'I think so, ma'am.'

'My regrets.' I squeezed tighter and felt him relax. 'Sorry,' I said again. I sat him back in his chair, wiped a little drool from the corner of his mouth, and angled his head so that it wasn't obvious, at least from a distance, that his neck had been snapped.

As I turned to go, I felt my blood freeze. A pair of eyes, bright as diamonds, stared out of the dark. A few feet in front of me, barred in shadow, was a Zygon.

I felt a surge of panic, and controlled it. This couldn't happen, not now! I had to be more careful. I closed my eyes and concentrated.

My earliest memory is of a bird standing on one leg, on a beach.

My saddest memory is of my father, sitting by a fireside, clutching a whisky. There were tears in his eyes, and my mother was snatching me away.

My name is Kate Lethbridge-Stewart.

When I opened my eyes, the Zygon was gone, and Kate was again looking back at me from the mirror. I dabbed the sweat from my face. In my anger and stress, I had let the body print slip, and that couldn't happen again. I had successfully penetrated a strategically significant target on planet Earth, and humankind's most powerful weaponry was in my grasp—now, more than ever, I had to maintain appearances.

I re-entered the Black Archive, and this time closed the door. I had been able to grant Atkins a death without fear, and I was very much hoping I'd be able to do the same for Clara Oswald.

EXCERPT ENDS

EXCERPT BEGINS

It's all a bit of a jumble at the moment, but writing it down will probably help. Or it won't. But I have to write it down anyway so, you know, here goes.

I remember being huddled in one of the corners, and I could hear them all moving about. There wasn't screaming any more, so I assumed they'd got everyone, and they'd find me eventually. I was so scared I thought might just shake into tiny pieces. But I was also cross with myself, and I think the Doctor would have been cross too. Because it was all my fault! I was the one who'd noticed. Why didn't I keep my silly mouth shut?

We'd been three floors down in the Under Gallery, and McGillop was being a bit thing, but I'd managed not to say anything about it. Not that he was grateful, of course, which was typical. I'd made a point of hiding my feelings ALL DAY but he kept not noticing anything.

The Doctor had told us to analyse the stone dust / rock powder / sand deposits, but the trouble was that the stone dust / rock powder / sand deposits really weren't very interesting, and McGillop kept going on about it. 'It's sand. Just sand. What does sand matter?'

Oh, I thought, look who's crossest pony in the paddock! But I decided to keep that sort of language to myself, because sometimes he's quite handsome (except short). The rest of the team had arrived, and there was equipment everywhere now, and cables straggling (is that a word?) all over the place. I think they were probably working away, but I wasn't sure because I couldn't remember most of their names and had to keep avoiding eye contact. Sometimes they stood right in front of me, which meant I had to shut my eyes. I don't think anyone noticed, but it's hard to tell when you can't see.

'What does the sand matter, Oz, got a theory?' asked McGillop, in his usual way, because he's Irish (which is fine).

'Why would I know?' I asked.

'Because one of us is pretty, and one of us is a genius, and, unfortunately for me, they're both you.'

He was probably being sarcastic in some clever way, but I couldn't work it out, so I decided I'd get cross about it later.

'I do actually mean that,' he said, with a nice smile (suspicious).

I decided to completely ignore him. And then I didn't. 'The composition is interesting,' I told him, running some of the stone dust / rock powder / sand deposit through my fingers. 'Marble, granite—lots of different stone, but none of it from the fabric of the building.'

'Okay. So?'

'So where did it come from? It's not from the walls or ceiling. These are secure premises, and we know all this sand wasn't here before. So how did it arrive?'

'Maybe something got broken?'

'Like what? Like what got broken? A great pile of different kinds of rock got broken, and then got distributed evenly over every floor in the Under Gallery? Even if there had been a pile of rocks here, which there wasn't, who smashed them up and who distributed the sand?' He was all frowny now, so I smiled at him ~~prettily~~.

'Maybe whatever came out of the paintings,' he said. 'But that doesn't make any sense. I know we're supposed to keep an open mind, but what lives in Elizabethan oil paintings that wants to break out and smash up rocks?'

It was then I started having thoughts. There weren't any rocks here that could have been broken up, but if you thought about it, there was an awful lot of stone.

'Can I pour you some tea?' asked McGillop.

'I'm not pouring you tea!' I snapped.

'No, you're not, *I'm* pouring *you* tea, because that's my job when you're thinking, and I can see you've started up the engines.'

I could hear him pouring, but I didn't look because my brain was going all fast. Now he was standing in front of me, offering me a cup. He held it with the handle towards me so I wouldn't burn myself when I took it, which probably meant he was burning his own hand as he stood there. I realised that was probably kind, but was it also patronising? I decided I'd make up my mind about that later, and send him emails. 'Thanks. Sorry. I'm just doing sums.' Then I took the cup from him, because I thought he might start crying.

'Do you want me to get your laptop?' he asked.

It didn't take long to run the numbers. I calculated the total floor area of the Under Gallery, estimated the average depth of the sand, and with a good idea of the cubic volume now present in the Under Gallery, modelled it into different shapes. I ran several possible distribution patterns, before realising there was enough sand in the gallery to make approximately fifty man-sized piles. I cross-referenced this with my file on the Under Gallery, and noted there were exactly fifty-two statues here. All of which were covered. Nine of which were surrounding us, in this corridor, right now.

'I said,' McGillop was saying, 'do you want me to get your laptop?'

I looked at the cup in my hand. The surface of the tea was quivering, like that bit in *Jurassic Park* when there's a dinosaur stomping about. It wasn't a dinosaur though, it was me, shaking. I looked at the sheeted statues lining the walls of corridor. I checked for exits. There was only one, twenty feet away, and you'd have to jump over all the cables and packing cases we'd brought in.

'Oz? Are you all right?' McGillop was looking at me, but I found I couldn't look at him, because I'd suddenly forgotten how to use my neck muscles. I concentrated on speaking.

'We have to go,' I said. 'Right now, this minute.'

'What's wrong?'

'The things from the paintings. I know why they smashed the statues.' My voice was a bit shaky, and I was already thinking I shouldn't be saying this out loud.

'Why?' asked McGillop.

'Because they needed somewhere to hide,' I ~~blurted~~ said.

Nothing happened for a moment—then all the statues under their sheets just seemed to relax and straighten up, like children at the end of a game of hide and seek. And then, slowly, all the covered heads turned towards us.

I was running before I even thought about it. 'Run first,' the Doctor always said, 'make time, think hard!' I jumped over the packing cases and raced up the stairs. All around me, sheets were falling from statues, and strange lumpy hands were reaching out of the dark. I ran and ran and never screamed once. I crashed into a cabinet, and suddenly the floor was all rats, skittering and scrabbling about, but still I didn't scream.

Now I was staring at a wall. 'Eventually,' the Doctor had said once, 'everyone runs out of corridor.'

I could hear it behind me. I turned.

It was about seven feet tall, and red, and wet-looking. Its skin was covered in suckers, and it had a huge baby head, and tiny, bright eyes. It looked like it was grinning, but I think it was just the shape of its teeth.

At the back of my mind a file opened. Zygons, Loch Ness, shape-shifters.

It came to a halt a few feet away, and just stared at me. At first I thought nothing was going to happen, then a droplet of yellow goo ran down between its eyes, leaving a track of slime, and with a loud crack the whole face started to split apart. As it opened, the flesh stretched like pizza cheese between the slowly separating halves. I didn't scream but the wall was suddenly pressing very hard against my back. The whole head had now flowered open, falling apart into segments, like a peeled orange, and with a horrible, sucking, gurgling noise a new head started to grow in the middle of the neck stump. At first it was the size of a fist, featureless with just a round mouth. Then it wriggled and grew, and a pair of little human eyes popped open and looked right at me. Features were now forming round the eyes, and in a few seconds I realised whose face I was looking at. 'Hello Petronella,' squeaked a rapidly growing replica of my own mouth, 'I'm Petronella.'

I closed my eyes because I didn't want to see the next bit. When I opened them again, a perfect duplicate of me was standing there. There was even a green chemical stain on the left sleeve of my lab coat, which was never going to come out. (Shut up, Mum!) I reached for my inhaler, then realised it was already in my mouth.

The other Osgood smiled, and held out her hand. 'Could I borrow the inhaler, please. I don't seem to have copied that. Rush job, sorry.' She gave the little wheezy cough that I knew so well. 'Oh, I do hate it when I get one with a defect.'

For a moment it felt as if I was in both our heads, looking out of both pairs of eyes. She was still live-linked with my mind, I realised, and probably still downloading me. She was stealing every last private little thing that was mine. Just pulling it out of my brain and taking it for herself. All my stupid secrets, all the things that made me ashamed. It was the first time I really wanted to scream.

The next bit was quite confusing. There was suddenly this terrible noise everywhere, and it took me a moment to realise that it was coming from the other me. She was screaming and screaming—not like she was scared, like she was furious. And then there was this mad look in her eye, and she lunged at me. I threw myself back against the wall, convinced I was about to die—but all she did was push right past me and run, still screaming, down the corridor.

For a moment, I thought I should follow, but then I found myself leaning against the wall, and a moment later, sliding down it. I sat there, huddled and shaking, and I wondered what I could possibly have done to frighten a Zygon away. Were my memories really that horrid? Was I so embarrassing? I had to be sensible, though—there might be something to be learned from this, and the Doctor would want to know. But I hoped it wasn't that incident with my sister and the dead turtles.

I don't know how long I sat there, but it was only McGillop who found me, thank God! 'The statues are all Zygons,' I told him, as he helped me to my feet. 'They're shape-shifters, they've copied me!'

'Yeah,' said McGillop. 'They copied me too.'

'What happened to your duplicate? Where is it now?'

McGillop gave me the sad smile that I'd always quite liked (but not really, just as a friend). 'Standing in front of you, I'm afraid. I'm the duplicate.'

Oh! This was pretty bad, I thought. And then I was a bit angry, and I was thinking that they'd better not have hurt McGillop in any way at all (because he is a valued colleague, like lots and lots of other people, including women).

'Okay,' I said, and fixed him in the eye, just like the Doctor would. 'Well, I've scared off one of you Zygon duplicates already, I can do it again.'

'No, I'm afraid you didn't.'

'Yeah, I did, it ran straight down that corridor. Screaming.'

He was still giving me the sad smile. 'Sorry,' he said. 'That was Osgood.'

I had the biggest *Gosh!* moment ever. Of course! Oh, of course! I wasn't Petronella Osgood at all—I was the Zygon!

It was tricky, sometimes, downloading all those memories through one little psychic link. Sometimes the donor mind could overwhelm you, especially if strong emotions were involved. Also, this mind was huge, I realised. Quite the largest mind I'd ever ingested. There were millions of random thoughts, bounding around all over the place, like a stampede of cartoon ponies. It was as much as I could do not to duck.

'We'd probably better kill Osgood super quickly,' I said. 'She's awfully, awfully clever, and there's hardly any room for me in here. Also, she took my inhaler.'

'It will be a pleasure,' said McGillop. 'But we have new orders—we have to join the Commander. The Black Archive has been penetrated, but the Doctor's associate, Clara Oswald, has gone missing from inside it.'

I was barely listening. The size of this mind, it went on and on. An intelligence like this couldn't just be switched off. 'No, wait, don't!' I said.

'Don't what?'

'Find Osgood, but *don't* kill her. As long as she's alive, I'll have a feed of her memories and abilities. And she's mega-tastic brillo-clever.'

'She talks like a moron,' said McGillop rudely.

'You don't have to tell me, Mr Grumpy Sausage! But, seriously. She's so smart she's officially listed as UNIT's number one tactical asset.'

'Really?'

'Yes, really. Well,' I added, with a shrug, 'in the absence of the Doctor.'

EXCERPT ENDS

EXCERPT BEGINS

For a moment it felt as if I was in both our heads, looking out of both pairs of eyes. She was still live-linked with my mind, I realised, and probably still downloading me. She was stealing every last private little thing that was mine. Just pulling it out of my brain and taking it for herself. All my stupid secrets, all the things that made me ashamed. It was the first time I really wanted to scream.

So I did. I screamed, right in her ~~stupid~~ face. She looked kind of shocked for a moment—and that was when I had the idea. If she was still linked with me, maybe she was feeling all the same fear I was feeling. Which you might think would make us equal, but that's wrong. Fear is only a disadvantage if you want to attack—it's brilliant if all you want to do is run away.

So I just sort of lunged at her. And I was right. She stumbled out of my way, looking all frightened, and I ran for it. And I made sure I kept on screaming and screaming.

155

'Scream when you're running away, and keep it going,' Sarah Jane Smith once told me (she was one of the Doctor's companions and easily my equal-second-favourite). 'That way they'll know exactly how far away you are.'

'Why's that good?' I asked.

'Because then you stop screaming and double back the way you came. A few minutes later, you'll see them dashing past your hiding place—they never bother looking properly if they think you're further away.' Then she said: 'Head down, dear, I think the eyes are hatching!'—but that's another story.

Sarah Jane was super-awesome—I'd grown up wanting to be her—and she was also right. A little while later I heard Other Me and Other McGillop walking right past the cabinet where I was hiding.

'Why the Black Archive?' I heard myself saying.

'Check your memories. That's where they store all the alien weapon tech—best arms dump on the planet.'

'Therefore the first place the Doctor will attempt to defend.'

Good point, other me!

'The Black Archive is TARDIS-proof, he can't get in there.'

Oh McGillop, I thought. Tell the Doctor there's a wall he can't climb over and he'll meet you on the other side.

'Oh McGillop,' Other Me was saying. 'Tell the Doctor there's a wall he can't climb over and he'll meet you on the other side.'

Oh, she's a clever one. 'Why are you calling me McGillop?' asked Other McGillop as their voices faded down the corridor.

I scrambled out of the cabinet. I knew exactly where I had to go now, because I had a theory, and I had to see if I was right. A little while earlier, I'd found Kate replacing the covering on one of the statues. She'd told me she'd seen nothing of interest under the sheet—but, logically, she should have seen a Zygon under there and I'm pretty sure Kate would have remembered seeing something like that (though she's always losing her phone, and vouchers). So, theory: that was a Zygon copy of

Kate. Question: what was under the covering I'd seen her replace?

It took me a few minutes to find the right statue. I pulled off the sheet. And oh my goodness, there was Kate!

She was bound up in horrid, red, rubbery stuff (like string, made of Zygon) and at first I thought she was dead. Then she moaned and I started yanking away at the stringy stuff.

'Kate! Oh my goodness, you're not actually dead,' I reassured her. 'That really is tremendously good news,' I said, to keep the positive feedback flowing.

'... Petronella?' Kate said, so weak. She only called me Petronella when she was stressed.

'That's right,' I said. 'Petronella. The Real Petronella, just like you're the real Kate.' The red stringy things were snapping quite easily, but I had to be careful because they were holding her up, and I didn't want her to fall on top of me and cause inappropriate sexual tension in the workplace (which I'm against). 'Those creatures, they're Zygons, they can turn themselves into copies of people. But I think they have to keep the original alive, so they can refresh the image, so to speak.'

'Where did ... where did they go?' she mumbled. She was spitting red stuff out of her mouth, which was a bit disgusting.

'Tower Base. The Black Archive.'

'What did you say? That's not possible!' Her head was almost complete free of all the yucky stuff, and she was trying to focus on me.

'It *is* possible, I'm afraid. They don't just steal your faces, they take your memories—bit embarrassing when you think about it—so anything you know, she knows. She can access the Archive.' I broke the last of the stringy things, and Kate collapsed forward. Fortunately I got out of the way, and she was able to hit the floor, uncompromised.

'That's right, you have a little rest down there,' I said as she scrambled to her feet and started dashing along the corridor. She really is tremendously ace at times. Basically, I've always wanted to *be* Kate. But then some days I just want to be anyone else except me, which is a bit sad when you think about it, so I don't (except now, accidentally).

'If those creatures have got access to the Black Archive,' she was shouting, 'we may just have lost control of the planet!'

'Probably best keep your voice down,' I said, mostly into my inhaler. 'This place is crawling with them.'

'No it isn't,' she snapped. 'They've been stuck in here for hundreds of years and they've just disposed of an armed UNIT response team. They're not going to hang around and play canasta! They'll already be at UNIT HQ, taking over.'

Kate is really very clever about all the military stuff, although she is mainly a science person (and gardening) and she was right (though I would have to look up canasta). The whole place was deserted. By the time we'd got to the top, Kate had called one of her special numbers, and a car came whizzing up, and me and Kate and McGillop all piled inside. (I forgot to mention I went and looked for McGillop when Kate was making the call, but only in case we needed any extra help. I found him under one of the statue sheets, on only my fourth attempt. He was all shivery and his eyes were really wide, but he was unhurt and Kate was basically fine about the tiny delay, and I probably shouldn't have shouted.)

'What are they?' McGillop kept asking, in the back of the car. 'What are those things?' I had my arm round him, but only because I thought he might be about to cry (Irish).

'Zygons. You must have read about them, they're in the files.'

'I haven't memorised all the bloody files, you know,' he said, rubbing away tears with his sleeve (which I do sometimes). 'I'm not like you.'

'Oh, stop it, I *did not* memorise the files,' I said. 'On purpose,' I added.

And then he looked at me and started laughing, in a really sort of high-voiced way, and I didn't know what do. But I held his hand, which seemed to be okay. I don't think I've ever wanted to be McGillop—although he is very popular and has lots of friends, so, maybe a bit.

The car was very fast (the driver missed a short cut, though, so I took his number to give him constructive feedback later) and we were at Tower Base in no time. But when we got down to the Black Archive, we knew that we were already too late. Atkins, who was always very nice, was sitting outside, as usual, but when he didn't stand up or say anything, Kate reached out and touched his arm. His head just flopped sideways onto his shoulder and it was horrible.

I'd never seen a dead person before so I'm afraid I was sick (in a waste bin). When I looked up again, Kate had covered him with her coat. 'The sad thing is,' she said, 'he thought he died on his first day.'

McGillop and I looked at each other, and he was as white as a sheet, and I think I was too (though he was trembling more). Kate had taken the spare key from Atkins's belt and was now unlocking the door. As it opened, we could hear a voice from inside. And it was totally weird because the voice was McGillop's.

'The equipment here is phenomenal,' he was saying, and they'd got his accent just right, even though it was regional. 'The humans don't realise what half this stuff does. We could conquer their world in a day. If I was from round here, I'd say it was Christmas.'

'No,' said Kate, striding ahead of us, into the Archive. 'I'm very much afraid you wouldn't.'

McGillop was looking at me. 'We have to go with her.'

'Do we?' I asked, which was wrong of me, but I was very scared.

'Because she needs you, and where you go, I go.' He'd taken my elbow, like he was going to guide me into the room. 'You're UNIT's number one tactical asset, remember?'

We didn't seem to be moving anywhere, and his hand on my elbow was shaking so hard. 'I think you'll have to push a little bit,' I said. 'Or we really won't get anywhere.'

159

'I know. I'm trying.'

'Tell you what. You keep hold of my elbow, and I'll tow.'

'Okay.'

We made our way into the room. UNIT's number one tactical asset, I was thinking. Not really. Not on a good day. Only in the absence of the Doctor.

EXCERPT ENDS

FEED CONNECTING
FEED CONNECTED
FEED STABLE
OWING TO THE RESTRICTIONS OF PSYCHIC PAPER
WE ARE UNABLE TO PRINT ANY OF THE FOLLOWING
WORDS:

... ... Oops, hello, sorry! Here you all are, again. Just, reminiscing. I'm an old man, memory is my television. Though, to be honest, so is my television.

Did you enjoy that one? No, hush, rhetorical. You can all go and write your reviews online, I don't want you wasting space here.

Zygon prose is always fascinating, I find. I can't get enough of picturing those big sloppy red hands wrapped round pencils. Though, in this case, that's not how it really worked. I'll explain later, I promise. Unless I forget, or can't be bothered, or I happen to notice a shiny thing.

I was just thinking about Alistair again. I do that a lot, because I enjoy smiling. I told him I was thinking of writing this book, of course, and I thought he'd be pleased. Instead he gave a sort of grim nod, and we carried on playing Risk in silence for a bit. (He always got to be the Daleks, which was a bit unfair.)

'What's wrong?' I said eventually.

'It's a security breach,' he said, through his crossest moustache.

'It's not my fault,' I protested. 'You left Italy undefended.'

'No, your book. Your book is a clear breach of security. There's classified material in there.'

'I've thought about that,' I said. 'And I have a clever plan.'

He rolled his eyes. 'Really?'

'I'm going to write "fiction" on the back.'

'Oh, for God's sake!'

'No, seriously. It will be released as fiction, and sold only in the fiction departments of bookshops. That way, everyone will think it's not true.'

'But it's not fiction, is it? It's fact.'

'Fact, fiction, same thing,' I told him.

'For God's sake, no it isn't!' He thumped the table with his big, silly fist, and all the little Daleks on the board jumped at once, like they'd had a fright. I think I laughed for five minutes.

'Fact and fiction are not the same thing. Please don't be so ridiculous.'

'Oh, Alistair, think about it. The Universe is vast, and it goes on for a very long time. And do you know what that means? It means that everything that can happen will happen somewhere eventually—that's the rule. That means every story you can make up, will actually happen one day, somewhere in space and time. The only difference between a factual book and a fictional book is that factual books are written after the event, and fictional books are written before the event. Which makes fiction much more useful, don't you see? When you're writing facts, you're just copying down. When you write fiction, you're seeing into the future.'

We just sat there for a bit, and he did a lot of glaring. I bent down and picked up the Dalek he'd thrown and put it back on the board. He'd got me right on the nose, though I have to admit it's not a difficult target.

'Why do the Doctor Papers exist?' he asked. 'Why write up that one adventure? Why not any of the others?'

I'd known he was going to ask that question, and I'd slightly dreaded it. 'To reflect, perhaps,' I said. 'Or to remember. The timelines were all tangled, it needed to be set down before it all faded from memory, possibly as a cheat sheet for next time. Though, of course, there's not a lot of use in a cheat sheet you don't know you have, because you can't remember writing it.'

I was standing at the window now, looking out over the grounds. Was I hiding my face, I wondered. I didn't like him seeing me unsure or troubled.

'There's more to it than that, isn't there?' said Alistair.

The sun was just starting to set, and a mother was leading a small boy along the path, away from the sad old building. I could hear their feet crunching on the gravel. The boy was clutching the string of a red balloon that bobbed along above them both, as if trying to escape. I stared at the little hand, with the string wrapped around it.

'The Doctor had to keep hold,' I said.

'Hold of what,' asked Alistair.

'The Doctor.'

'You're not making any sense.'

I sighed. How to explain? 'It wasn't an adventure,' I said. 'It was a day. A day that went on for a very long time, and happened over and over again.' The boy had twisted round to look back at the building. I thought about all the windows he could see from down there, and wondered if he was thinking about all the people behind them, tucked up in their beds, fading slowly from their lives. I gave him a smile and a wave, to show him it wasn't so bad, but he just turned to look ahead again, and kept marching away down the path. Quite right, I thought. Get away from here, have a laugh, play a game, make mistakes, and never, ever stop running. Time enough for this place, I thought. Time enough.

'What are you talking about?' said Alistair. 'Not an adventure, a day—what is that supposed to mean?'

I looked at the sunset, and pulled myself together. 'It was the day the Doctor understood who the Doctor always had to be.'

Alistair didn't say anything for a long moment. Then a Dalek pinged off the window next to my head.

… ah, I'm sorry. Lost in memories, I did warn you. So very old now, hard to keep hold of myself. Where were we? Ah, yes, Chapter Five. Written by the Doctor this time. Ah, but which one? Which one?

Chapter 5

The Wedding of the Doctor

'At first I thought she just fancied me,' said Clara Oswald, and then broke off. It was beyond strange, she thought. She looked around the three of them: the grumpy old one who seemed to carry the smoke of battle with him; the angry, pacing one, who knew he was cooler than the other two; and her one, who was currently lost in contemplation of his own knuckle joints. As long she'd known him, he'd seemed to view his fingers with a degree of suspicion, and sometimes even jumped when they moved. It was ridiculous, she thought, looking again from one to the other, but somehow you could tell, without even trying, they were all the same man. So different, and yet all so clearly and obviously *him*. She couldn't even give them different names in her head. They were just the Doctor, the Doctor, and the Doctor.

'Clara, you okay?' asked the Doctor, and she had to check it was her one.

'Yes, sorry ...'

'You were explaining about Kate Lethbridge-Stewart?' said the pacing one.

'Yeah, yeah I know.' She forced herself to concentrate. 'Okay, so at first I thought she just fancied me, or something. It was honestly weird. Every time I said anything, or even just made a face, I could feel her just *looking* at me. It was kind of like when someone thinks you're hot. You know, when someone's into you? And every time you laugh or speak, or do anything, you can feel their eyes just glom on to you? You know what I mean??'

'Not, I'm afraid, a solitary syllable,' sighed the Doctor.

'I find people *always* act like that,' grinned the Doctor.

'Yeah, I get that all the time too,' frowned the Doctor. 'Especially, when I knock over things.'

The Doctor glanced at the other two, with unconcealed contempt, then turned back to Clara. 'Am I to understand, from that apparently random collection of words, that you thought this Kate person was … *attracted* to you?' His face had creased into a sort of fastidious regret, as if these matters had become slightly distasteful to him at his time of life. The other two rolled their eyes and turned away.

'Well, yes, I guess.'

He nodded. 'And then you concluded she had to be an alien duplicate. I see.'

'No, I concluded maybe we should get a drink sometime. But when I thought about it, something was wrong. Because when we first met, she'd barely looked at me. So what was different now? People don't suddenly start fancying you out of nowhere, because you happen to hang around for a bit. Except in romcoms. Written by stalkers.' A succession of baffled winces had passed over the old man's face. She suppressed a smile. 'So when she stepped out for a moment, well, I watched what she did.'

'Good, intelligent work—it's a delight to meet you, Miss … Oswald, wasn't it?' said the Doctor. When he smiled, his eyes almost disappeared in the crinkles.

'Call me Clara.'

'Dangerous, but proactive, Clara—I approve. So you witnessed the Zygon transformation. An alarming sight, I know.'

'Bit weird.'

'You are to be congratulated on your bravery and your insight. First class! I needed a few more men like you in the field.'

'Down boy,' said the other two Doctors simultaneously.

'So I ran for it,' continued Clara, 'but there was nowhere to go. Then her phone beeped—she'd left it in a sort of dock on the wall—and I saw she'd got a text. A photo.' She pointed to the numerals the Doctor had carved into the stone. 'Of those numbers, right there. So I figured it was the activation code for this.' She held up the vortex manipulator, on her wrist. 'And boom, here I am.' She prodded the charred leather. 'Think it's blown out, though.'

'Excellent. You have done extremely well. Whichever of these young men is travelling with you, they have made an excellent choice.' She noticed he was wearing a bandolier round his chest—it suited him, she thought, but one day he was going to wear a bow tie. She glanced over to where that bow tie was now, and saw the face above it was looking at her, smiling.

'You okay, Clara?' he said.

'Just getting my head straight. So both of these guys are you?' she asked him.

The Doctor glanced at the Doctors. He shrugged and smiled. 'Yes, I'm afraid so. Previous editions. Captains Grumpy and Swagger. My exes. Well not my exes. But my exes if you see what I mean. We don't actually know why—'

'I came here tracking a migratory Zygon hive,' the Doctor interrupted. He was still pacing, faster now, as if his feet were getting angrier by the step. 'But according to what you've just told us, there are Zygons active in the twenty-first century too. How does that work? They don't have time travel.'

'You boys seem to have forgotten what the Time War was like,' snapped the Doctor. 'Gallifreyan technology got stolen all the time. Plenty of people ended up with time travel, who weren't supposed to.'

'So!' said Clara. 'Three of you in one cell. Three Doctors in one little room—and none of you thought to try the door? Not one of you, not even a little bit?'

There was a complicated succession of glances among the Doctors that seemed to suggest they were all about to start blaming each other, before each of them figured out how pointless that would be.

'It's hardly our fault,' said her Doctor. 'The door should've been locked. Why wasn't it locked?'

'Because,' came a clear, high voice, 'I was fascinated to see what you would do upon escaping.' They all turned to the doorway. There was a whirl of gold in the shadows beyond it and a flame-haired woman in a blazing dress was stepping into the room.

Clara stared. There was only one person this could be.

'Though you seem remarkably disinclined to go anywhere,' Elizabeth said, raking them all with a glance. 'What timidity is this? One recalls a better class of prisoner.' She skewered the Doctor with a look. 'What say you, my betrothed?'

'I have standards,' he said. 'I only escape through locked doors. And by the way, dear, don't call me your betrothed. I proposed to Queen Elizabeth, not a Zygon in a big dress.'

She stared at him for a moment, then stepped closer to him, examining his face, as if for the first time. 'I understand you have a fondness for this world,' she said at last. 'It's time, I think, you saw what is going to happen to it.' She turned and swept out through the door. 'This way,' she called behind her. 'It is dead of night, and something is stirring below England.'

Elizabeth led them deeper and deeper into the Tower. She walked at speed through the pitch darkness, never missing a step or a turning. When one of the Doctors had attempted to light the way with his screwdriver, she had snapped at him to switch it off. 'We do not wish to attract attention. If your feet are unsure in the shadows, follow me—I do not suffer the inconvenience of mortal eyes.'

Clara plucked at her Doctor's arm, and only realised she'd got the wrong one when she heard his voice. 'Yes, my dear?'

'I've been down here before,' she whispered.

There was a fruity old chuckle. 'So you've just been telling us—but in fact you haven't. Technically, you haven't been down here *yet*.'

'But this is the way to the Black Archive.'

'No. It *will* be. The Black Archive will not exist for hundreds of years. We are about to see where UNIT chose to build it. Which raises intriguing questions, don't you think?'

Ahead of them, Clara's Doctor had been listening. 'More like the *red* archive now.' He was pointing. At the end of the corridor, there was a door; blood-red light spilled round its frame. In front of it, Elizabeth was turning to face them, her hand on the handle.

'I suggest you compose yourselves. You are about to see the darkest secret in the Kingdom. Beyond this door, a seed is being planted which, in times to come, will flower into the doom of all England.'

She opened the door.

It was like stepping into a giant mouth. First there was a hot, wet reek, like rotting orchids, then the walls and floor curved round them, pink and wet and alive, like a tongue tumoured with suckers and hanging nodules. The Zygons themselves were barely visible for a moment, slow and silent in the rising steam of their flesh-base, like so many foetuses drifting round a womb.

Foetuses with teeth, thought Clara, as one of the Zygons turned towards them. Even from a distance, its tiny eyes glittered. As it saw them, its lips drew back in seeming rage— but then its gaze fell on Elizabeth, and it appeared to hesitate. After a moment, it made what could be mistaken for a small bow.

'Attend your given tasks,' commanded the Queen. 'There is much to be done if England is to be ours.' The Zygon turned back to its work.

'Zygons,' said the Doctor, straightening his bow tie, as he always did in the sight of the enemy. 'A whole Zygon hive.'

'Yeah, Zygons, what have I been telling you,' replied the Doctor. 'I followed them here, that was my mission.'

'We know all about your mission! Venom sacs in the tongue.'

'Shut up!'

They were interrupted by an ill-tempered grunt from the Doctor. 'The Zygons lost their home world in the first year of the Time War. Perhaps, if we could all stop wittering on, we might receive an explanation as to what they're doing here.'

'A new home is required,' said Elizabeth.

'So they want this one?' asked Clara.

'Not yet,' she replied. 'Far too primitive.'

'Yes, that makes sense,' grumped the Doctor. 'Zygons do insist on a certain amount of comfort.' His mouth creased on the word 'comfort' as if the idea was more disturbing to him than conquest. He looked to Clara. 'So, my dear—the walls, what do you observe?'

'They're like … flesh, or something. Wet flesh, like this place is made of gums.'

'Quite, yes, very well put. A living support chamber for the Zygons. Once abandoned, however, it will calcify into a shiny black rock-like substance. Ring any bells?'

'The walls of the Black Archive.'

'Precisely, Miss Oswald. They carved their idiot archive out of the sediment of this place. The Black Archive not only contains alien technology, it is built out of it.'

Elizabeth was now staring at him, stony-eyed. 'Old man, why do you treat your current danger as if it were an educational opportunity?'

'Because, ma'am, I have never encountered a danger that wasn't.'

Her eyes narrowed, but she was interrupted as another Zygon came padding over to them. Up close, the smell was overpowering and Clara felt her eyes stinging. The Zygon gave a little bow to Elizabeth and spoke in a scraping whisper: 'Commander, if I may ask—why are these humans here?'

'I say they should be, therefore they are. Just because I am presently in human form, do not presume to question my judgement, or I shall put out your eyes. As you know, I have already had to do that once today, and I dislike to repeat myself.'

'My profound apologies, Commander.'

'Noted. How many have been processed now?'

'Almost all, Commander. I am the last of the invasion brood.'

'Very good,' nodded Elizabeth. 'I will remain with the others to ensure your safety. It is time you too were translated.'

The Zygon lowered its head in assent, and Elizabeth placed a hand on its arm, as if comforting it.

'Do not fear this strange world you go to now,' she said. 'For you will be the commander there, not I. It is my place only to open the door. You shall step through it into glory.'

If a Zygon could look moved, this one did. 'Commander,' it breathed.

'To your mission, brave voyager,' she said, sterner now. 'There are humans present, as there will be in the future—you must maintain appearances at all times.'

'It shall be done,' hissed the Zygon. It began making its way towards the wall behind them. Turning to watch, Clara saw what she had missed before. All the landscape paintings from the Under Gallery were arranged haphazardly round the door through which they had entered, each of them gripped in place by a fibrous sucker extruding from the flesh wall. 'Landscapes *with* figures,' said the Doctor, next to her now. 'You see? Those are the same paintings we saw in the gallery, but with figures still in them.'

'Not as bad as you made out,' she said.

'Who isn't?'

'You weren't.' She nodded to the old man who was now examining the paintings.

'Observe this, Doctor,' Elizabeth was saying. 'I believe you will find it fascinating.'

The Zygon had stepped towards a fibrous nodule growing out of the floor. The nodule ended in a ring of fingers, which gripped hold of a gleaming, silver sphere.

The Zygon placed its hand on the sphere. There was a rapid series of clicks, the air around the Zygon seemed to glitch for a moment, and then the whole Zygon simply folded out of existence and was gone.

'Well, what do you think? Does my betrothed approve?' asked Elizabeth, slipping her arm into the Doctor's.

'That's Time Lord technology,' the Doctor snapped back at her. 'Stolen Time Lord technology.'

'And to think, you *date* these people,' said the Doctor.

'You boys really don't have memories, do you?' sighed the Doctor, querulous as ever. 'As I have already reminded you, lots of our technology got stolen during the war, it was one of the principal dangers. Perhaps if you pair spent less time flapping your hands about and posing dramatically you might develop some kind of useful recall.'

'But where did the Zygon go?' asked Clara.

'Look to the paintings,' said Elizabeth.

As Clara looked, one of the landscapes glowed. The lumpen figure of the Zygon was materialising on a hillside.

'That's him? That's the Zygon, in the picture now.'

'It's not a picture, my dear,' said the Doctor, crinkling a smile at her again—the old man seemed to enjoy explaining things to her. 'It is, in fact, a Stasis Cube. Time Lord art, you see? Frozen instants in time, bigger on the inside. Like a three-dimensional photocopy of a four-dimensional event. But as you can see, you could store living matter inside it too. Though why would you want to?'

'Suspended animation!' shouted the Doctor. He turned to Elizabeth, who was still wrapped around his arm. 'Oh, that's very good. First class. Your Zygons all pop inside the pictures, wait a few centuries till the planet is a bit more interesting, then out they come. Blimey, you lot—you won't invade anywhere that doesn't have decent broadband.'

'Yes, yes, yes!' yelled the Doctor, his hands now whizzing about at each other, as if he were signing an aerial dogfight for the deaf. 'You see, Clara? They're stored in the paintings in the Under Gallery, like Cup-a-Soups. Except you don't add water, you add time. You add time-water to the painting-soup. If you can picture that. Nobody could picture that. Forget I said Cup-a-Soups.'

'Okay, I get it,' said Clara. 'Back in the future, when we went to the Under Gallery, the Zygons decided the world was finally worth conquering. Basically the alarm went off, and they climbed out of the paintings.'

The Doctor was now disengaging his arm from Elizabeth's. He looked at her, cold now. 'Right, well, seeing as that's all settled, it's time I told you something,' he said. 'Do you know *why* I know you're a fake, Queenie? Because the fact is, you're such a bad copy. It's not just the smell, or the unconvincing hair, or the atrocious teeth, or the eyes just a bit too close together or the breath that could stun a horse—it's because my Elizabeth, the *real* Elizabeth would never have been stupid enough to reveal her own plan. Honestly, why would you do that?'

For a moment, Elizabeth said nothing. Then she leaned in a little closer to them all, and lowering her voice, spoke in the sweetest tones. 'Because,' she said, 'it is *not* my plan, and I *am* the real Elizabeth.'

There was a silence. For the first, second, and third time in his life, the Doctor could find absolutely nothing to say.

'So, it would appear that my Kingdom is infested with demons that may steal the faces of mortal men and that England is doomed to suffer their dominion in the years to come; that the man whose proposal of marriage I have just accepted is a spy from another world who believes me to be a demon in disguise;

and that the odour of my breath might stun a horse. I am of the firm opinion that this has *not* been a good picnic.'

They were in the Queen's bedchamber, and Clara was amused at the way the Doctor had arranged himself around the room. The old man sat in a chair at the side, with the air of a presiding dignitary. He glanced around from time to time, seeming either faintly amused or faintly disgusted by everything he saw—except when he looked at Clara, when he always crinkled a smile and nodded. This hated phantom from the Doctor's past seemed to like her and, to her surprise, she discovered she liked him too. Just as she thought that, he glanced at her and then away again, as if he had overheard her. She knew her Doctor would sometimes take peeks inside her head, and wondered if his previous selves ever did that too.

The Doctor who had proposed to Elizabeth was striding about the room, agitated, his hands rammed in his pockets, like a sulking schoolboy. Dear God, that man could pace. It was as if every floor he stood on was too hot for his feet. He was issuing a constant stream of explanations and excuses and apologies, which no one seemed to be listening to, least of all him.

Her Doctor was sprawled on the bed, as if exhausted by the efforts of his previous self, eyes shut, and apparently dozing. She wondered what he remembered of being in this room, twice before. Mostly he seemed surprised by what was happening around him, but now and then she caught him glancing at the others, clearly haunted by a memory. She lay on the bed next to him, with her head propped on her hand, and her eyes kept returning to the remarkable woman who had brought them all here.

The Queen had arranged herself on the window seat, with the rising sun behind her. Somewhere, a portrait painter was missing a majestic opportunity.

'Yes, yes, okay,' said the Doctor, suddenly opening his eyes, and interrupting the flow of excuses, 'But you still haven't explained what happened to the other one. Where's the Zygon version of you?'

'I was talking!' said the Doctor.

'You still are,' replied the Doctor.

'My twin is dead in the forest—as I believe I told you.'

'You didn't tell us how she got that way,' said the Doctor, wriggling up to a sitting position on the bed. 'They don't just pop like balloons, Zygons.'

'One begs to differ,' said Elizabeth. She had produced a dagger from somewhere inside her dress. 'Whatever a balloon is.' She flicked a look to the Doctor. 'I was having a picnic with a strange man, naturally I took precautions.'

'I took sandwiches.'

'My dear, you took a Zygon and here we all are. Once I returned here, the other Zygon creatures never even considered that it was me who survived the conflict rather than their own commander. The arrogance that typifies their kind.'

'What, Zygons?' asked Clara.

'Men,' said Elizabeth.

Clara grinned. 'And you actually killed one of those things. Like, in hand-to-hand combat?'

'I may have the body of a weak and feeble woman—but at the time, so did the Zygon. I was therefore able to take the command of the others, without difficulty—'

'Sorry, wait, wait, wait, *wait!*' protested the Doctor, stopping pacing for a moment. 'You're saying you just took command of an entire Zygon hive from outer space?'

'Whatever their aspect, they are soldiers. Like all soldiers they have the character defect of obedience, which they mistake for the higher purpose of duty. It is easy to command those accustomed to orders. In many ways it is a kindness.'

'But from *outer space*,' he repeated.

The Doctor was now chortling away on his chair. 'I did notice, your Majesty, that they appeared to have taken up bowing. Haven't seen Zygons do that before.'

'I confess that was my innovation.'

He laughed even harder. 'Your Majesty, I am greatly looking forward to meeting you.'

Elizabeth glanced briefly at him; then she looked again, harder. She pointed to the gleaming sphere that rested on the writing desk next to where the Doctor was sitting. 'That is from the Zygon lair.'

'Yes, your Majesty. I stole it as we left.' He picked it up and tossed it in his hand. 'It belongs to my people. A family heirloom, you might say.'

'But when did you steal it? I saw nothing.'

'With respect, your Majesty, that is what you may expect to see when I steal something.'

She narrowed her eyes. 'Your arrogance is familiar,' she said, then rounded on the Doctor, who was still reclining on her bed. 'As is yours, sir—you help yourself to the comforts my bedchamber, as if you belong here. I feel there is something of importance I am failing to perceive.' She looked around the three men with a gathering frown.

'Okay,' said Clara, to break the silence. 'But if you're in charge of the Zygons, why didn't you just order them off the planet, or something?'

'That would have been unexpected, and therefore questioned. One should not stimulate one's enemies into thought, while in the midst of a deception. In any event, the greater number of them were determined to put themselves inside those strange pictures, where I understand they intend to remain for many hundreds of years. I encouraged haste in this project, in the knowledge that we would be safer with them gone. I have resources enough to dispose of the few that have stayed behind.'

'No, no, *no*!' said the Doctor, 'Come on, I know you, you've tortured me. You don't *dispose* of people! Those creatures are stranded here, you have to find a way to make peace.'

'The only peace they will find on English soil is underneath it.'

'No, I forbid this—'

'You forbid it, sir? Be less bold. Your eyes are pretty enough where they are, and I have a sufficiency of earrings. Henceforth please try to remember—' her voice rose to a bellow—'*I am in charge here!*'

For a moment it seemed to Clara that the windows rattled. Then, in the silence that followed, Elizabeth refolded her hands in her lap, and her smile resumed its former sweetness.

'Hang on. Eyes,' said Clara. 'Downstairs you said you'd put out a Zygon's eyes ...'

'It was a disciplinary matter, I had to behave as their commander.'

'That's what Zygons do?'

'I have no idea, I was forced to improvise.' She turned her gaze on the Doctor. 'Can I expect you to do your duty, beloved?'

'Depends on what you think my duty is.'

'I will deal with the Zygons that remain here, and arrange for the paintings to be locked away, where they may do no harm. You will travel to the future and deal with whatever devilry they intend to unleash, upon emerging.'

The Doctors exchanged glances, clearly worried. 'I may be a dab hand at a picnic,' said the Doctor, at last, 'but who said I can travel in time?'

'You did. You have made many flippant remarks about other times you have visited. Flippancy is so often a concealed truth flaunted by an over-confident man. And I seem to be surrounded by three of those.' She now rose to her feet. 'Doctor!' she said to the man on the chair. 'Doctor!' she said to the man sitting on the bed. 'And Doctor,' she said to the man, now staring back at her astonishment. 'The future of my Kingdom is imperilled. Can I rely on your service?'

'You've let this place go a bit,' grouched the Doctor as he entered the TARDIS with the Doctor.

'It's not my TARDIS, it's his one,' replied the Doctor, nodding to the Doctor, who was racing round the console, slamming levers, and powering up. 'I've refurbed a couple of times since this version,' he went on. 'Dumped the coral, went a bit metal, you'll love it.'

The Doctor grunted in reply. 'There better be more round things,' he muttered.

Elizabeth had lost no time in making the necessary arrangements. The TARDIS had been transported from the forest, where it had been parked for several months, and after a brief ceremony, the Queen had sped them all on their way. 'England depends on you. Remember your promise, Doctor!'[2]

'So where are we going?' asked Clara, as the TARDIS roared into life. 'The Black Archive? Because there's a Zygon in there right now. Well, right then. Well, in a few hundred years.'

The TARDIS lurched and they all grabbed on to the console.

'Unfortunately,' said the Doctor at the controls, 'the Black Archive is the one place on Earth we can't go.'

'But I thought the TARDIS could go anywhere.'

'Anywhere,' he replied, 'except the Black Archive.'

The Doctor found himself a chair at the side of this disgracefully grubby version of his TARDIS—really, was a quick dab with a sponge out of the question?—and contemplated the two boys, racing around the console, squeaking and bouncing like cartoon boffins. Really, he kept thinking. *Those?*

One of them was wittering on about phasing the TARDIS through the sub-dimensions, and the other one was disagreeing,

---

[2] What promise? Indeed, what ceremony? Is the Doctor omitting certain details here? We shall return to this subject after the chapter is concluded. The section does seem strangely rushed, doesn't it?

because they'd be better off adapting the chameleon circuit, but none of it was worth listening to. Nothing would suffice, the Doctor knew. For these boys, the Time War was too long ago. They'd forgotten that TARDIS-proofing *worked*.

He sighed. Why had the Moment brought him here? What was the purpose? Seeing his future had changed nothing about his predicament. Soon he would have to return to the barn, and commit mass murder, and end the war. And then, apparently, he would descend into his second and third childhoods. Nothing had been altered by this visit, except that he now understood that he was doomed to survive.

The Doctor frowned. And yet something *had* changed. Something inside him was different now, but for the moment he couldn't quite put his finger on what it was.

'Why can't the TARDIS get into the Black Archive?' asked Clara. She had joined him, sitting on the arm of his chair, and seemed equally bemused by all the jabbering around the console. 'Kate said the Tower was TARDIS proofed, or something. Well, Zygon Kate.'

He looked at her for a moment. Splendid girl. He'd found himself glancing inside her mind, from time to time, which was an atrocious habit, of course, and one he would have to cut out. But there was something almost familiar about her, as if they were already fellow travellers. 'Fear makes companions of us all,' he said, aloud, and she frowned at him.

'What do you mean?'

'Sorry, my dear, I don't know why I said that. Something in your voice brought it to mind. I'm an old man, my memory is a terrible jumble.'[3]

---

[3] For an explanation of the Doctor's confusion, see *Doctor Who: Listen*, available in early 2195.

'Not as old as you're going to get,' she said, glancing at the other Doctors.

Or as young, he thought, then remembered she'd asked him a question. 'In the Time War, many species became adept at proofing themselves against the intrusion of a TARDIS—it's easier to scramble the engines than you'd think. The Zygons were particularly good at it.'

'And the Black Archive was built inside the remains of the Zygon base!'

'Just so. Their reasoning seems clear. They wanted to avoid the attention of the Beverley Sisters over there'—he nodded towards the other Doctors—'who most certainly would not approve of them stockpiling alien technology.'

'I'm not an expert,' replied Clara, 'but weren't there three Beverley Sisters?'

'I feel you are making a point, but I'm afraid it is eluding me.'

'Then I'm not making it very well. So there's no way we can get into the Archive?'

'Oh, but we have to, my dear. The Zygons are in there, they must be stopped.'

'But you just said we can't get inside.'

'Can't?' twinkled the Doctor. He held up the silver sphere he had taken from the Zygon lair. 'No such word as can't,' he grinned. He got to his feet, and approached the other two, who now seemed to be tearing the console apart.

'This wiring's a right mess, you should sort it out,' Bow Tie was complaining.

'Well, apparently I'm going to.'

'Yeah, leave everything to me.'

'Well that is roughly what's going to happen.'

'Gentlemen,' interrupted the Doctor. 'Enough of this chatter. We can't beat the TARDIS-proofing, but there is another way.' He tossed the silver sphere in his hand. 'Cup-a-Soup!' He frowned. 'What *is* Cup-a-Soup?'

'What are you on about?' demanded Bow Tie.

'Isn't it time,' said the Doctor, 'that we our turned our enemy's choice of weaponry against them? That is our M.O., is it not? We are the Doctor, after all.'

His ears hummed, the blood stood still in his veins, and he nearly dropped the sphere. That was it! That was what had changed! But when did he start doing that? *When had he started calling himself the Doctor again?*

'You got an idea?' Daddy's Suit was asking.

'Share with the class, why don't you?' said Bow Tie.

He could feel it inside himself. It had all come back, like it had never been away. He was ready to ride to the rescue, make some jokes, nick some stationery and trick the monsters into their own traps! He had looked the other way, and left a door open; and in that moment, look who'd snuck back in. He was the Doctor again. He should have been outraged, of course, but someone somewhere had started laughing, and to his astonishment, he realised it was him.

'Have I missed another funny thing?' asked Daddy's Suit.

'Seriously have you got a plan, Grandad?'

'A plan? Yes, I've got a plan! Of *course* I've got a plan! I've *always* got a plan, I'm the Doctor. But I should warn you, boys,' he said, and wondered if the smile on his face would ever stop growing, 'it's a little bit timey-wimey!'

And he started to roar with laughter again. The other two stared at him, clearly thinking he'd gone mad, but he didn't mind a bit. Because in that wonderful moment, spinning through time and space in the TARDIS, with the Doctor and the Doctor and Clara Oswald, there was exactly one thought going round and round in my head.

Doctor once more!

FEED CONNECTING
FEED CONNECTED
FEED STABLE
PLEASE STORE THIS BOOK IN THE CLOSED POSITION TO STOP THE WEEPING ANGELS CLIMBING OUT.

So what are we to make of that? Perhaps the hottest topic in Doctor scholarship (or, more likely, perhaps not) is this: did the Doctor marry Elizabeth I? What was the nature of the ceremony he so briefly alludes to? Was he his own best man? Did he also give away the bride? Obviously by now you've read the Doctor's Best Man speech in Chapter Nine—yes, you did, I'm sorry, settle down—and while it is extremely funny, extraordinarily moving and even revealing in quite unexpected ways (Susan!), it's possible, I suppose, that it's a fake. So what concrete evidence do we have for history's least likely union?

There is considerable doubt about how much time the three Doctors and Clara Oswald spent in Elizabethan England, before setting off on their mission to the future. You might suppose they were in a hurry, but since their transport was a time machine, time itself was not an issue. So did the Doctors linger and, more importantly, did the Doctor dally?

Many have pointed out that something *must have happened, because the Doctor is clearly being evasive when it comes to the* 'ceremony' and the exact circumstances of his departure. One cannot avoid a subject unless there is a subject to avoid. There is also the issue that Elizabeth addresses him as 'husband' in her letter of instruction.

For many, it is beyond doubt that the Doctor is lying, but consider: this doesn't necessarily mean that the marriage ever happened—only that the Doctor believed it did.

Consider also Elizabeth: a woman of immense accomplishment and intelligence, used to manipulating the many egos competing for her attention. Is it possible that she could have faked a secret wedding ceremony, just to tether the Doctor to her service?

We may never know for sure, of course, but I have my suspicions, and once I shared them with an old friend. Miss Clara Oswald often pops round for tea these days. I know her of old, though I like to pretend I can't remember why, and she is happy to play along with that. I asked her once if the Doctor, a Time Lord of renowned intelligence and insight, could really have been so easily bamboozled, even by Elizabeth.

'Yeah, I know what you mean, but trust me on this,' Clara said, 'she was a phenomenal kisser.'

Our next chapter, Dearest Petronella, is in the form of letter. The circumstances of its composition will be clear in the reading.

Chapter 6

Dearest Petronella

Dearest Petronella,

Hello you. Or Hello me. It's Petronella here. By the time you read this, I think, you'll be about to abandon your human form—but I wonder if you would mind waiting just a little? Could you read this letter, while you're still me? There's something I want to explain.

We have so many memories in common, don't we? All my life in your head. How embarrassing! But let's not dwell, you know all the stuff I'm talking about. Your face will be red enough when you're back to Zygon. Oops, shape-shifter humour, right? But just between us girls.

If you are a girl, really? Are you a girl? Are Zygons girls and boys like we are, or just all the same? I think all the same would be so much better. Think of the bathroom-space we could save. Honestly, what the human race could have achieved if we didn't have to double up on plumbing!

Anyway—drifting, drifting. You know me. Well, gosh, you really do know me, don't you? No one's ever known me like you do. Which is sort of the point of this letter.

As I write, you're still unconscious. It's funny, looking at you, because one thing you never see in the flesh is what you look like asleep. There's no drool, which is a relief, but you're snoring a bit. I keep apologising on our behalf, which is a bit weird, but I had no idea I was so loud!

You-know-who says the effect might take longer to wear off for you lot, because you're shape-shifters, and a bit more complicated. Also, your memory of what happened might not fully restore, because ... well, you've got twice as many memories as any of us. All mine on top of all yours.

So in case you've forgotten what went on in the last few hours, and what we said to each other, here it all is. From my point of view. Which, for now, is your point of view too.

RECAP. (I love those, don't you? Well, I KNOW you do.)

So we'd just found Atkins dead (very hard to forgive, sorry to mention) and Kate had gone striding into the room, because she always does that—you know, I think I want to be Kate the most—and McGillop had taken hold of my elbow, to be protective. Unfortunately, he couldn't move his legs, because of all the terror, so I had to sort of pull him forwards, while he kept protecting my elbow.

END OF RECAP.

As we made our way through the door, I could hear Kate talking.

'I am not armed. Neither are the two people now entering the Archive. It is against our code of conduct, and our inclination, to initiate any harm against an off-world visitor, and if you doubt my word on that, please consult the memories you have downloaded from my head.'

We could see them now. Kate was standing in the middle of the room, opposite an exact duplicate of herself. That was freaky enough, but behind her was another McGillop, and next to him there was ... well, you. Or me. Or you/me. You turned and saw me, and you gave me a weird kind of look, but I couldn't tell what it meant. Then I realised something. No one ever learns to read their own face, do they?

The real Kate looked over her shoulder. 'Petronella, I want you to lock the door please. No one must come in.'

She was calling me Petronella! That wasn't a good sign! She'd left the key in the door, so that was easy enough, but my hands were shaking so badly it took me ages. McGillop tried to steady my hand, but he wasn't any better, and we just rattled away together like a drinks trolley during turbulence. Behind us, I could hear the other Kate replying.

'Having downloaded your memories, I'm also aware of the resident population's general attitude to visitors. You have enough difficulty with your own species, let alone ours.'

'If I may point out: you are invading.'

'My Zygon duplicates are already taking command of UNIT. The invasion is nearly over.'

'With the weaponry in this room, you would be unstoppable.'

'I agree.'

'So I regret to inform you that you are about to be stopped. You don't mind if I sit down?' There was a meeting table, right in the middle of the room, and Kate just pulled out a chair and sat down. She smiled at her double, and waved her into the seat opposite.

Copy Kate didn't move for a moment. 'You are not armed. We are Zygons—we were *born* armed. This room is ours, therefore so is your planet.'

Kate just shrugged. 'Technically, the planet is yours, yes. I hope you enjoy your reign, as you're going to be dead in a little over five minutes. Please, do have a seat.'

Copy Kate was frowning now, and I knew that look; somehow control was slipping from her hands. After a moment, she pulled out a chair and sat opposite Kate. Then the other McGillop moved into position at her shoulder, and then you came and stood at her other shoulder. It was like a movie poster about a family business or the mafia (or cross TV presenters).

McGillop and I looked at each other. Oh well, we thought, and we went and stood in exactly the same positions behind the real Kate. It was all very scary, but it was kind of ridiculous too. Movie posters facing each other.

I glanced at you, wondering how you were feeling, and you were already looking at me, and it was so funny, because at the exact same moment we both made the big wheezy noise. We reached for our inhalers, but of course only I had one. I hope I didn't look too smug, but I think I probably did.

Kate was speaking again. 'If you search the memories you've taken from me, you will realise there are protocols protecting this place. The weaponry in this room cannot be allowed into your hands, or we will lose control of our own planet. Osgood?'

This was my bit, though I wasn't looking forward to it. 'In the event of alien incursion, the contents of this room are deemed so dangerous it will self-destruct in—' My mouth just gummed up! I couldn't say it!

Kate had her phone out, and she clicked something. On the wall, big red numbers lit up. I looked at them, but I was so scared, I couldn't make sense of them. They just sort of jumbled about in front of me, like my eyes were jumping up and down.

'Five minutes,' Kate said.

Copy Kate had her phone out too, and was looking at it. We were all about to die, and suddenly all I could think was, how could she have a phone? Did Zygons copy phones too? Was that a phone made of Zygon? Active hologram shell, I thought. Good theory, I thought, impatient with myself, but never mind that now.

'This is some of the most sophisticated powerful equipment in in the seven galaxies,' Copy Kate was saying. 'Your explosives would barely scratch it—oh!'

'Exactly,' said Kate. 'I see you've just remembered that there's a nuclear warhead twenty feet beneath us. Are you sitting comfortably?'

'You would destroy all of London?'

'To save the world? Yes, I would.'

'You're bluffing.'

188

'Do you think so? Somewhere in your memory is a man called Brigadier Alistair Gordon Lethbridge-Stewart.' I couldn't see her face from where I was standing, but I knew she was doing *that* smile. 'I'm his daughter.'

Copy Kate narrowed her eyes, like it was the annual performance evaluation, and leaned back in her chair a bit. She was drumming her fingers on the table now. Then she smiled. 'So am I,' she said.

This is mad, I thought. This is ridiculous, and pointless.

'Then I fear we have an impasse,' said Kate.

'Not for long,' said Copy Kate.

This will destroy everyone, I thought. They will murder millions. Us too!

What? What did I mean, us too? Why was I thinking that? Except, hang on, I *wasn't* thinking that! Those thoughts were just popping into my head. But where from?

Of course, that's when I looked across the table and saw you. And you were staring at me through your funny big spectacles. How can you have spectacles, I wondered. Were the spectacles made of Zygon?

I told you—active hologram shell.

Oh, that was you?

Of course it was me.

We're still linked then? Psychically?

I reopened the connection, yes.

You can do that?

Not normally. This is different.

Why?

Because I was able to figure it out. Your brain is amazing, Petronella. I've never been anywhere so huge.

Seriously? You like it?

I love it. How do you cope, though? All these thoughts! It's like chasing a herd of ponies.

I love ponies.

I'm aware. Shall we return to the end of the world?

Oh, okay, yes, sorry.

Copy Kate was speaking. 'The order can be cancelled, of course. One word from you would stop the detonation.'

I glanced to the counter on wall, and so did you. Oh God! We had three minutes.

'Quite so.'

'Keyed to your voice print.'

'And mine alone.'

'Not any more,' said Copy Kate. 'Cancel the detonation,' she shouted.

'Countermanded!'

'*Cancel the detonation!*'

'*Countermanded!*'

Copy Kate stared at herself. She was shaking her head. 'We only have to agree to live.'

'Agreed. All you have to do is surrender all your troops to mine.'

'Never!'

'Then we can only agree to die.'

They were both on their feet now, staring at each other. Kate was the most stubborn person in the world; she never backed down from anything. That stubbornness had saved so many people, so many times, but now she was face to face with herself. Unstoppable force meets immovable object, I thought; then realised that was from you.

You were looking at me again. Do you think he's got a plan, you asked.

Who?

Who do you think?

The Doctor can't even get in here.

You shook your head. Tell the Doctor there's a wall he can't climb—

—and he'll meet you on the other side, yes, I know. But how could he do it?

Look over my shoulder, you said.

When I looked all I could see was a painting propped against the wall. No, hang on, not just any painting. It was the *Gallifrey Falls* painting from the National Gallery. The one we'd shown to the Doctor just a short time ago.

But what's that doing here, I asked. It can't be moved, except on the specific orders of Kate Lethbridge-Stewart.

Or the Doctor, you reminded me.

But when could the Doctor have done that? I asked

You glanced at the Copy McGillop, and I noticed he was staring at me too. We've copied your colleague, McGillop, you explained, so we've got all his memories as well. We're going to send you a memory graft of something that happened a few hours ago.

Copy McGillop was staring and staring at me now, and I was about to ask what a memory graft was when—

I was back in the National Gallery, when we'd shown the painting to the Doctor and Clara for the first time. It was all exactly the same, except I was standing in a slightly different place, and my mouth tasted a bit funny. I was feeling a tiny bit hungover (hang on, I don't drink) but I was still looking forward to seeing Angus and Ferdinand that evening— except I didn't know who Angus and Ferdinand were. And then I realised! I was McGillop. I was standing inside his memory. This was a memory graft, and I was him. And oh my! Everything was so different! Even colours and smells and the feel of my feet on the floor—nothing anywhere was the same. When I looked at the Doctor, he wasn't called the Doctor any more, he was called Git-In-Bow-Tie. When I looked at Clara Oswald she was suddenly Bossy-Munchkin. When Kate started talking she was Cheer-Up-Dear. Then I was having a big sad thought, and thinking (in an Irish accent), 'Oh she can't take her eyes off him, can she?' I didn't understand that at first—who couldn't take their eyes off who?—and then I found I was looking at myself, and, yes, I was staring at the Doctor. And goodness me, all of a sudden I was called Princess.

Princess? Why was McGillop calling me Princess? I had a quick look round his memory—*gross!!*—and there was simply tons of me in there, and I was always called Princess! Didn't he know I was against all constitutional monarchy (except Prince Harry)? Mind you, I had to admit, he wasn't saying it in a mean way. He was saying it in a nice way. Actually, a very nice way. I didn't quite know what to do with myself. I'd have blushed if I'd had my own face. Did this mean he liked me? At the exact moment I asked myself that question, I realised I was looking at my bottom.

No, no, no, I thought! Oh, McGillop, cut that out. It was going on and on, and frankly it was embarrassing.

Git-In-Bow-Tie had just finished the Queen's letter. 'What's happened?' There was quick glance over to the Doctor as he spoke, then whoosh, back to my bottom.

'Easier to show you.' A quick glance at Cheer-Up-Dear, then whoosh, bottom! Oh, control yourself, McGillop! Was this what had been going on all these years? Was he objectifying me every time I turned my back (which seemed to be a requirement, in fact)?

Thankfully, my phone rang—no, I mean McGillop's phone rang. A familiar voice said, 'Take a look at the number on your phone, and confirm who you're talking to.'

The phone screen said that the Doctor himself was on the line. But how was that possible? I—no, McGillop—glanced at Git-In-Bow-Tie who was walking right past him, following Cheer-Up-Dear out of the room. Now Princess followed right behind him. Whoosh, bottom! Oh, *McGillop!* What did he think I kept back there?

'But that's not possible, sir,' McGillop was saying. 'He's right here.'

'Yeah, I know I am, I remember,' replied the Doctor on the phone. 'I'm a time traveller, figure it out. I am currently in flight, in the TARDIS, and I need you to get the *Gallifrey Falls* painting sent straight to the Black Archive. Priority Buffalo One. And tell absolutely no one this has happened.'

'Understood, sir.'

'Not even me. Do you still understand?'

'Why am I doing this, sir?'

'Because the future of Planet Earth depends on it,' said the Doctor and the line went dead. McGillop look down the corridor, where he could still see us walking away, and *whoosh*—

I was back in the Black Archive. I looked at the counter. I'd been gone for less than a second (well, not really gone, but you know what I mean).

'All you have to do is leave this planet,' the real Kate was saying.

'Fine, we'll go. But we're taking all this equipment,' said Copy Kate.

'So you can burn us up from space?'

'No, to stop you shooting us down as we leave.'

'We won't.'

'You've done it before. Why should we trust you?'

'You invaded us. Why should we trust *you*?'

'We have a problem, then.'

'A mutual problem.'

'But not for much longer.'

'For exactly a hundred and nineteen seconds, I fear.'

'I fear also,' said Copy Kate, with the saddest smile.

I looked at you. So it was the Doctor who moved the painting here, I said.

Are you thinking what I'm thinking?

By definition, you said. If the Doctor has found the ability to place himself inside the painting—

Do you remember that you never finished that thought? There was the most tremendous sound of shattering glass and the front of the painting exploded into the room. The air was suddenly filled with a strange, screaming, zooming noise, which made you scared just to hear, followed by a low drumming thunder, so deep you could feel it in your tummy, and then a spinning blue tunnel blasted like the beam of a searchlight through the picture frame, swirling and howling as it filled the room. I shaded my eyes and looked down the tunnel. I could see, silhouetted against the kaleidoscope of tumbling blue shapes, three men striding out of the painting, towards us.

I have the most stupid feeling that there might have been a tear in my eye, which you probably think is silly (or maybe you don't, of course, being me). But, you see, I knew what it meant. It's hard to describe, but I knew, even then, that everything was going to be absolutely fine—like it was suddenly Christmas Day, and Santa Claus was landing on the roof. I also knew I wasn't UNIT's number one tactical asset any more.

We were no longer in the absence of the Doctor!

Do you remember any of it, Petronella? I think it will start getting tricky now, because of what the Doctor did to us all. But I hope you can remember those three men climbing out of the painting and just striding into the room. I knew, straight away, they were all the Doctor. I've studied him all my life, but that wasn't the reason: you could just see it somehow. The Doctor and the Doctor and the Doctor!

There was the one we met today, all goofy and adorable, with his bow tie and swirly hands. And there was the one with the tight (!!) suit and the Converse. My mum saw a photo of him once, and told me that she would (which was a bit gross, wasn't it?). And there was another one I'd never seen in any pictures. The mysterious extra Doctor! It was like finding a secret Top Trumps card that no one else knew about! He was very different from the other two. Sort of older and more crumpled. When he looked at you it was like he was grand and frail at the same time. It was still him, though, there just wasn't any doubt. He wore a bandolier round his chest, which

I thought would be difficult to replicate, so I'd probably be hitting the antique shops.

'Hello,' they all said.

'I'm the Doctor.'

'I'm the Doctor.'

'I'm the Doctor.'

Honestly, I could hear my tattoos cheering (apologies for those, by the way).

'Sorry about the mess,' said the old one.

'And the showing off,' said a voice. I looked round to see ~~Bossy Munchkin~~ Clara Oswald climbing out of the picture too.

'Kate Lethbridge-Stewart, what in the name of sanity are you doing?' said Doctor Bow tie. (He said it to the wrong one, but I suppose when there's three of you in the room, you stop worrying about that sort of thing!)

'There's a protocol for when this place is breached—' began real Kate.

'I know all about your idiot protocol,' said Doctor Converse. 'I just never thought anyone would be idiot enough to activate it.'

'The countdown can only be halted at my personal command, there's nothing you can do.'

The Doctors all looked to the numbers on the wall. We had a bit over a minute. I'd read every file there ever was on this man—I knew he'd keep going to the last second, just for dramatic effect.

'I'll tell what we can do about it,' said Doctor Converse. 'We can make you both agree to halt it.'

'Not even for three of you,' said Kate.

'You are about to murder millions of people,' snapped Doctor Old.

'To save *billions* more,' said Kate. 'How many times have you made that calculation?'

'If you'd never had this stupid, dangerous collection in the first place—'

195

'*Irrelevant!*' shouted Kate. 'I repeat: how many times have you made that calculation?'

The Doctors all looked at each other, and there was something awful in their faces.

'This is not a decision you will ever be able to live with,' said Doctor Converse. (When he said that, I noticed Doctor Old glancing at him, and there was a look in his eyes that was so big and so sad, I almost went and hugged him.)

'Well then,' Kate replied, 'lucky thing I won't have to. Doctor, *how many times?*'

The Doctors looked at each other. I knew the answer they were going to give. Never! That's what they didn't want to tell her. Maybe because they didn't want to seem superior, or as though they were judging her, but if being the Doctor counted for anything, I knew that—

'Once,' said the Doctor.

The floor swayed at my feet. What did he say?

'Once,' he repeated. It was the Bow Tie one talking. I wanted him to stop, because what he was saying could not be—could never ever be—true. 'Once, long ago, I did exactly what you're about to do now, and told myself it was okay.' Stop talking, I wanted to scream, shut up, shut up, *shut up.* 'It turned me into the man I am today. And I'm not even sure who that is any more.'

'You tell yourself it was justified. All the time, every minute, you tell yourself that.' It was Doctor Converse now. He was all blurry, and my eyes were stinging. 'But it's a lie. What I did that day was wrong. Just wrong.'

I wiped my eyes on my sleeve. A few feet behind Doctor Converse, I could see Doctor Old. He had put a hand out to support himself on the wall, and his face was turned away. He looked weak suddenly, and I wondered if he was crying too. As I watched, he sort of crumpled into a chair, and held his head in his hand. Remember I said you could sort of tell he was the Doctor? Well, it was strange, because suddenly that wasn't true any more.

'So, anyway, here's the point,' said Doctor Bow Tie. 'Because I got it wrong, I'm going to make you get it right.' Suddenly he was all lively again, like nothing he'd just said mattered. 'How long have we got, Doctor?'

'Oh, about forty seconds, Doctor,' said Doctor Converse. 'Shall we get started straight away, or have a cuppa first?'

'Nah, let's get it done now, Doctor, we can spin it out to fill up the time.'

I looked at the clock. They didn't have forty seconds, they had about thirty. Were they lying on purpose to make it more dramatic?

'Assets, Doctor?' said Bow Tie.

'Well, incomparable genius, screwdrivers of varying sizes, and of course, the light fittings.'

'Ah, yes, the amnesia light fittings. We can work with that, can't we, Doctor?'

'I should say so, Doctor!'

Oh, try hard and remember this bit, Petronella. In exact unison, like they'd been practising, they pulled out two chairs at the end of the table, sat themselves down, banged their feet, one at a time, on the table top, and then leaned back and beamed at us all. The clock on the wall kept flicking the time away, and they were deliberately wasting it, just to show off. It was so 'Doctor' I almost forgot about what they'd just told us.

Across the table, the two Kates were staring at each other, as if they each expected the other to do something about this, but neither had a clue what.

'Now then!' said Doctor Bow Tie. 'Let us tell you what's about to happen.'

Kate stepped forward, like she wanted to protest, but couldn't think of anything to say.

'Any second now, you're going to stop that countdown, both of you, together!' said Doctor Converse.

Copy Kate stepped forward too, but nothing came out her mouth either.

197

'And then you're going to negotiate the most perfect treaty of all time.'

'Safeguards all round, completely fair on both sides.'

'And the key to the perfect negotiation …'

'… is not knowing what side you're on.'

They slammed back their chairs, and then they both leapt up onto the table. They spun their screwdrivers in their hands, then aimed them at the light fittings.

The Kates looked at each other, bewilderment in their faces.

'For the next few hours …'

'… until we decide to let you out of here …'

'… no one in this room will be able to remember …'

'… if they're human …'

'… or if they're Zygon.'

Both screwdrivers buzzed, and both Doctors laughed.

It was such a funny thing, because nothing really seemed to happen. The lights just got brighter for a moment, everything went a bit milky, and suddenly there we all were, just standing like we had before. For a moment, I wondered if something had gone wrong. But when I looked at you, I realised I couldn't remember which of us was which. (It's an odd feeling, writing this—remembering not remembering.) One of us was a Zygon and one of us was a human—but I didn't know who was who, and I could tell, by the look in your eyes, you didn't know either. Then we both looked to the timer on the wall, just as it clicked to zero.

'Cancel the detonation!' shouted two Kates at once.

The next few hours were as strange as you can imagine. You must have bits and pieces of it in your head, I would think. The two Doctors prowled around like prison warders, as all six of us sat at that table, and oh, how we negotiated. The Doctor was right, of course: if you're given the job of dividing something in half, but aren't told which half you're going to end up with, you make an extra special effort to get it right. He knew we were only cruel because we were selfish and afraid—so he used our fear and selfishness to force us to be kind.

Now and then I'd see one of the Doctors pause by a shelf, and pocket something, or zap it with a screwdriver, or pull out a power pack. I wondered if the Black Archive would ever be quite such a problem again.

The other Doctor, the old man, just stayed where he'd crumpled into his seat, his head still in his hand. He glanced at me once, and I swear his eyes were wet. Which one was he? Where did he come in the numbering?

We had a chat, you and I, during one of the breaks, and I suppose that's really what I want to talk about. I was saying that if I was a Zygon with an active hologram shell, did that mean my shoes were holograms, and if so, how did I clean them, and what if I picked up the wrong pair at the bowling alley. You laughed, and the laugh turned into the dreaded wheeze. I reached for my inhaler, and passed it to you. And we both froze, of course. Because that meant I was the human one, and you were the Zygon, and the secret was out. I wondered if everything was going to fall apart in that moment. But you just smiled, pressed your finger to your lips, and took my inhaler. It was rather fun to save the world together, over something so small and silly.

'You look a bit sad,' I said, a few minutes later. 'At least I think that's my sad face. Is that my sad face?'

'I like being you,' you said, with one of my shrugs, when I'm trying to say I'm basically fine but I'm really not. 'I suppose I'm going to have to stop now.'

And that's when I realised something very important. Oh, Petronella! We are not the same!

You just stirred and mumbled there. I don't think you'll be asleep much longer, so I'd better hurry up and get this written. Once we'd hammered out a sort of treaty—ten hours, it took—the Doctors zapped the lights again, to restore our memories.

This time, it knocked us all out, and I'm afraid (no offence) the humans all got better quicker than the Zygons. So here I am, writing by your bedside.

I learned a lot today, Petronella. The Doctor has always been my hero, but it's silly and wrong to expect him to be a hero every day, because that's not the truth about him. Just as I know I can never be with McGillop, because he thinks I'm a princess and that's not the truth about me either. I've never understood why people want to be loved like that, because you're bound to be a disappointment in the end. But if we're not heroes, or princesses, I suppose we can do a bit better with what we've got, can't we?

I said we're not the same. Here's why. All my life, every day, I've wished I was someone else. I've wanted to be Kate, or Sarah Jane Smith, or Amy Pond, or anyone really. But you're a shape-shifter, you've been lots of other people—and you want to be *me*. I think that makes you a much better Petronella Osgood than I am.

I think I'd like to be a better version. If the Doctor can't always be a hero, we're going to need a few more, right?

Dearest Petronella, if you like being me, why not just carry on? Stay. Please stay, be my friend and teach me, if you can, how to be you.

All my love,
Petronella Osgood (well, one of them)

FEED CONNECTING
FEED CONNECTED
FEED STABLE
*PLEASE DO NOT LEAVE THIS BOOK UNDER YOUR
BED AS IT GETS HUNGRY AT NIGHT.*

*There is a saying that if the ravens ever the leave the Tower of
London, then England will fall. Lot of nonsense, of course. And
anyway the real ones left ages ago. I'm afraid the ones there now
are robot replicas. (Sorry, the tourist board asked me, and semi-
retirement gets boring now and then.) But never mind birds—
excellent theoretical physicists though they are—what about
Osgoods? Since that day there have been two Petronella Osgoods on
duty at the Tower, keeping the world safe. I truly think humanity
might fall if either were to leave.*

*Serious students will know (and if you do not, it is my
sadness to inform you) that one of the Petronellas died in the line
of duty a few years later. No one has ever known which of them
perished, and Petronella herselves is quite firm about never
telling anyone. I say 'herselves' because another Earth resident
Zygon took the fallen Petronella's place, so that there could be
two of them again.*

*All that matters is this: Osgood lives—and so long as the fangirls
stand guard on the gates of humanity, so will we.*

To this day, there are Zygons living among the humans, in peace—and, it must be admitted, in secrecy. Not ideal, but better than fighting. And Kate Lethbridge-Stewart finally has some first-class holiday cover. The Zygons find her a bit exhausting, though, and take it in turns to be her. The important thing is, you can never see any difference in the handwriting!

We now approach Chapter Seven. I hope that this volume so far has given you the skills you need to grapple with the questions of authorship you are about to encounter, as you embark on The Day of the Doctor.

(As usual, I'll be here when you're finished. And keep the noise down when you're reading, I'm trying to wire up my webcam. With any luck, I'll have a special treat for you.)

Chapter 7

The Day of the Doctor

At the table, negotiations had entered their ninth hour, and both Kates looked ready to flop face down. Clara noticed that the Osgoods were taking a break with each other, and appeared to be sharing the same inhaler, which surely presaged well for peace on Earth. The two younger (older?) Doctors were wandering about the shelves, fiddling with things, and occasionally gossiping about some photographs of their various companions which they'd found pinned to a noticeboard. There had been an ugly period when they discovered a VHS tape of the movie *Daleks: Invasion Earth* and had insisted on watching it. They nearly derailed the negotiations by shouting, cheering and joining in, and then had spent the next hour calling each other Dr Who and talking like Peter Cushing. Clara had a sinking feeling that her Doctor might stick that way. 'I love his bandy legs!' he'd said, imitating Dr Who's walk by making no apparent change at all.

'I can tell!' said the other one.

'How?'

When they'd found a DVD of the other movie ('Remastered!') they'd tried to get the old man to join in, but he'd smiled, and waved them away.

Clara frowned, thinking of the smile. You can only really tell how sad someone is when they smile, she reflected. So as the ninth hour began, she made a cup of tea and went to sit with him.

'You've been peeking inside my head again,' she said.

'I'm terribly sorry, yes, I have,' I replied. 'I will stop immediately, you must forgive me. Please understand, I would never look at anything personal.'

'I know,' she shrugged. 'My Doctor does it too, sometimes. Usually in a crisis, though. Why were you doing it?'

'I was looking for the Doctor,' I admitted. 'I wanted to understand him.'

'But you *are* the Doctor.'

No, I'm not, I wanted to tell her. Instead, I said, 'I came here to discover the man I would become. I found him in your mind.'

'So that's what this is all about? That's why you showed up?'

'Well done, yes. The boys seem to have forgotten to ask that question. The disadvantage of their permanent sugar high, one imagines.'

Clara smiled. 'It was the movies that did it. I think they're on the phone to Peter Cushing now, pitching a third one.'

'I think my future selves crave distraction from memories they cannot lose.'

'I know they do,' she replied. 'Mine does, anyway. I've always known that.' She cocked her head at me, as if weighing up the words she was about to say. Then she hesitated.

'Is there a problem?' I asked her.

'The Doctor—my Doctor—he's always talking about the day he did it. The day he wiped out the Time Lords to stop the war.'

'One would,' I nodded, a little evasive. How could I tell her I knew nothing of the Doctor's regret, because it was all in my future? How could I explain that this was still the last day of the Time War, and the murder of 2.47 billion children still lay ahead of me. She was staring at me now. If I'd looked inside her mind then, I think I'd have seen only my own thoughts, so intently was she studying my face.

'You wouldn't,' she said at last. 'Because you haven't done it yet; it's still in your future.'

It seemed to me, for a moment, there was only Clara Oswald in the world, and that everything around her was falling into darkness.

'You're very sure of yourself,' I said, and wished the same could be said of me.

'He regrets it,' she said. 'I see it in him every day, he'd do anything to change it.'

'Including saving all these people,' I said. 'How many worlds has his regret saved, do you think? Look over there. Zygons and humans, working together in peace. That is the Doctor's regret in action. That is the penance I will serve, and the saving of so many.'

There were lights around her now, but not the lights of the Black Archive. Instead, dimly at first, I saw shafts of sunlight slanting through cracks in an old barn wall. I'm ready, I thought. I am ready for this.

'How did you know?' I asked her.

Clara seemed to be squinting at me now, as if I was becoming harder to see. 'Your eyes,' she said. 'You're so much younger.' And the barn grew brighter, and though she didn't move, Clara seemed further and further away.

'Then all things considered, it's time I grew up,' I said.

Clara raised her hand as if to grab hold of me and stop me leaving. 'Don't,' she said, and was gone.

The heat of the barn closed round me, and the box that would slaughter the children of Gallifrey was again at my feet. There was something new on top of it. I stood in the baking air and the drone of the flies, and stared at the new addition.

'Well,' said the Interface in my ear, 'you wanted a big red button.'

I have no idea how long I stood there. An hour perhaps. Or a minute, or a day. Time takes on a different meaning when it is measured in the heartbeats of the billions you are about to destroy.

The Interface stood across from me, and I could have been mistaken but there seemed to be compassion in her eyes. Could the control interface of the deadliest weapon in the universe truly have compassion?

'One big bang,' she was saying. 'No more Daleks, no more Time Lords. Are you sure?'

'I was sure when I first came here. I am sure now,' I said. 'There is no other way.'

'You saw the men you will become.'

'Yes, I did.' I thought about it for a moment. 'And they were extraordinary,' I continued, suddenly realising it was true. 'They were brave and kind and brilliant, and everything they needed to be.'

'They were *you*.'

I shook my head. 'No. They are the Doctor.'

'Don't you understand, even now?' Was it possible for a weapon interface to get impatient? 'You're the Doctor too!'

'No,' I told her. 'Great men are forged in fire. It is the privilege of lesser men to light the flame.' I raised my hand to the big red button. 'Whatever the cost.'

I thought of the children all over Gallifrey. I hoped it would be quick, and they wouldn't be afraid.

'Before you do this,' she said, 'I want you to swear something.'

'Swear what?' I said. What could matter now?

'You know the sound that the TARDIS makes, when it lands? That wheezing, groaning?'

'Yes.'

'I love it. Don't you.'

'Of course I love it.'

'Then swear this,' she said, taking my hand. 'Swear that wherever that sound is heard, it will bring hope.'

'I swear it.'

Her grip on my hand was tighter now. 'No, swear it and mean it. Swear that anyone, anywhere, who hears that sound will turn and look, and know they're not alone.'

I smiled at the thought. It was such a good dream. I could hear the TARDIS engines roaring in my head. The Doctor, in the TARDIS, riding through the stars to the rescue. I could never be that man, of course, but I could set him on his way.

'I swear it. I swear on both my hearts, and all my lives, that whoever hears that sound will know they are not alone.'

She smiled. 'I believe you. And I know you mean it. And above all, I know you will keep your word. So, my dear little breakable mortal … you have earned this.'

'Earned what?'

She leaned towards me, and her voice was a whisper. 'Turn, Doctor,' she said, 'turn and look.'

I turned. I fear, in that moment, my eyes were hot, and my face was wet. I confess I may have trembled.

The sound of the TARDIS engines had not been in my head: not one, but two, beautiful, blue police boxes stood at the other end of the barn, and in front of each box, stood a man who was also me.

It was the last day of the Time War. It was the worst day of my life. But I was not alone.

That moment seemed to turn and hold in the air, and I stood frozen, unable to speak. Then Clara Oswald came bounding out of the TARDIS. 'You see, I told you,' she said, 'he hasn't done it yet!'

Her voice broke my trance. I cleared my throat, and hoped my disarray was not obvious. 'Gentlemen, your presence is appreciated, and your support more so. But this is for me, and for me alone. Return to your appointed times and places, with my every blessing.'

It was the kind of request I'd ignored all my life—and now I learned I was always going to.

'These events should be time-locked,' said the one in the suit. 'We shouldn't have been able to come here.'

'So something let us through,' said the one in the Bow Tie.

'Clever boys, aren't they?' whispered the Interface in my ear. 'Don't worry, they can't see me—they'd be very confused if they could. Especially Pinstripe.'

Pinstripe, I thought! Bow Tie and Pinstripe, that worked. In other circumstances I might have laughed, but instead I turned my back on them both. If they couldn't remember the fear I was feeling now, I didn't want to remind them by letting them see my face.

'Go,' I said. 'Go back to your lives. Go and be the Doctor I could never be. Make it worthwhile.' I placed my hand on the button. It was time for them to go, and I knew they wouldn't want to stay and witness this.

For a moment, there was no movement behind me. Then I heard them both approaching.

'All those years, burying you in my memory,' said Pinstripe.

'Pretending you didn't exist,' said Bow Tie. 'Keeping you a secret, even from myself.'

'Pretending you weren't the Doctor, when you were the Doctor more than anybody else.'

'You were the Doctor on the day it wasn't possible to get it right.'

They were either side of me now, with the box between them. I couldn't look either of them in the face, so I kept my eyes on my hand, resting on the button.

'But this time ...' said Pinstripe, as his hand appeared and rested on top of mine.

'... you don't have to do it alone,' completed Bow Tie, as his hand came to rest on top of the other two.

I should have told them to run. I should have ordered them to get away from this place, and leave me to my duty. But I was old and tired, and about to kill billions.

So all I said was, 'Thank you.'

I looked to the Interface, and saw she was staring at me. It was impossible, of course, but it seemed to me there were tears in her eyes. For a moment, I could see nothing except her face.

Many years later, wearing a brand new body, I met Rose Tyler and wondered, for a long time, why her face haunted me.

Later still, I found myself trapped on Floor 500 of the Game Station, as the Dalek Emperor mocked me. 'Are you coward or killer?' it had demanded. I thought about the barn, and what I had done that day—and then I stepped away from the levers that would have unleashed death on Daleks and humans alike. 'Coward,' I said, 'any day.' I remembered the big red button under my hand, and wept, because I knew it hadn't always been true.

On the planet Messaline, I held a gun to the head of a murderer, as my daughter lay dead by his hand, and then spared his life. 'I never would,' I told him. 'Do you get that? I never would!'

I'm the man who never would, I told them all, but I knew I was the man who had.

So many years passed, and in time I found myself back in that barn, trapped again in the last day of the Time War. I laid my hand over the hand of the man I'd once been. I remembered being a coward not a killer, I thought of being the man who never would. And then I said, 'What we do today, is not out of fear, or hatred—it is done because there is no other way.' And as I said it, I still knew it to be true. Despite everything I'd ever done, or tried to believe, there was still no other way.

And then came Amy Pond and Rory. I escaped the Pandorica, and I fought the Silence. I discovered the true name of River Song, I met Clara Oswald, and I saw my grave on Trenzalore. I tried to be the coward, not the killer, and every day I told myself I was the man who never would. But I knew, in every moment, I was lying—because the man I was had stood in a barn, twice over, and made a terrible mistake.

Centuries passed, and I was back in that barn for the third time. Again, I laid my hand over the hand of the man I'd once been. I took a breath, I prepared myself, and I said: 'This is done without joy or triumph, in the name of the many lives we are failing to save.'

We looked at each over the gap of the centuries, and nodded. We were ready. We were making a mistake—but there was no other way, and there never had been.

And then, for the second time that day, Clara Oswald said, 'Don't.'

She was staring at me, tearful now. As if tears could make a difference on a day like this.

'Don't?' I said. 'What do you mean, "don't"? What good is saying "don't"?'

'I don't know,' she said, her words tumbling out. 'Just don't, don't do this. This is not you. This can't ever be you. Just don't do whatever it is you're doing.'

'Clara,' I said. 'This happens. This has always happened. I've never lied about it, I've always told you what I did, and this is it, happening now.' She had flinched away from me, and I realised I'd been shouting. In the silence that followed, she just looked at the floor. In all the time I'd known her, she'd never avoided my gaze.

'What is it?' I asked her, gentler now.

'Nothing,' she said, but she didn't look up.

'No, it's something,' I said. 'Tell me.'

She still wouldn't look at me. 'You told me you'd wiped out your own people, I knew that. I just never … I never pictured you doing it, that's all.'

'Look at me!'

'No.'

'Why not?'

'Because you're not here,' she said, her voice breaking. 'Because the Doctor is not in the room.'

'The Doctor is …' I began. 'It's just a name, it's not …' I began again. I calmed myself, ordered my thoughts. 'I'm a Time Lord, my name is … it's just a sort of promise. And you can't always keep your promises. Clara, *look at me!*'

'Okay,' she said, and raised her eyes from the floor. But instead of looking at me, she looked right over my shoulder. 'I

210

see an old man who thinks he's a warrior.' She moved her eyes. 'I see some other bloke who thinks he's a hero.' Then, finally, she turned her gaze on me. 'And I see you.'

I was stepping towards her now. I wanted to keep her looking at me, because it scared me when she couldn't. 'And what am I?' I asked.

'Have you really forgotten?'

'Yes. Maybe, yes.'

'We've got enough warriors,' she said. 'Any old idiot can be a hero.'

'Then what do I do?' I sounded pathetic in my own ears, like a terrified child.

'What you've always done. What you do every day.' Her eyes had dropped to my bow tie. She reached out and straightened it, as if somehow that would fix everything. Then she looked up at me again, and this time she smiled. 'Be a doctor,' she said.

I tried to speak, but found I had nothing to say.

'If your name is a promise,' she continued, 'tell me what the promise was.'

Again, I tried to speak, but I still couldn't.

'Never cruel, never cowardly,' came a voice from behind me. The hero.

'Never give up, never give in,' said the warrior.

Clara's eyes never left mine. 'This is the day you keep your promises. Because this is the day your promises were *for*. Doctor,' she said, 'be a doctor.'

And strangely enough, after four hundred years, that was all it took. The floor rocked below me, the air swelled in my lungs, and the Doctor was back in the room.

We stood there for an hour or so, Clara and I, though possibly it was only a few seconds. I reached to straighten my bow tie, but discovered it was straighter than it had ever been. I gave Clara a wink of approval, and turned to face the others. I think I must have been smiling, because they looked at me in horror.

211

'You're not suggesting …' began Captain Swagger.

'Suggesting what, dear?' I asked.

'I was just wondering if you were about to suggest that we change our own personal history.' His eyes were wide and he looked dumbfounded. It was a good look for him. Especially the mouth.

I shrugged. 'We change history all the time. I'm suggesting something far worse.'

'What exactly?' demanded Captain Grumpy, and he looked so serious, I nearly tickled him under the chin.

'Gentlemen,' I said, 'I've had four centuries to think about this. To hell with changing history, I'm changing my mind.' I pulled out my screwdriver, aimed it at the wooden box, and zapped it. The big red button snapped out of sight, like the box had just gobbled it up.

For a moment, in that barn, there was the most beautiful silence. We looked at each other. Everything was different now. A new reality was snapping into place around us. We were suddenly off the map, and we didn't know what the hell would happen now. I suppose that's why we all started to smile.

'I hope you realise,' said Captain Grumpy, forcing a frown back on his face, 'that there are still a billion, billion Daleks up there, attacking us.'

'Yes,' said Captain Swagger, who was starting to lose control of a big old grin. 'But there's something those billion, billion Daleks don't know!'

'What?' asked Clara, who wasn't really keeping up, poor dear. 'What don't the billion, billion Daleks know?'

'This time,' I said, 'there's three of us.'

'What difference does three of you make?' asked Clara, who could always be such a downer at moments like this, and really needed to buck her ideas up. (I have a vague sense I'm being a bit unreasonable here, but it was all very exciting.)

'Oh, I don't know,' I said. 'But, basically, we've got about twenty minutes to halt the biggest Dalek attack in history, save Gallifrey, and end the Time War forever.'

'Yeah,' said Captain Swagger. 'In view of the urgency of the situation, I'm not even going to suggest putting the kettle on.'

'Will you two take this seriously!' thundered Captain Grumpy.

'We *are* taking it seriously,' I said. 'This is *how* we take it seriously. We assume everything is going to work out, then work out how it's going to work out. You know the M.O.'

'But *how* do we work it out?' he demanded.

'You tell us,' I said. 'You're the military genius. You're the finest general I've ever been. How do we pull this off?'

'How do I … How could I possibly …'

I thought he might just splutter himself to death, if I didn't interrupt. 'Look, just shut up and figure it out, Grandad! What are our assets, what have we got? And stop thinking like a boring old warrior—think like a Doctor!'

He was halfway through drawing breath to tell me what an idiot I was, when I saw an idea catch fire in his eyes. 'Oh!' he said, and smacked himself in the forehead so hard I thought he might fall over. 'Oh!' he said again. 'That is good! That is very, very good!' Whatever the idea was, it went burning down through the years and lit up inside Captain Swagger.

'Oh, I'm getting that now,' he said. 'That's brilliant! That's totally, totally brilliant!'

The idea went barrelling on and hundreds of years later went off like a bomb in my head. Suddenly I was leaping and shouting and punching the walls (mostly accidentally). 'Awesome. That is awesome!'

'What,' pleaded Clara, 'is awesome?'

'She didn't show me any old future,' Captain Grumpy was raving away. 'She showed me exactly the future I needed to see. She showed me the answer! She showed me how to fix it! That's what all this was about! She was *helping* me!'

'Please, please tell me,' said Clara. 'Anyone, just tell me what you're talking about!'

213

The old boy rounded on her. 'The Dalek fleets are surrounding Gallifrey, firing on it constantly. The sky trenches are holding, but here's a thought. What if the whole planet just disappeared?'

'Tiny bit of an ask,' said Clara.

'Yeah, but if you could do it, just imagine what would happen,' said Swagger. 'If there's suddenly no planet, the Daleks would be firing at each other. All those warp drives in all those ships, caught in the same firestorm. Supernova! They'd destroy themselves in their own crossfire.'

'Gallifrey would be gone, the Daleks would be destroyed, it would look to the rest of the universe like they'd annihilated each other,' said Grumpo.

'And where would Gallifrey be?' she asked.

'Frozen!' he told her. 'Frozen in an instant of time, safe and hidden away!'

She looked at me. She was hoping so hard, but she still wasn't getting it.

'Like a painting, Clara,' I said. 'Like a 3D oil painting.'

In fairness, the General was already having a bad day, and he'd known for several hours it would be his last. The Time War was coming to an end and it wasn't going to be good. That morning, the warrior formerly known as the Doctor had left a message for Daleks and Time Lords alike, that the war was over for them all. The tone had sounded ominous, and the intent, apocalyptic—especially as the Doctor had broken into the Time Vaults and stolen the deadliest weapon in the universe. Armageddon was imminent, the General was sure, but in the shuddering chaos and falling masonry of Gallifrey's last surviving war room he tried not to let it show in his face. Keep them focused, keep them fighting, he always said. But whether the end came from the Daleks massing in the sky, or the Doctor destroying Daleks and Time Lords alike, it would be here very soon.

'Not soon enough,' he caught himself, muttering under his breath.

So when Androgar approached him to say there was another message from the Doctor, he barely felt a flicker of interest.

'You're sure the message is from him?' he asked.

'Yes, sir,' Androgar replied. The Under-Colonel had been in the disintegrating war room so long, he looked like he was carved out of solid dust. 'It's definitely the Doctor.'

'What did he say?'

'See for yourself.'

The General turned to see two words spread in shimmering holograms in the dust-filled air above the war table. He blinked in astonishment. 'What's the mad fool talking about now?'

GALLIFREY STANDS, flickered the holograms.

'Gallifrey stands,' he sighed. 'What's he talking about. We've already fallen!'

'Hello!' came a cheerful voice, filling the room. 'Hello, Gallifrey High Command, this is the Doctor speaking.'

One of the screens fizzed, and there was a smiling, youthful face above a ludicrous choice of neckwear.

'Hello, also the Doctor, can you hear me?' On another of the screens, another smiling young idiot.

'Also the Doctor!' And there he was on another screen, the battered old warrior the General knew so well, with his leathery face and his slitted eyes. Odd, thought the General—he didn't normally call himself the Doctor. 'Standing ready,' the old man said.

The General felt himself leaning against the table. 'Dear God,' he said, 'three of them! All my worst nightmares at once.'

'Standing ready for what?' Androgar asked.

'General, we have a plan,' said one of the two younger Doctors.

'In fairness,' said the other one, 'it is a fairly terrible plan.'

'And almost certainly won't work.'

'I was happy with "fairly terrible".'

'Sorry, thinking aloud.'

The old warrior was rolling his eyes. 'Gentlemen, time is pressing—can we just get on with it?'

'Sorry, Grandad,' said one of the young ones, adjusting his neckwear. 'General, we are flying our three TARDISes into the upper atmosphere of Gallifrey.'

'We're positioning ourselves at equidistant intervals round the globe.' It was his turn to straighten his neckwear. '"Equidistant"—so grown up!'

'And we're just about ready to do it,' said the old man.

'Ready to do *what*?'

There was a beat of silence, as if none of them wanted to say. It was the one with the ridiculous neckwear who finally spoke. 'General, we're going to freeze Gallifrey.'

'... I'm sorry, what? You're *what*??' said the General.

On the screen, Neckwear was holding something up, so they could see it. A silver sphere. 'Got my hands on one of these,' he said. 'Using this, and our TARDISes, we're going to freeze Gallifrey in a single moment in time.'

'You know—like those Stasis Cubes,' said the old man. 'A single moment in time, suspended in its own pocket universe.'

'Except we're going to do it to a whole planet. And all the people on it.'

The General looked round the three faces, each alight with the confidence of madness. 'Even if that were possible ... which it isn't ... why would you do such a thing?'

'Because the alternative is burning!' said the old man.

'And I've seen that,' said one of the young ones.

'And I don't want to see it again,' said Neckwear.

'We would be lost in another universe, alone forever,' protested the General. 'We would have nothing.'

'You would have a chance,' said Neckwear. 'And right now, that's exactly what you don't have.'

The General was suddenly aware of everyone in the room, staring at him, and there was something terrible in their faces. It was hope, he realised. Oh, Doctor, don't give them hope—don't be cruel!

'It's delusional,' he said. 'It can't be done. To translate every detail of a whole planet, an entire population—it's impossible.'

'My TARDIS could do it.'

'Not in the time you have. The calculation alone would take hundreds of years.'

'Oh, hundreds and hundreds.' said the other young one. 'But don't worry—I started a very long time ago!'

Another voice was echoing round the room now. 'Calling the War Council of Gallifrey! This is the Doctor. I am on final approach now, this is the Doctor!' Another screen fizzed into life, and there was an old man with long white hair. 'Do you hear me? This is the Doctor. I have received your message, and am here to assist.'

The General stared. He knew that face from centuries ago. The dark-eyed child who claimed he lived in a barn. The adolescent who kept disappearing into the mountains. The student who had broken into the deepest levels of the Cloisters and never spoken of what he'd seen. The young man who had stolen the moon and the President's wife. He looked older and sterner now, as if he was trying to appear respectable, but the General remembered the crisis that had ensued the day this man had fled Gallifrey, not just because he had stolen a TARDIS, but because he had taken with him—

'That's the original, isn't it?' said Androgar, cutting across his thoughts. 'The first one, the first Doctor?'

The General rolled his eyes. The Doctor had become the obsession of the entire military and they knew all his faces by hearts. Aloud he said, '*Four* of them!' and sighed heavily.

'Commencing calculation,' said the original Doctor.

Androgar was gripping the General's arm now. 'Do you see what he's done, sir?'

Yes, of course I bloody do, thought the General.

'He's spread the workload across his timeline. He'll have time to do it. His TARDIS computer will have centuries to complete the calculation, *he can do it!*'

'Listen to me, please, listen!' The General was now shouting at all four faces on the screens. 'Do you understand what translating an entire planet into another dimension will do—the havoc it will cause? The poles could switch. There will be earthquakes, tidal waves. We could lose half the population. We could lose *everyone!*'

'I'm aware of the dangers,' said Neckwear. 'I'll get to it later.'

'Later? When's later?'

'The calculation is complete—thank you, Doctor Number One! Sorry, General, we're moving the TARDISes into position now. Translation will begin in two minutes. Brace yourselves.'

All four screens winked out.

The General thumped his fist on the war table. 'Brace ourselves? How are we supposed to do that? He'll tear Gallifrey apart faster than the Daleks!'

'He said he was going to do something later.'

'There is no later,' snapped the General.

'Then how about now?' I suggested.

Both men turned. It was the first time they'd noticed I was in the room and they stared at me aghast. It might have been my eyebrows, they often had that impact.

'Doctor?' said Androgar, while the General just mumbled something about 'Five of them.'

'Sir, you can't be here,' continued Androgar.

'Oh, do you think so?' I said, mostly because it sounds really good in a Scottish accent. 'Well, that's bad news, because here I come.' I glanced up and they followed my look.

The large screen on the highest part of the wall was filled with a view of the sky over the Capitol, and now, down through the fire and smoke, tiny blue objects were spinning towards us.

'I put the word out,' I explained.

Androgar was staring at the whirling objects. 'What are those?'

But the General already knew. 'How many now?' he asked faintly.

'Hard to say,' I replied. 'Loads, lots. From all over my timeline. What is the collective noun for those anyway? How about a blizzard? Do we like "blizzard"?' Nobody replied; they just stared upwards. 'Okay, to work. Gallifrey is about to disappear down a plughole, and it's going to be a helluva ride. I'll need a continuous live feed of every disaster area on the planet. I am literally—*literally*—all over this.'

For a moment, they said nothing. They just stood and stared up, as the war-torn skies of Gallifrey were filled with a blizzard of police telephone boxes.

It took the better part of a day to translate the world of Gallifrey from one plane of reality to another, and the General was right. The planet screamed and burned and raged.

There was a town, on the southern shore of Lake Calasper, ripped apart by a giant earthquake. No one should have survived, but everywhere the people ran, they found a police telephone box standing in front of them, opening its doors.

A tornado tore through a tiny village, till a ring of blue boxes spun round the storm in the opposite direction, shrinking it into the ground.

As cities and towns and villages burned all around the planet, blue boxes came hurtling through the smoke, rescuing people from windows and rooftops.

A sky transporter, plunging towards the heart of the Capitol was suddenly being piloted by a funny man with big ears and a black jacket. Everyone on board stared out of the windows, as he climbed along the wing, to rewire one of the engines.

A ship on the high seas, about to capsize, was suddenly captained by a strange little man in a frock coat and check trousers, who kept offering people gobstoppers and complaining about his aunt being giddy.

There was a man with a ridiculous umbrella, who evacuated a school as a mountain crumbled towards it, and kept everyone laughing as they ran. A gentle cricketer took command of a hospital on fire, rescued the patients and completed an operation, as the flames licked at the theatre door. A man with a cloud of white hair and a swirling cape stood on a beach and, with a tiny silver rod, froze a whole tsunami as it thundered towards a town. A laughing joker in a colourful coat led a party of miners out of the tunnels that had come crashing down around them. Four children, trapped on the side of a cliff face, knew beyond doubt that no one was coming to their rescue, till the end of an absurdly long scarf dangled down in front of them.

I was everywhere I was needed that day, across all my lives, and I believe I have never run so fast. If I sound proud, forgive me: it is the inverse of the shame I carried for so many years. This was the last day of the Time War, but it was no longer the worst day of my life. Instead, this was the day the people of Gallifrey rose up and put 2.47 billion children safely to bed. This was the day I remembered who I was, and swore never to forget again.

This was the day of the Doctor.

FEED CONNECTING
FEED CONNECTED
FEED STABLE
WARNING: IF THESE WORDS ARE VISIBLE ON THE PAGE YOU ARE WITHIN TEN FEET OF A CYBERMAN.

For the people of Gallifrey, the translation from one dimension to another took many hours—rather longer than the Doctor had estimated, in fact—but for the surrounding Daleks, active in a slower gradient of time, the planet vanished in a little under two seconds. As the Doctor had planned, once their target disappeared, the Daleks were engulfed in the firestorm of their own weaponry, and the final battlefield of the Time War was marked by a supernova that burned for over a thousand years.

Now, the fact is, there are many historians out there, shaking their heads and frowning—and not just because they're a funny, cross bunch of people who can only see time in one direction, and think that's worth boasting about. It's not even because a weekly Cheese & Wine Social is the only way they can think of to meet new people. No, it's this: how, historians demand of each other, could all the Daleks have been destroyed? Most them certainly. Maybe nearly all of them? But is it credible that this explosion, massive though it was, could have ended the life of every last Dalek in the universe? Surely some of them must have survived? This question has caused heated debate at the highest level, and froideur at the Cheese & Wine.

The truth is, of course, we know that a number did survive, and that they continued to plague the Doctor in the years that followed the end of the Time War. But still, say the historians, can this account for the likely number of survivors? Perhaps not.

It might help, though, to imagine what happened from the Daleks' point of view. Their campaign had been going well up to that moment—they had driven the Time Lords back to their home world, which they had then surrounded and were on the verge of destroying. With victory in their grasp, picture what the Daleks then saw: in two accelerated seconds of time, their most dreaded enemy, the Doctor in the TARDIS, was flying everywhere at once, filling the skies of the world they were about to destroy. For a moment, there was a planet full of Doctors, and before they had time to react, their entire battle fleet blew up.

That many of them perished in the explosion is certain. That a few of them survived to regroup is known. It is my strong suspicion, however, that the remainder are still running for their lives.

Now! I promised you a treat. Everybody settle down, and just wait a moment. Talk among yourselves.

Shh!

No, really, shh!

I'm back, but you've got to be very quiet. I've got the webcam on, they might hear us. I've popped it in the flower in my buttonhole, and I feel rather like a spy. Exciting, isn't it? Now keep your voices down, they're just around the corner.

Who's around the corner, you ask silently (thank you!).

I'll explain in a moment. First of all, let me explain how this webcam works. I've switched on the automatic prose translator. That means everything the camera reads, you will read. No, sorry, I'll try that again. Everything the camera reads, you will read. Oh, dear, there's a problem. Any time I say the word 'read', the prose translator automatically turns it into the word 'read', if you read what I mean.

Oh, never mind. What a bother!

Okay, once the Doctors and Clara Oswald had saved Gallifrey, they did what Doctors and Clara Oswalds always do. They went for a cup of tea. As it happened, they all went to the National Gallery for another look at the Gallifrey Falls *painting, which had started the whole thing. And that's what they're doing round the corner from me, right now. To be honest, that's the real reason I waited all this time to write my bits of the book. So I could give you a live experience for the last of our sessions together!*

Hush, listen!

'I don't suppose we'll ever know if we really succeeded. We pushed Gallifrey into another dimension, and kept it safe in transition— but how long can they survive? Where are they all? Still, at worst we failed trying to do the right thing, as opposed to succeeding in doing the wrong.'

Oh! That was the War Doctor (as we'll call him to avoid confusion).

'Life and soul, you are.'

Oh, cheeky. That's Clara Oswald, of course. Oops, sorry, she's still going on.

'Something happened. And at least the Daleks blew up.'

'At least they did that.'

Shall we take a peek round the corner? If I can just position my spy-button-hole …

Oh, there they are. There's the goofy one with the bow tie, standing next to the painting. He looks rather dashing, really, doesn't he?

Also next to the painting is the one in the tight suit. Goodness, it is tight, isn't it? No wonder he stands like that.

And, oh, sweet, they've got their glasses, so they can look clever. I think it works, don't you? As a matter of fact, I have glasses like that.

That's the War Doctor, sitting on the bench, and that's Clara Oswald next to him. Yes, I know, she's very pretty. Settle down, boys and girls. Along the far wall, you can read a very rare sight.

Three police box TARDISes, standing in a row. The same box, three times. Brings a tear to one's eye, doesn't it? Sorry if there's smudging.

Notice there's a lot of abandoned teacups around the place. I think we have missed quite a few people. Look, someone's left their umbrella. Yes, you're right—the handle is in the shape of a question mark! Rather stylish, don't you think? I'll pop it in Lost Property later, I'm sure you-know-who will be back for it.

Hang on, I think they're about to start talking again. Shall we listen? Look, Tight Suit is examining the painting.

'What's it actually called?' he says.

Look, there's Goofy, sniffing like an art critic. 'There's some debate. Either No More, or Gallifrey Falls.'

'Not very encouraging.' Oh, that was the War Doctor, sipping his tea. I'm sure he feels he ought to join the other two at the painting, but I think he rather likes sitting next to Clara, don't you?

'How did it get here?' asks Tight Suit.

'No idea,' says Goofy.

'There's always something we don't know, isn't there?'

'One should certainly hope so,' says the War Doctor. Oh, dear, the old sausage is putting his tea down, and getting up. Looks like he's off, don't you think? Now, keen students may have already noticed a sort of flickering light on his hand. What do think that might indicate? QUIETLY please.

'Well, then. Gentlemen,' he's saying, 'it's been an honour and a privilege.'

'Likewise,' says Tight Suit.

'Doctor!' adds Goofy, as if he's bestowing a compliment.

Ahh, look at old War Doctor. He gets the point Goofy's making, doesn't he? And he's so thrilled to be called the Doctor again. I think I'm having a sniffle. Oops, he's about to make a big old speech, I think! He's straightened up, and he's looking at the other two, all serious.

'If I ever grow to be half the man you are ...' Look at those two boys preen! Oh, but the War Doctor is turning away from them towards ... 'Clara Oswald, I shall be happy indeed.'

Ha! He got them there, didn't he? But Clara's loving it, isn't she? What a smile!

'That's right,' she says. 'Aim high.'

Oh, look at the old boy go! The War Doctor is kissing her on the cheek now, the naughty devil. And look at the boys! I think they're trying to out-sulk each other. Ah, now the War Doctor has turned back to talk to them. Oh, he's frowning. Good at frowning, isn't he?

'I won't remember this, will I?' he asks.

'The time streams are out of sync, you can't retain it, no,' says Goofy.

The old man looks sad, but then he manages a smile. 'So I won't remember that I tried to save Gallifrey, rather than burn it. I will have to live with that. But for now, for this moment ... I am the Doctor again. Thank you.' He's looking at the row of TARDISes. Is he having a senior moment? 'Which one's mine?'

Oh dear, this could be a bit embarrassing. But no, he's laughing. He was joking. Oh, the dear old soul, he's a laugh-a-minute now, isn't he? Look at him, chortling away, as he steps back into his TARDIS. Shame he's about to cease to exist.

And there's the wheezing, groaning noise, and off he flies.

Sorry, what? Cease to exist? Well, yes, of course. The flickering light on his hand? He's far too old, he's been holding off regeneration for years. I shouldn't think he's got much time left at all. Now don't worry, settle down, he'll be fine. He'll go a bit northern, and his ears won't know when to stop, but after a while he'll be the same silly old dear he always is.

Ah, now the other two, are having a bit of confab, aren't they. If I can just turn up the volume ...

Oh, sorry, did he say Trenzalore—

* * * * *

Sorry about the asterisks, I just had to turn off the camera for a moment. Trenzalore is a bit of a security issue, and in any event, not on the syllabus for today.

You haven't missed much. Tight Suit is just saying goodbye to his future self. 'Good to know my future is in safe hands!'

Oh, that was a nice thing to say, wasn't it? Goofy's all pleased—he'll be at that bow tie any second. But Tight Suit has turned to Clara. 'Keep a tight hold of it, Clara.'

Oh! Ouch! There's Goofy's second aborted preen of the day. And now Tight Suit is kissing Clara's hand (they're all at it, aren't they?) and stepping to the TARDIS.

'Trenzalore!' he's saying. Oh, I didn't hit the mute button in time, pretend you didn't read that. Secret, secret, secret! 'We need a new destination. Because I don't want to go.'

Oh, pay no attention, he always says that. And there's his TARDIS, dematerialising.

Goofy looks sad for a moment, then smiles. 'He always says that.' Oh, snap!

'Need a moment alone with your painting?' asks Clara.

Interesting. Why is she saying that? But look at Goofy. He looks like he's going to cry. 'How did you know?' he says.

She's stroking his face now. 'Those big sad eyes—I always know. I guess you can sit here as long as you like. You're the Curator, after all.'

And she gives him a little kiss (there's just too much of this these days, isn't there?) and she's off into the TARDIS. Bye, Clara, I think that's her last bit in the book. No, don't applaud—she'll hear! Now Goofy is alone. Oh, shall we just start calling him the Doctor, since he's the only one left? Okay, we're going to hang around a bit, because from what I understand, something very interesting happens now. According to Myth and Legend (lovely girls), the Doctor is about to meet a Mysterious Stranger. Possibly from his past, possibly from his future. Possibly from both. Shall we wait and read who turns up. Oops, hello! The Doctor has started talking to himself (I suppose he should be used to that by now!).

'Yeah,' he's saying, 'I could be a curator. I'd be great at curating. I'd be the great curator. I could retire and do that.'

Oh, listen to him! Silly old Doctor.

'I could retire and be the curator of this place,' he says.

Ha! Do you know, Doctor, I really think you might!

Oh! Oh, dear! He's turned and looked at me. He just looked right at me. I must have said that out loud. Oh, I've been incredibly silly. Let's just wait and see if he stops staring. No, sorry, he's keeping going. And now he's getting up and walking towards me. Oh, I really am hugely sorry about this, everyone. I've gone and accidentally fallen into the book. This is strictly against the rules, I'm not supposed to get involved in the narrative.

He's staring right at my face now. To be honest, he has reason to. He used to have a face exactly like this. Well, it was a bit younger then, but basically the same.

'*I never forget a face …!*' *he says.*

Sorry, you lot, we're all in this together now. I'm going in!

'*I know you don't.*' *That's me talking now.* '*Of course you never forget a face. And in years to come, you might even find yourself revisiting a few. But just the old favourites, eh?*'

I'm giving him a wink. Sorry you can't appreciate it from that angle. And sorry if my nose is looming at all, it does that. Oh, he's staring at me, all surprised. Don't really blame him in the circumstances.

'*But you … are you …?*' *he says.* '*But you can't be!*'

'*You were curious about this painting, I think. I acquired it in remarkable circumstances.*' *Ah, yes, I probably should have mentioned—I own that painting. It's an astonishing piece. Of course, no one really understands how a painting of the Time War can exist, or who the artist could have been, or how Elizabeth knew about it. Well, I do. But that's another story. Oops, hang on, I think the Doctor is waiting for me to speak.* '*What do you make of the title?*' *I ask him.*

'*Which title?*' *he says.* '*There's two.* No More *and* Gallifrey Falls.'

'*Ah, no, that's where everybody's wrong,*' *I tell him.* '*It's all one title:* Gallifrey Falls No More. *Now what would that mean, do you think?*'

Oh, look at his face, look at all that hope. '*That Gallifrey didn't fall? It worked, it's still out there?*'

'I'm only a humble curator, I'm sure I wouldn't know.'

'Then, where is it?'

'Where is it indeed?' I say. 'Lost, perhaps. Things do get lost, you know. Now you must excuse me—you have a lot to do.' Well, I've got this book to finish, for a start.

He's excited now, isn't he? 'Do I? Like what? Is that what I'm supposed to do now? Go looking for Gallifrey?'

Brace yourselves, everyone, I'm going for wise and enigmatic. 'Oh, that's entirely up to you. Your choice. I can only tell you what I would do, if I were you. Perhaps I was you, of course. Or perhaps you were me? Or perhaps it doesn't matter either way. Who knows. Who knows ...'

Right, come with me, we're off. I want to get out before this book gets completely out of control. We'll all end up in the sequel if we're not careful. No, don't look back, keep walking! Round the corner, that's right. Down the stairs, though the door, past the desk with the giant pot plant (if the plant winks at you, just wink back).

Phew! I don't think he's following. Everybody, deep breath and relax.

Well then, I hope you all enjoyed that. Because I'm afraid that's me for the day. Yes, no, sorry. Time for tea and scones with Ohila and Elizabeth. I'll leave you to read the last chapter for yourselves— it's only a little one.

Oh, just tiny thing before I go. Did you all guess who I am? Go on, did you?

Yes, well done, that's right! I'm the Curator of the Under Gallery. Of course I am. Who else could I be?

Sorry, what was that? Yes, fair point, I suppose. The Doctor is the Curator of the Under Gallery. So does that mean I'm the Doctor? Well you already know the answer to that one, don't you?

It's complicated.

Chapter 13

The Doctor

'Was he a friend of yours?' I asked. 'A relative?'

Cass Fermazzi didn't reply, but she took the bandolier I held out to her, and strapped it round her chest. She was looking at the sky, and there was something fierce in her eyes.

'You look like you're ready for a fight,' I said.

'Been ready all my life,' she said. 'I'm just admitting that now.' She flashed a bleak little smile at me. 'Thanks for looking after him,' she said, and started climbing out of the crater.

'What do you mean, all your life?' I called after her.

'Oh, you know,' she said, without turning.

'No, I really don't.'

She turned at the lip of the crater, and sighed. 'It's going to sound stupid.'

'Good. I hate things that don't.'

'When I was a kid I was in therapy.'

'Weren't we all?'

'We weren't rich though. I had one of those bots. Looked like a clown—God knows why. It was supposed to take away some of my memories, but it was so full of someone else's, they all just kept spewing out.'

I felt my stomach turn over. It was exactly what I'd figured out, but it was chilling to hear it. 'What kind of memories?'

'Just vague stuff. About always fighting for what's right, but trying never to hurt people. Never be cruel, never be cowardly, that kind of thing. Cheesy stuff, but it got to me.'

Yeah, I thought, me too.

'Time to go and do like the clown says, I guess.' She flashed another sad smile, and was gone.

I could never save her, I knew that. She was too wrapped up in my own timeline. But at least, just once, she'd looked at me without hating me.

And you can't save everyone, I reminded myself. You just have to save all the ones you can. Was that what the Moment had wanted to teach me?

I thought about the Moment a lot, and I knew it sometimes irritated her. Once, sitting on a bench in Henry VIII's third-favourite garden, I was brooding away on the subject, and suddenly she just sat down next to me.

'Will you stop thinking about me all the time,' she said, still in the form of Rose Tyler. 'It's getting annoying!'

'But why did you do it?' I asked. 'What was in it for you?'

She smiled at me, as flirtatious as always. 'I may be the interface of the deadliest weapon in the universe, but I still want the same thing from a relationship.'

'Which is?'

'Not to be used.' And she winked and was gone.

The next time I saw her she was standing knee-deep in a fountain, at the heart of the Villengard banana groves. It must have been a year later but she resumed the conversation as if there had been no interruption.

'I did it because the universe needs the Doctor to be the Doctor, and you were in danger of stopping. You have no idea how necessary you are.'

'Don't be daft,' I said.

'Truly, Doctor. If you didn't exist we would have to dream you.'

'The Doctor doesn't exist—just a stupid idea in my stupid head.'

'No, no, no, you're always getting this wrong!' She was stamping and splashing now, impatient with me. 'The Doctor isn't who you try to be—you are the Doctor, *because* you try.'

'Are you absolutely sure you're a weapon interface,' I asked her. 'You sound a lot like a Christmas cracker.'

'Oh shut up,' she said, and vanished, crossly.

She might have been flattering me, I thought, as I climbed out of the crater. But did weapon interfaces do that?

Well, anyway, enough brooding, I decided. The day of the Doctor was over at last, and it was time to get my head back in the game. Somewhere there's danger, somewhere there's injustice, and somewhere else the tea is getting cold. Come on, Doctor, work to do.

So it was me who set off across the muddy battlefield towards the TARDIS, but it was the Doctor who opened the door, stepped inside, and slammed it shut behind her.

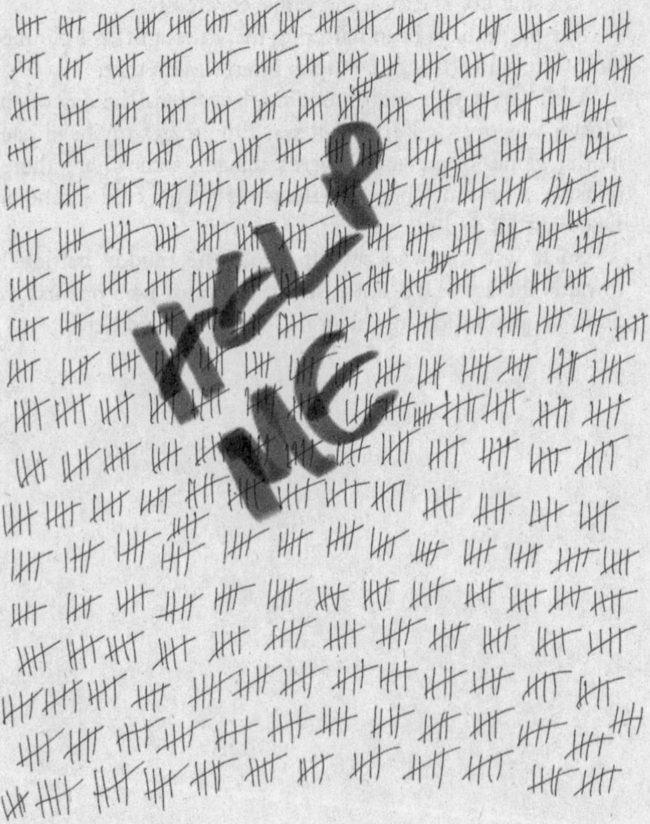
HELP
ME